"Sylvia's not even from Alabama—she's from one of those Yankee states, Kansas or something."

"She's only lived here twenty years, a newcomer. And she has the nerve to ask me to decorate her house." Hillary laughed. "But I guess that at least shows she's got good taste."

With a slam of the brakes and a yank on the steering wheel, Hillary pulled the car into the shaded driveway of a two-story white frame house. "This is it." They walked up to the double doors and rang the doorbell. No answer. Hillary frowned and knocked on one of the doors with enough force that it swung partway open. She gave Jane a questioning look, then pushed the door open and peered inside.

"Sylvia?" Silence. Hillary took a step into the foyer, and Jane followed reluctantly. "Sylvia?" Hillary called again. They walked through the foyer into the living room. In unison they audibly sucked in their breath.

"Oh my god! Mauve cushions with red drapes!" said Hillary.

Jane couldn't speak at all. The dead-white face and life-less, still-open eyes of Sylvia Davis, who lay on the floor, had robbed her of her voice. A mauve sofa pillow partially covered her face.

MORE MYSTERIES FROM THE
BERKLEY PUBLISHING GROUP ...

DOAN AND BINKY MYSTERIES: San Francisco's dazzling detective team is back and better than ever. These detectives have a fashion sense to *die* for ... ''An entertaining cozy with a nineties difference.''—*MLB News*

by Orland Outland
DEATH WORE A SMART LITTLE OUTFIT   DEATH WORE A FABULOUS NEW FRAGRANCE

DOG LOVERS' MYSTERIES STARRING JACKIE WALSH: She's starting a new life with her son and an ex-police dog named Jake ... teaching film classes and solving crimes!

by Melissa Cleary
A TAIL OF TWO MURDERS	DEAD AND BURIED
DOG COLLAR CRIME	THE MALTESE PUPPY
HOUNDED TO DEATH	MURDER MOST BEASTLY
FIRST PEDIGREE MURDER	OLD DOGS
SKULL AND DOG BONES	AND YOUR LITTLE DOG, TOO

SAMANTHA HOLT MYSTERIES: Dogs, cats, and crooks are all part of a day's work for this veterinary technician ... ''Delightful!''—*Melissa Cleary*

by Karen Ann Wilson
EIGHT DOGS FLYING	COPY CAT CRIMES
BEWARE SLEEPING DOGS	CIRCLE OF WOLVES

CHARLOTTE GRAHAM MYSTERIES: She's an actress with a flair for dramatics—and an eye for detection. ''You'll get hooked on Charlotte Graham!''—*Rave Reviews*

by Stefanie Matteson
MURDER AT THE SPA	MURDER AT THE FALLS
MURDER AT TEATIME	MURDER ON HIGH
MURDER ON THE CLIFF	MURDER AMONG THE ANGELS
MURDER ON THE SILK ROAD	MURDER UNDER THE PALMS

PEACHES DANN MYSTERIES: Peaches has never had a very good memory. But she's learned to cope with it over the years ... Fortunately, though, when it comes to murder, this absentminded amateur sleuth doesn't forgive and forget!

by Elizabeth Daniels Squire
WHO KILLED WHAT'S-HER-NAME?	WHOSE DEATH IS IT, ANYWAY?
MEMORY CAN BE MURDER	IS THERE A DEAD MAN IN THE HOUSE?
REMEMBER THE ALIBI	

HEMLOCK FALLS MYSTERIES: The Quilliam sisters combine their culinary and business skills to run an inn in upstate New York. But when it comes to murder, their talent for detection takes over ...

by Claudia Bishop
A TASTE FOR MURDER	MURDER WELL-DONE
A PINCH OF POISON	DEATH DINES OUT
A DASH OF DEATH	A TOUCH OF THE GRAPE

LEADING AN ELEGANT DEATH

PAULA CARTER

BERKLEY PRIME CRIME, NEW YORK

LEADING AN ELEGANT DEATH

A Berkley Prime Crime Book / published by arrangement with
the author

PRINTING HISTORY
Berkley Prime Crime edition / February 1999

All rights reserved.
Copyright © 1999 by The Berkley Publishing Group
This book may not be reproduced in whole or in part,
by mimeograph or any other means, without permission.
For information address: The Berkley Publishing Group,
a member of Penguin Putnam Inc.,
375 Hudson Street, New York, New York 10014.

The Penguin Putnam Inc. World Wide Web site address is
http://www.penguinputnam.com

ISBN: 0-425-16733-X

Berkley Prime Crime Books are published
by The Berkley Publishing Group,
a member of Penguin Putnam Inc.,
375 Hudson Street, New York, New York 10014.
The name BERKLEY PRIME CRIME and the BERKLEY PRIME CRIME
design are trademarks belonging to Berkley Publishing Corporation.

PRINTED IN THE UNITED STATES OF AMERICA

10 9 8 7 6 5 4 3 2 1

LEADING AN ELEGANT DEATH

1

Something smelled funny. Jane noticed it while she was trying to figure out how to make the washing machine stop dancing and thumping around the laundry room. Now the lid was flopping and suds were oozing out.

"Stop!" she yelled at the frenzied machine as she pushed button after button on the control panel. In desperation, she reached behind the washer and pulled the plug. The motor stopped with a sickly whir. That was when she noticed the smoke coming from the kitchen.

"Oh, my God! The roast!" she cried as she ran to the kitchen, which was now engulfed in a thick cloud, like pictures she'd seen of wars in the Middle East. She felt her way along the counter to the oven. A woman's voice oozed a Southern accent from the small television set Jane kept on the counter, but the smoke cloud was too thick to see a picture.

"Using your glue gun, carefully attach the first nut to the frame you have constructed from a wire hanger and a bit of masking tape. Don't burn yourself, now, and remember, it's not always easy working with nuts," the disembodied voice admonished.

Jane found the stove and lifted the lid of the pot. An even thicker cloud of smoke escaped.

"When the nuts are all in place, you're ready for the shellacking . . ."

Jane switched off the burner, then stumbled to the window and finally managed to get it open. She ran for the portable fan in her bedroom, found it under a mound of dirty clothes, rushed back to the kitchen, and plugged it in.

". . . colorful feathers for the wings, which I have my husband, Billy, bring me when he goes duck hunting . . ."

Enough smoke had escaped that Jane could see the pot on the stove. She pulled it off, lifted the lid, and peered inside. The small black lump in the center of the blackened pot was all that was left of the pot roast. She'd planned it as a surprise for Sarah tonight—a special dinner. And it had taken half her grocery budget to buy it.

"And there you have it—the perfect centerpiece for your Thanksgiving table."

Jane turned toward the television set, visible now that some of the smoke had cleared. A dark-haired woman wearing artfully applied makeup and an expensive, chic suit was smiling at her and holding up an effigy of a turkey made of walnuts. Jane had caught a glimpse of the show once or twice before, but she always switched it to another channel. Hillary Scarborough's weekly thirty minutes on how to be the perfect homemaker bored her.

The woman continued to speak as background music swelled and credits rolled across her face and her walnut turkey. "This is Hillary Scarborough saying good-bye until next week, when our program will focus on how to plan for your fall cleaning. We'll take another look at all those cupboards and cabinets that haven't been reorganized since last spring."

"Oh, I can hardly wait!" Jane said with no attempt to keep the sarcasm out of her voice. She picked up the remote control to switch channels to her favorite local talk show known as *The Sylvia Davis Show*, but before she pressed the button, something Ms. Scarborough said caught her attention.

"And don't forget, if you're interested in the executive assistant position, apply at the address shown on your screen now. In the meantime, I wish you a week of elegance!"

Crawling across the screen were the words: "Apply in person at Elégance du Sud, 336 South Main. Call 555-8755 for appointment."

Jane forgot sarcasm and forgot to switch channels. She fumbled for something to write down the message. There was a pen next to the telephone but no paper. The only thing she could find was the slightly bloody Styrofoam carton that had once held the now-ruined roast. She took down the number, poking holes in the Styrofoam as she wrote.

When she had dialed all the digits, she heard, "Elégance du Sud." French with a Southern accent. Jane told the voice she wanted to apply for the position advertised on television. She was given an appointment for the following week and told to send in a résumé.

Jane was both surprised and elated that it had been so easy. She hung up the phone and punched one fist into the air, crying "Yesss!" It was the first appointment for an interview she'd had since she'd started her job search three weeks ago. The only other ads she'd seen in the classified section of the paper were for accountants, hairdressers, pipe fitters and, of course, other executive assistant positions. The latter were the only positions she was even remotely qualified to do, and it seemed her qualifications were even more remote than she had imagined since she'd never even been called for an interview at any of the places she'd applied.

What would it be like working for the superwoman of domesticity, she wondered. But it was too early to think of that. She only had an appointment for an interview, not an offer. It didn't matter really what working for Ms. Scarborough would be like, however. She needed a job. Desperately. She had to do her best to impress the woman.

Just what did an executive assistant do, anyway? And what did Elégance du Sud mean? French for elegant suds? Did Hillary run a laundry on the side? Or a bar? Seems she did have a business somewhere in town. But it was a home decorating business called Scarborough's, wasn't it?

She'd find out soon enough. The interview was scheduled for Monday, which meant she had to get a résumé in the mail tomorrow.

It had been more than ten years since she'd held a job, and now the thought of going back to work gave her a lump in her stomach. She'd have to tell Sarah about the interview, and she'd have to give her the other not-so-good news at the same time.

Elégance? That had to be French for *elegance.* That probably meant she couldn't wear her faded jeans and twenty-year-old Grateful Dead T-shirt when she went for the interview. What did people wear to interviews these days? Could it really have been ten years since she'd had a job? Could she ever have been twenty-something with so much hope for the future? That was before she married Jim Ed Ferguson from Birmingham, the cute boy who'd won her over with his Southern charm when they were both at Stanford. That was before she'd put him through law school. Before he'd moved her here to hot, humid, magnolia-scented Prosper, Alabama, from where she'd grown up in California. Before he divorced her.

Would the aqua blouse look all right with a brown suit? Or was it pink you were supposed to wear with brown? Maybe Sarah would have some ideas; she always did. It was almost five o'clock, and she'd be home from her music lesson any minute now. She'd have to hurry to make her that special dinner; then she would tell her the news.

Jane threw out the burned roast and dumped a ready-made salad into two mismatched cereal bowls and was thawing out a frozen pizza in the microwave when she heard the front door open.

"Hi, Mom, I'm home!" Sarah, ten years old, corn silk hair and blue eyes, all knees and elbows. The light of her life.

"I'm in the kitchen, hon."

"The kitchen? You're cooking? Something stinks. Like you burned something."

"Of course I'm cooking. Isn't that what mothers do?"

Sarah put her violin case down and gave Jane a quick kiss on the cheek. "I don't want to hurt your feelings, Mom, but when you cook, it's usually a disaster. Like that pizza. I bet you zapped it too long and the crust will be, like, rock hard by now." Sarah opened the microwave, slipped the pizza out and onto a pan, then popped it in the gas oven.

"OK, so I'm not the world's greatest cook." Jane hadn't meant to sound hurt or petulant, but she couldn't hide it from her daughter.

Sarah turned to her with a look of alarm. "I'm sorry, Mommy," she said. "I didn't mean to hurt your feelings. Maybe you're not the world's greatest cook, but you are the world's greatest mom." She gave a little fanfare. "And someday, you'll be the world's greatest prosecuting attorney."

"I want to talk to you about that, Sarah. That and some good news."

"Good news?"

"I've got a job interview later next week."

Sarah's face lit up, and she jumped twice with enthusiasm before she threw her arms around her mother's neck. "A job interview? Way to go, Mom! If you get a job, does that mean I can have a new bike and I can take karate lessons?"

"Of course it does," Jane said, feeling a little joy for her decision at last.

Sarah sobered. "But how are you going to work at a job and go to law school at the same time? Won't that be kind of hard?"

"That's something else I want to talk to you about." Jane pretended to be busy tossing the already-tossed salad. "I'm—well, I won't be going back to school this term."

"You're dropping out?" Jane heard disbelief and disappointment in those words, just the thing she had dreaded. She felt her own disappointment keenly enough. Two years ago, she'd finally talked Jim Ed into keeping his end of the bargain and letting her go back to school. They'd made the bargain when they first were married that she would help him get his law degree, and then he would help her. By the time Jim Ed had his degree, they had Sarah, though. Then they had to skimp while he got his practice launched. "We can't afford for you to go back to school yet, darlin'," he'd told her every time she brought it up. Finally, though, he relented, and she had driven two hours every day to Tuscaloosa to attend the law school there. She was halfway through her second year when he left. Went back to Birmingham with Leslie Ann Thornberry. Changed his name to James Edward Ferguson III, in spite of the fact that there never had been a James Edward I or II. Leslie Ann was a twenty-four-year-old lawyer who had once been Miss Alabama and who had joined the firm where Jim Ed was an associate, just to get a little experience so she could eventually become a part of her very rich daddy's law firm in Birmingham. She and Jim Ed both were members of that firm now. He'd left Jane with the house and the mortgage and a meager child-support check each month. If she'd been a semester farther along in law school, as she was now, she would have known how to get more.

Jane took a deep breath and told Sarah what she had been dreading. "I can't afford to stay in school, sweetie. We're down to our last hundred dollars. I have to get a job."

"But, Mom, you always wanted—"

"Look on the positive side, Sarah—no more after-school programs three days a week while you wait for me to get home, and now that I won't be busy with law school, I can do all the things a mother should. You know, clean the house, cook decent meals, make Barbie doll clothes for you . . ."

"I don't mind the after-school stuff, and why would I want you to make Barbie clothes? I could buy them at Wal-Mart if I ever wanted any. Besides, you know you hate doing all that stuff. You love going to school. You're smart. You'll make a terrific lawyer.''

"We have no more money, sweetie. We have to eat. That means I have to get a job. Maybe eventually I can take a night course or something.''

"But . . .'' Jane saw tears in Sarah's eyes, and that was more than she could bear. She pulled her daughter to her and held her close. "It will be all right, Sarah, you'll see.'' Sarah clung to her, and Jane stroked her hair. She could never get enough of this child, could never quite get over being awestruck at the idea that the beautiful creature was her daughter.

"What kind of a job is it?'' Sarah asked, finally.

"Executive assistant. Some place called Elégance du Sud. Ever hear of it?''

"Oh my goodness, Mom!'' Sarah's expression alarmed Jane.

"What? Is there something wrong with that? It's not like it's an escort service.''

"What's an escort service?''

"It's—never mind. If you know what this place is, tell me.''

"It's that Hillary Scarborough place.''

"I know. That woman on TV who talks about gardening and cooking and how to have a perfect house. The Martha Stewart of the South.''

"I didn't know you ever watched her show.''

"Well, I've seen it a time or two when I was flipping through the channels looking for a ball game. I like the talk show opposite her on channel seven. Sylvia Davis.''

"Oh yeah, I heard of her. My friend, Shakura, told me about her 'cause she was going to have her brother on her show one time, but she never did. I watched her once, and it was like totally boring. Nothing but politicians sweating because she was talking about stuff they did wrong.'' Sarah was opening a package of Oreos.

"Put those away until after dinner, Sarah.''

"Just one won't hurt.''

"Sarah.'' A warning.

Sarah took on a petulant look, but she tossed the cookie package aside.

"Ms. Scarborough owns a decorating business, too, but that's not Elegance of Suds or whatever, is it? I thought she just called it Scarborough's."

"She used to call it Scarborough's. Now it's Elégance du Sud. You know what that means, don't you? Southern Elegance?"

"Of course I knew that. You think I'm a slob *and* an idiot?"

"I don't think you're either one, Mommy," Sarah said with more tenderness than defensiveness. There were times now, since Jim Ed left, that Sarah was more the mother than the child.

"How'd you know what it meant?" Jane asked.

"Hillary said on her show that's what it means," Sarah said, taking a peek at the pizza.

Jane turned away from her and sat down heavily on one of the kitchen chairs with a sigh of despair. "I know what you're thinking, though, and you're right. Hillary Scarborough would never hire me. I can't even cook frozen pizza. And as far as decorating, look at this place!" She swung her hand toward the living room with its mismatched sofa and chairs, which she had bought at Goodwill after Jim Ed took her Ethan Allen living room as a part of the divorce settlement. All of it was cluttered with her schoolbooks and papers.

"Oh, now, Mom . . ."

"And look at me!" She pulled at her jeans and T-shirt. "I look more like Agony of the Slums than Elegance of the South."

"We could fix that, if—"

"They film some of those shows at her house, you know. It's perfect. She's perfect. She even bakes her own bread. Probably grows her own wheat, and—what do you mean we could fix that?"

"I mean, if you really want the job, we can make you look great. You've got the clothes. Maybe a little out of style, but not bad. And she doesn't have to know that you can't cook or what our furniture looks like.''

''Oh, honey . . .''

''I want you to be a lawyer, Mommie, but—''

''I will someday. I've just got to have a job for now, and I can do the job, I know. Executive assistant. Probably you just have to keep things running smoothly. I can do that.''

''That's what you always tell me. That I can do anything I want to do.''

''And I believe that. I believe I'll eventually go back to school and finish my law degree.''

Sarah gave her mother a smile. ''Promise?''

''Promise.''

Sarah cocked her head, studying Jane's face. ''Maybe you ought to get your hair cut. A short do looks nice on older women.''

''What do you mean, older women?''

Sarah hadn't heard her. She was off to the bedroom to pull things from Jane's closet. ''It's a couple years old, but it's got style.'' Sarah held up the brown suit on the hanger and studied it. ''Why don't you wear it with that beige silk blouse? That always makes your eyes look golden.''

''You don't need Barbie dolls to dress when you've got me. Where'd you learn all that, anyway?''

''Tracy Andrews's mother gets *Cosmopolitan.* Last month, they had something on career dressing.''

''*Cosmopolitan*? Oh, my lord, Sarah, you're too young to . . .''

''Your shoes should match your hemline. Don't you have some low-heeled brown pumps?''

''All I can find are those old sneakers. They've turned kind of brown,'' Jane said, digging into a mound of shoes in her closet. ''What am I going to do if she asks me for my favorite recipe?'' She found a brown pump in the pile of shoes and tossed it out over her shoulder. ''And why do you want karate lessons?''

• • •

On Tuesday, Jane arrived at Elégance du Sud a few minutes early for her appointment. She'd lost weight since the last time she'd worn her brown suit. Law school had kept her too busy to eat regularly. But it improved the fit of her suit, and she actually felt pretty for the first time since Jim Ed had left. She hadn't had time to get the short haircut Sarah had recommended, but her light brown hair was pulled back from her face in a smart French twist that she had managed with Sarah's help.

Nevertheless, she was nervous as she opened the door to 336 South Main and stepped inside to the reception area. The sweet, heavy scent of vanilla potpourri greeted her as she entered. The room was decorated in an antebellum style with massive cherrywood furniture, diamond-tufted upholstery, and portraits of women looking wan and delicate in lace. The potpourri was in a large basket tied with a pink and green ribbon and sitting beneath one of the portraits on a gleaming antique cherry sideboard.

A receptionist, looking anything but wan and delicate, glanced up at her from the computer. She was at least fifty pounds overweight with dark hair and perfect skin. An airbrushed Rosie O'Donnell. Jane had never seen her before, and Prosper was a small enough town that she was used to knowing practically everyone. Well, maybe it was just as well that she didn't know her. At least she wouldn't be asking her about Jim Ed or the divorce.

"Are you the nine o'clock?" the receptionist asked.

"Yes," Jane said, feeling a little nonplussed at being referred to as a number on a clock.

"Ms. Ferguson?"

"Yes," Jane said again.

The receptionist glanced up at her from the appointment book. "You're not the one who used to be married to Jim Ed Ferguson, are you?"

"Well—yes," she said, because she couldn't think of anything cutting or clever. The receptionist shook her head in a slow, pitying way, then said softly, as if she needed comforting, "Ms. Scarborough will be with you in just a minute."

Jane had just started leafing through a copy of *Architectural Digest* when she saw Hillary Scarborough standing in the doorway of her office. She looked much like she did on television: attractive and well into her forties, a fact she couldn't completely disguise with her careful makeup. The expensive teal cashmere suit was tailored in a way to help hide the ten extra pounds she carried, and in spite of the fact that the style of her heavy dark hair would have looked better on a younger woman, she still managed to look terrific. It was a look of extreme femininity Jane had come to think of as Southern Chic.

"Jane Ferguson?" Hillary asked in the long, soft drawl that still sounded foreign to Jane's Californian ears.

"Yes, I'm Jane Ferguson." She stood, ready to follow Hillary into her office, but Hillary walked toward her and extended a well-manicured hand. "It is so nice to meet you, Jane. Are you the Ferguson who used to be married to Jim Ed?"

"No, Jim Ed is my cousin."

"Well, I declare! I didn't know Jim Ed had any cousins outside of Birmingham. Well, anyway, I hope you will excuse me for not conformin' to standard procedure, but I misread my appointment book, and I scheduled a meeting with a client this mornin'. Would you mind terribly if I asked you to come along, and we did the interview on the way?" She had pronounced *I* each time as if it were *ah*.

"Not at all," Jane said, eager to escape the potpourri.

Hillary's car was in the parking lot—a two-year-old gold Cadillac with leather upholstery and the words ELÉGANCE DU SUD inscribed in small letters with an abundance of curlicues on each of the front doors.

"The neighborhood has really gone down since that pawn shop moved in the vacant building next to me. We have to share the same parking lot," Hillary said, glancing at the car parked next to her Cadillac. She was referring to Jane's six-year-old, faded maroon Toyota with the empty pop cans on the floor. Jane gave her a weak smile and sank into the plush seat of the luxury car.

Hillary backed out of her parking space with a lurch, narrowly missing the already dented fender of Jane's Toyota. "Your résumé was interesting," Hillary said, using the Southern pronunciation: *ina-RES-tin'*. She turned out into the street, pulling in front of a delivery truck. "A B.A. in comparative literature, two years of law school, and some experience in management at a radio station," she continued, ignoring the truck's blaring horn.

"Uh huh," Jane said. Her knuckles turned white as she gripped the armrest and the edge of her seat. A red light glared ahead of them, but Hillary showed no signs of slowing.

"What was your position in management?"

"Executive assistant to the station manager." Hillary's briefcase slid to the floor as she slammed on her brakes behind the motorcycle, which was stopped in front of her at the light. Jane had been, in fact, a secretary and general flunky at the radio station, the only job she could get with a B.A. in literature, but Al, her boss, would have called her an executive assistant if she'd asked him.

"You've seen my television show?"

"Oh, yes, many times."

"What do you think of it?"

"It's very—interesting."

"Interesting?"

"Yes. I especially liked the one you did on decorating with nuts."

"It's amazing what you can do with nuts."

"Isn't it, though."

"I run a catering business as well as my interior design business, you know. Plan parties, receptions, that sort of thing? Sometimes I make the hors d'oeuvres myself. I would need someone with an expert touch to help me. How are you on cooking and menu planning?"

"My daughter says there's no one else like me."

"I would also expect you to act as a producer for my television show. Ratings are important, you know, even

in a town like Prosper. There's a show on channel seven
opposite me. Have you seen it? Sylvia Davis? A local talk
show?''

''Well, maybe once.''

''My station manager tells me she's cutting into my
ratings. I don't believe it, of course. He's just being tacky,
telling me he'll have to cancel my show if I don't get my
ratings up. Can you imagine such ignorance?'' Hillary
took her eyes off the road, directing all her attention toward Jane, and, as a result, she ran a red light. One car,
coming through the intersection from Jane's right, stopped
inches from Jane's door. Hillary ignored the cacophony
of horns and screeching tires. ''People have only been
turning on her show out of curiosity. But they'll come
back to me because they need what I offer. Style and
substance.''

Jane felt a nervous breakdown was a real possibility.

''I can't believe the nerve of that woman,'' Hillary continued, changing lanes without a signal. ''She's not even
from Alabama. I mean, she's from one of those Yankee
states, I don't know, Kansas or something. And she thinks
she can talk about *local* issues? Why, she's only lived
here twenty years. A newcomer. No offense, hon. I mean
just because she was the mayor's campaign manager for
the last three terms, does that make her a celebrity? And
get this, Jane, she had the nerve to ask me to decorate her
house.'' Hillary laughed her throaty laugh. ''But I guess
that at least shows she's got good taste.'' She took her
eyes off the road once more, glancing in the mirror on
the sun visor and flicking at her hair with the Revlon Red
tips of her fingers. ''She came by the office last week and
picked up some carpet samples and some sofa pillows and
fabric swatches for drapes. Everything in mauve. Made
an appointment for me to come out for a consultation
today. That's where we're going now: Sylvia Davis's
house. She wants it redecorated. Don't you wonder what
kind of a house a person who likes mauve would have?
I mean, really, that's last year's color.''

''I just wonder if we're going to get there.''

"What?"

"Soon. I wonder if we're going to get there soon. I mean, I'm eager to see it. Her house." Jane was sweating in spite of the fact that the Cadillac's air conditioner was blasting its arctic wind at her.

"Well, don't be so impatient. It's probably tacky, anyway."

With a slam of the brakes and a yank on the steering wheel, Hillary pulled the car into the shaded driveway of an attractive two-story white frame house. "This is it," Hillary said, reaching to retrieve her briefcase from the floor.

They walked up the steps to the double doors and rang the doorbell. No answer. Hillary frowned and rang again.

"It would be just like her to not keep her appointment and never notify me," Hillary said. She knocked on one of the doors with enough force that it swung partway open. Hillary gave Jane a questioning look, then pushed the door open more and peered inside.

"Sylvia?"

Silence. Hillary took a step into the foyer, and Jane followed, reluctantly.

"Sylvia?" Hillary called again. She and Jane walked through the foyer into the high-ceilinged living room. In unison, they audibly sucked in their breath.

"Oh, my God! Mauve cushions with red drapes!" said Hillary.

Jane couldn't speak at all. The dead-white face and lifeless, still-open eyes of Sylvia Davis, who lay on the floor, had robbed her of her voice. A mauve sofa pillow partially covered her face.

2

"What on earth has she done to my sofa pillow?" Hillary's high-heeled pumps clicked on the gleaming hardwood floor as she moved toward Sylvia.

"Hillary! Don't . . ."

Hillary turned to look at Jane, the sofa pillow in her hand.

". . . pick up the sofa pillow," Jane finished after it was too late.

"Well, I'm certainly not going to leave it here on the floor," Hillary said.

"That woman's dead, and you're worried about sofa pillows?" Jane said. She stood in the foyer, a knot of desperation and fear tightening in her stomach.

"Nonsense. She can't be dead," Hillary said, peering down at the body on the floor. "She's just trying to get attention. I know her type, she's . . . Oh dear, she does look a little bit odd, doesn't she?" She stared at the woman a moment longer, then her eyes widened as she glanced up at Jane. Her mouth opened, but no words came out. For once she appeared speechless.

"We've got to call the police," Jane said.

Hillary nodded, still unable to summon speech.

"There's probably a phone in the kitchen."

Hillary nodded again, mutely.

Jane waited. Hillary didn't move. "You should be the one to call," Jane said. "You were the one who had the appointment with her."

Speech returned to Hillary. "I—I wouldn't know what to say." She shook her head.

"Just tell them we found her when we came in to—"

"Honey, would you mind doing it for me? I'm just too—" Hillary's hand went to her forehead. "Well, I have never seen anything like this before, and you're from California so I think you should be the one to do it."

"What does my being from California have to do with it?" Jane's voice was edged with tension.

"Well, you know, all those Hollywood people. They have connections with the Mafia, don't they? I mean, they make movies about them, so they know about dead people. You probably rubbed shoulders with that kind of person every day, so you—oh, just go call the police. You'll know what to say. You're practically a lawyer anyway, aren't you?"

Jane couldn't think of anything to say at the moment. It wouldn't do any good to argue with that kind of logic. She turned aside, looking for the kitchen.

"Don't leave me in here alone with that dead woman!" Hillary screeched. Her high heels clicked a desperate staccato on the wood floor as she hurried after Jane.

The telephone sat next to an answering machine on the kitchen counter. The machine flashed two quick flashes over and over again, signaling that the dead woman had two messages. Jane reached for the telephone but yanked back her hand before she touched it.

"What's wrong?" Hillary asked.

"I can't have my prints on that phone," Jane said. "What if whoever killed her used this phone to call someone? My prints would mess up the killer's prints."

"What do you mean, killer?" Hillary's voice rose to a squeaky pitch. "Nobody killed her. She just died, that's all."

For a moment, Jane let herself believe that was a possibility, but her better sense told her it wasn't. She shook her head slowly, sadly. "I don't think so."

"Oh my lord!" Hillary's face registered shock and disbelief, then a sudden change. "Oh, Jane, in all this excitement, I forgot about my cell phone. It's in my handbag. I left it on the floor next to that god-awful sofa. Did you see it? French provincial? Only a cretin would think that goes with antique mahogany." She was clicking her way back to the living room, checking over her shoulder to make sure Jane was following. She hesitated slightly just as she approached the body, then made a wide arc around it to retrieve her purse.

She dug into the depths of the stylish bag, brought out the phone, and pushed it into Jane's hand. Jane took it reluctantly, then dialed 911. A dispatcher answered—a woman who sounded as if her vocal cords had been accosted for years by too many cigarettes.

"I need to report a—a dead body." Jane's voice shook, and her head pounded.

"What kind?"

"What do you mean, what kind?"

"Well, is it pig or cow or raccoon or what? I need to know how big a truck to send."

"Oh God, this isn't roadkill." Jane couldn't seem to get enough breath in her lungs. "I'm talking about a woman. I think she's been murdered."

"Well, my lord," the dispatcher said. Obviously dead bodies were not common in Prosper. "I reckon I ought to let you talk to Detective Jackson," the woman said. "Hold on."

It took a while for Detective Jackson to come to the phone, and Jane paced nervously back and forth from the living room to the foyer while she waited.

"Jackson here," a male voice said at last. He had pronounced the last word, "heah."

"I want to report a dead body. Sylvia Davis. I think she's been murdered."

"Who is this, and where are you callin' from?" The

Southern accent didn't keep Jackson's voice from sounding crisp and professional. There were several more questions. Why was Jane at the Davis residence? How long had she been there? Was anyone with her? Had she spoken to anyone else? Had she touched anything?

Jane continued her pacing while she answered the questions, distracted and unaware of Hillary, who was still in the living room. When at last Jane hung up the phone, she saw that Hillary was in the process of moving one of the chairs from the window to the fireplace.

"My God! What are you doing?"

Hillary glanced at her, then put her hand to her chin as she studied the placement of the chair. "I thought I'd just tidy up a little bit before the police arrive, and I was just thinking, this chair here next to the fireplace would give the whole room a much cozier—"

"You did what? You tidied up?" There was that squeak in Jane's voice again.

"It looks better, don't you think? With those pillows on the other end of the sofa? And all that stuff she had on the coffee table just gave the room a cluttered look, so I—"

"Don't tell me any more!"

"What ever is wrong with you? This nervous habit you have concerns me. I can't have an assistant who—"

"Sit down, Hillary. Just sit down. Here on the sofa. No! Don't move that pillow." She grabbed Hillary's arm. "Better yet, we'll wait in the car."

"Wait? Wait for what?"

"For the police, for Christ's sake. They'll be here any minute. Don't say a word to them about moving the furniture around." Jane, still holding Hillary's arm, pulled her toward the door.

"What is wrong with you, Jane? You're acting like moving furniture is a crime," Hillary said as Jane hurried her to the car.

"It is." Jane opened the driver's side door for Hillary. She shoved her inside, then went around to the passenger side to open her own door.

"What do you mean, 'It is'?" Hillary said when Jane had sunk into the plush leather seat of the Cadillac.

"What you just did—moving that furniture, that sofa pillow, all that stuff on the coffee table. You could be charged with interfering with a crime scene and tampering with evidence."

"You don't mean it!" Hillary's face had gone pale.

Jane nodded her head gravely.

"Oh my lord!"

"Don't say anything when the police get here," Jane said. "Just let me do the talking."

"You're sure about this? After all, you only had two years of law school."

"I'm sure."

The police siren screamed at them from a distance and grew louder as the squad car got closer. They saw the flashing lights from four blocks away, and Jane noticed curtains move slightly in two of the large old houses across the street as the car came to a stop in front of Sylvia's home. A man got out of the car, sandy-haired, medium height, with broad shoulders: a square-jawed, clean-cut look. He was dressed in a suit and tie.

"Why that's Beaumont Jackson," Hillary said. "I did his house last year. Braided rugs, antique distressed oak, country prints. Beautiful. They loved it. I don't have a thing to worry about." She was already out of the car, waving. "Beau! Beau! It's me, Hillary Scarborough."

Jackson was walking toward the car, his movements quick and self-assured. His only acknowledgment of Hillary as he drew closer to the Cadillac was a curt, "Ms. Scarborough," and a slight nod of his head. He had walked up to Jane's side of the car and was now looking down at her through the open window.

"Ms. Ferguson?"

"Yes."

"You're the one who called." A statement not a question.

"Yes," Jane said.

"Would you get out of the car, please."

He stood back while she opened the door. Cautious. As if he expected her to have a gun.

"Which one of you found her?"

"She did," said Hillary from the other side of the Cadillac. "We both did," Jane said at the same time.

Jackson gave each of them a questioning look.

"Well . . ." Hillary said. "Jane saw her a few minutes before I did."

"Come inside with me while I have a look," Jackson said. He had already started for the front door. Jane and Hillary followed. "Who unlocked the door?" he asked, when he saw that it was still partially open.

"It was that way when we got here," Hillary said.

Jackson turned to look at both of them. "Did you touch the doorknob?"

"No," Hillary drawled. "It opened when I knocked."

"Wait here in the foyer," Jackson said when they were inside. He walked into the living room and glanced at Sylvia lying on the floor, then he stooped over her and touched her at the pulse point just below the jaw. *As if those dead, open eyes didn't say it all,* Jane thought.

Jackson stood and looked around the room. "Did you touch anything?" he asked.

"No!" Jane said a little too quickly. She glanced at Hillary. A dangerous look. "I mean no, no I didn't," she said, her voice quieter this time.

Jackson looked around the room, before he came back to the foyer and went down the hall, looking in all the rooms, including the kitchen.

"You really don't think he's going to mind if he finds out I did that tidying up, do you?" Hillary whispered.

"Shh!" Jane said. She moved cautiously toward the kitchen but stopped before she got to the door. She pressed herself close to the wall, hoping Jackson wouldn't see her. She could see his back, however, and she could see that, just as she expected him to, he had spied the blinking answering machine. She continued to watch as he pulled his handkerchief from his pocket, placed it over the end of his finger, and pushed the play button on the machine.

"This is Cy. I got you a sweetheart of a deal, sweetheart. Give me a call," the first message said.

There was a beep and the next message began. A different male voice said simply, "We need to talk," then there was a click and two beeps signaling the end of the messages.

As Jane turned around to hurry back to the foyer before Jackson saw her, she bumped into Hillary. She hadn't known she had followed her. Jane put her finger to her lips again and signaled for her to move away. By the time Jackson came out of the kitchen and headed for the stairs to check the rest of the house, the two women were in the foyer again.

"She certainly didn't have a very interesting life, judging by those phone messages," Hillary said.

"You just never know," Jane said.

"What do you mean by that?"

"Something in her life was interesting enough to get her killed."

"Hmmph!" Hillary said.

In a little while, Jackson came down the stairs and into the foyer where Jane and Hillary waited. He pulled a notebook from his hip pocket. "I want to get your names," he said. "Hillary Scarborough and Jane Ferguson?"

"Yes," they both said.

"Scarborough? You're the one has that TV program?"

"That's right," Hillary said, beaming.

"On channel four. Same time Miss Davis was on channel seven."

"Yes," Hillary said again.

"Her show was getting better ratings, I understand."

"Who told you that? You can make statistics say anything you want, you know. My show has quality and substance, not just a lot of blather about nasty old politics and—"

"I heard there was some hard feelings between the two of you."

Hillary's eyes widened, and for just a moment she looked like a frightened animal, but she quickly caught herself. "I don't know what you're talking about." She smiled sweetly and added, "You do remember me, don't you, Beau? I did your house. Distressed oak, country prints, the kitchen all in pink and green. Your wife is such a charming woman. Such good taste, and I'm sure you're—"

"She's not my wife anymore, and it's not my house anymore, either."

"Oh, I see. Well, your wife wasn't *that* charming, but I—"

"What were the two of you doing here?" Jackson asked.

"Miss Davis made an appointment with me to talk about doing her house," Hillary said. "She must have heard of my reputation. I'll give her credit for wanting quality, even if she did have that dreadful show—"

"She was here to see about redecorating Miss Davis's house," Jane said quickly before Hillary could talk herself into even more of a pickle.

"And you," Jackson said. "Why were you here?"

"I was interviewing for a job, and Hil—Mrs. Scarborough asked me to come along."

Jackson was busy writing notes on his pad as they spoke, but he quickly flipped it closed and said, "I'm going to have to ask you to come down to the station so I can question you further."

"I'll be glad to drop Jane off, if you can take her home when you've finished questioning her," Hillary said, her voice bright.

"I meant both of you," Jackson said with his usual short manner. His Southern accent did little to soften his tone. "You're not under arrest yet, so you can follow me in your car," he said, walking past them. He swung the door open and held it while Jane and Hillary walked out. Jane suspected it was as much to make sure they didn't touch the door as it was an act of chivalry.

"What did he mean, we're not under arrest yet?" Hillary whispered as they followed him out the door.

"I don't know," Jane whispered back.

Jane was grateful that the drive to the police station was a short one. She thought that having to endure a long stretch of Hillary's erratic driving after the emotional trauma of finding a dead body would have been more than she could take.

Jackson called Hillary into his office first. The time she was inside seemed interminable to Jane. There were no magazines in the waiting area to leaf through, and the only activity in the office occurred when a drunk was brought in. He'd been picked up in the Shoney's parking lot panhandling the tourists who habitually stopped there on their way to Panama Beach, just across the state line in Florida.

That was the way Prosper, Alabama, was supposed to be, Jane thought, a small town that no one noticed on the road to somewhere else, yet a pleasant enough place to live for its fifty thousand or so inhabitants, complete with its quaint little antique shops, fast-food chains, antebellum homes, sprawling modern ranch-style houses, a Civil War cemetery, and a water park. A place where the biggest crime was an occasional drunk or maybe a small-time burglary. Not a place where people were murdered.

Finally, forty-five minutes after Hillary had gone into Beaumont Jackson's office, Jackson opened the door and held it while Hillary, looking harried and tired, walked out.

"Wait out here, please, Ms. Scarborough. Ms. Ferguson, will you come into my office, please?"

Jackson's office was sparsely furnished with a large metal desk and a row of filing cabinets. His desk was cluttered with stacks of papers, pink telephone messages, a couple of books, and what was once a white mug, turned brown from coffee. A small bouquet of roses—yellow, red, and pink—sat on one corner of the desk in a water-filled canning jar. The only photograph on his desk was of a horse—sleek and beautiful.

"Have a seat," he said, indicating the straight-backed chair upholstered in orange tweed that sat in front of his desk. When he was seated behind his desk, he said, "Now, tell me exactly what happened." Here was a man who took his job seriously, Jane thought, noticing the perpetual worried look he had, the way his hazel eyes seemed to be scrutinizing her for suspicious signs, the quick, practiced movement of switching on the tape recorder.

"Well, it's like I told you before. When we got to Sylvia's house, Hillary knocked on the door several times, but there was no answer, and since the door was partially open, she pushed it open all the way and called her name. When there was still no answer, we walked inside and found her on the floor."

"She was dead when you arrived?"

"She looked dead to me."

"Did you touch anything?"

"No, I didn't," Jane said, her heart pounding, hoping he wouldn't ask her whether or not Hillary had touched anything. She didn't want to lie, but she didn't want Hillary in any trouble, either, since what she had done was done innocently. Or perhaps ignorantly.

"How long have you known Ms. Scarborough?"

"I just met her today. Like I told you, I was interviewing for a job with her, and she asked me to go along with her to Miss Davis's house to talk to her about redecorating."

"Had Ms. Scarborough ever been to Miss Davis's house before?"

"I don't think so. She seemed surprised at her decorating scheme, so that led me to believe she'd never been there before."

"How well did you know Miss Davis?"

"Not at all. I mean, I've seen her TV show a time or two, but I've never met her."

"How well did Ms. Scarborough know her?"

"I don't know. I assumed she didn't know her at all. They were . . ." Jane suddenly knew where these questions were leading, and she didn't want to continue.

"They were what, Ms. Ferguson?"

"Nothing."

"Were you maybe about to say they were rivals?"

"Well, that's what you said, but I—I really don't know if they . . ." Jane was beginning to sweat, and she had that knot forming in her stomach. She wasn't sure how much more she should say.

"They were on at the same time on local channels, weren't they?"

"Well yes, but—"

"And wasn't Miss Davis cutting into Ms. Scarborough's ratings?"

"I'm not sure. I mean, I don't keep up with television ratings. I've been too busy going to school and raising my kid, but surely you don't think—"

"Going to school? Aren't you a little old for that?"

"Lots of people go to law school when they're older."

"Law school? Up in Tuscaloosa?"

"Yes."

"Long drive every day, isn't it?"

"Well . . ."

"I've got a second or third cousin with the same last name as yours who went to law school there. Jim Ed Ferguson. Know him?"

"I've heard of him, yes."

"Criminal lawyer. Used to defend all the deadbeats I brought in."

"Ummm."

"Never met his wife. I heard they divorced. Jim Ed moved to Birmingham."

"Did he?"

"Yep. I also heard he's out of criminal law. Now he's representing insurance companies. Gettin' rich, I guess."

Jane was thinking that he probably was, but it certainly wasn't reflected in his child-support payments. Jackson was still talking.

"You wouldn't be his ex-wife, would you?"

He'd caught her off guard, but she recovered quickly. "It's better than being his current wife."

For the first time, Jackson laughed. "Ol' Jim Ed always was a son of a bitch, pardon my French." He scrutinized her again. "You're not from around here, are you?"

"No, I'm from California."

Jackson was still giving her a long, penetrating look while he tapped his notebook with his pencil. "Well, Ms. Ferguson from California, if you recall anything you may not have told me, particularly anything Ms. Scarborough did or said, I would appreciate it if you would give me a call."

"Is she a suspect?"

"Let's just say I would appreciate it if neither one of you left town for a few days."

"You mean I'm a suspect, too?"

"You both found the body, Ms. Ferguson. I may need to question you again."

"Look, you've probably known Hillary Scarborough all your life. You must know she couldn't do anything like that."

"How do you know that?" he asked. The slight frown had returned to his forehead. "I thought you said you didn't know her."

"Well, I don't, but—"

"As a matter of fact, I haven't known Ms. Scarborough all my life. She grew up in a little town thirty miles from here."

"Oh, so that makes her suspect, does it? That must mean I'm really in trouble, being from California."

"Did you have a reason to want Sylvia Davis out of the way?"

"Of course not, and neither did—"

"Why are you protecting Ms. Scarborough?"

"I don't know what you mean."

"Why didn't you tell me she moved that furniture around when I asked you?"

He had once again caught her by surprise. She opened her mouth to speak but could think of nothing to say that wouldn't get her into even more trouble.

"I saw the indentations on the carpet where the chair used to be. Was there a reason for moving it? Was she trying to cover up something?"

"I—I don't think so. She just thought the chair would look better there, and—"

"I may have to hold you both for tampering with a crime scene."

"Both? But I didn't touch—"

"Like I said, Ms. Ferguson, don't leave town." He was out of his chair, opening the door for her, and she seemed to have no choice but to leave.

Hillary stood up as soon as Jane entered the waiting area.

"What did he say to you? Did he ask you questions about me?" she whispered.

"Let's go to the car," Jane said.

When they were both inside the Cadillac, Hillary turned to her with a worried look. "Well?" she said.

"I think we're both suspects," Jane said, "but I think you top the list."

"But why would he suspect *me*?"

"Because you and Sylvia were professional rivals, and because he thinks you may have tampered with the crime scene, and because there doesn't seem to be any other suspects or any other motives at the moment."

"But that's ridiculous. We're the ones who called the police—"

"The investigation's just begun, Hillary. Try not to worry."

"That's easy for you to say. You're not the number-one suspect. And besides, what does that Beaumont Jackson know? Did you see that office of his? Doesn't he know orange went out with harvest gold in the seventies?" She started the car and pulled out of the parking space with a lurch. "You've got to help me, Jane," she said.

"Help you? What do you mean?"

"Well, if you're going to be my executive assistant, I'm going to expect you to help me prove I had nothing to do with this."

"Hey, wait a minute, I haven't accepted the job yet,

and besides, your ad didn't say anything about helping you prove your innocence in a murder.''

"Jane, don't get bogged down in technicalities. My reputation is at stake. You know I had nothing to do with killing Sylvia Davis. You were with me when we found her. And besides that, you're a lawyer.''

"I'm not a lawyer. I'm a former law student, and I don't want to get mixed up in this.''

"Help me, Jane. I'm desperate. I'll—I'll up the salary two hundred a month.''

"The first thing we have to do,'' said Jane, "is try to find out who might have wanted Sylvia dead.''

3

Jane was in the kitchen, sitting at the table, looking at a new crop of bills, when the front door slammed and Sarah called to her.

"Hi, Mom. I'm home."

Sarah's arrivals sometimes reminded Jane of the whirlwinds that she used to see sweeping across the desert in California. Her daughter's Rollerblades made a rackety-rackety sound as she glided into the kitchen. She dropped her schoolbooks on the table, then sat on the floor to remove her skates.

"Hello, sweetheart," Jane said. She pushed the bills aside and began absentmindedly leafing through a cookbook.

"Did you get the job?"

"Did I get . . . ? Oh, yes. Yes, I did," Jane said, distracted. It was hard to keep her mind focused when she kept remembering the dead body on the floor of that big house.

"Mom? Are you all right?"

For the first time, Sarah had her full attention. "Of course, why do you ask?"

"You seem so—I don't know—zoned out or something. Aren't you *glad* you got the job?"

"Of course. The hours are flexible so I can be home when you need me. The pay's not bad. Much better than I expected."

"Then why aren't you happy?"

Jane looked at her daughter, marveling at her perception. "Well, I guess I had a—well, a sort of upsetting day."

"You had another argument with Daddy."

"Oh, no, nothing like that. It was—do you remember we were talking about Sylvia Davis and her TV show?"

Sarah nodded.

"Well, Sylvia had called Hillary to redecorate her house, and I went with her today, and . . ." Jane stopped, constricted.

"And what, Mommy?" Sarah wore a look of deep concern.

"We found her dead."

Sarah sucked in her breath. "You mean, like, not breathing?"

Jane nodded.

"Oh, Mommy!" She ran to Jane and wrapped her arms around her waist. In a little while, she pulled away from her. "You remember when my friend Shakura's brother died?"

"Yes, of course."

"Her mom went to a therapist up in Montgomery. It seemed to help her. I can get the therapist's name for you if you want."

Jane gave her daughter another hug. "That's very sweet of you, honey. Just give me some time. I don't think I'll need a therapist. This isn't quite the same thing. Not like a relative dying." Jane remembered how Shakura Young and her mother had grieved when young Rashaud drove himself off an embankment near Landry Lake, supposedly after a night of drinking. He had been working late as a busboy at a restaurant out by the lake, then, according to news accounts, had several drinks on the way home from work, and there had been a bottle found in his car. She remembered the funeral—the first time she had ever been to a black religious service in the South—and how Thelma Young had refused to believe her son could have been drinking at all, much less drinking enough to drive himself into a lake. No, this was not like that at all. The death of one's own child would be far, far more difficult to bear.

"Did she have a heart attack or something?" Sarah asked, slathering peanut butter on a piece of bread.

"What are you doing?" Jane asked. "You won't eat your dinner if you eat that."

"Peanut butter's high in protein. It's good for me. And, anyway, did she die of a heart attack?"

"No, she was—murdered."

Sarah dropped the knife on the floor. "No way!"

Jane could only nod. Gravely.

"Do they know who did it?"

"Well, they have a couple of suspects."

"Who?"

"Uh . . . I don't think the police are releasing any names."

"You really found the body, Mom? Did you have to go to the police station and make a report and get finger-printed? Did you look at one of those lineups where all the criminals walk in front of you behind a window and there's always a cop in the lineup to throw you off, and—"

"Sarah, you watch entirely too much television."

"Well, gosh, I guess this means everybody will go back to watching Hillary Scarborough's show again, won't they?" Sarah said as she reached down to retrieve the knife she'd dropped.

"Odd that you should think of that."

Sarah let that remark pass and sauntered over to the table. "What's that you're reading?"

"Oh, just a cookbook."

"A cookbook? Geez, Mom, you're not going to try to cook again, are you?"

"No, I'm not going to cook, but I have to produce a

television show next week, and Hillary wants me to find a recipe for coq au vin. So far, I haven't found one. Guess I'll have to make one up."

"That should be interesting," Sarah said.

Jane closed the cookbook and used it to give Sarah a playful tap on her bottom. "Get your shoes on, and I'll take you to Morrison's Cafeteria. You need a balanced meal."

"Couldn't we just have a pizza delivered?"

"We had pizza last night, Sarah, and anyway, our telephone's been turned off."

"You didn't pay the bill again?"

"I *couldn't* pay the bill again. But don't worry. Now that I have this job, things will be different."

Morrison's was a short five-minute drive away. *Quicker and certainly easier than cooking*, Jane thought. She had hoped to keep Sarah's mind off of Sylvia Davis and her death while they ate, but Sarah seemed determined to play detective.

"There must be lots more than a couple of suspects," she said, munching the salad that Jane insisted she eat. "I mean, she must have had a lot of enemies. She was always having some politician on her show and asking him stuff about how he spent money and if he had affairs. That's why I didn't like to watch her. It was kind of boring."

"Try not to think about any of this, Sarah," Jane said. "The police will handle it just fine, I'm sure." She was thinking about what Sarah had just said, though, and making a mental note to see if she could manage to view tapes of some of Sylvia's shows to get an idea of who, besides Hillary, might have had a grudge against her.

It was easier than she had thought. She had simply to call the television station and make an appointment to see the tapes. The station kept them on file for one month, so she asked to see the entire month.

"It's going to take at least two full days," Jane said to Hillary as she sat in her office.

"Of course you have to do it," Hillary said. "Your

daughter is right; she must have made lots of people mad at her. I just wish I could go down to channel seven with you and see the tapes for myself, but that would look tacky, wouldn't it?''

''It would, Hillary. It would look tacky.''

''Most stations will sell you copies of the tapes for thirty dollars or so. If there are any you think I should see, just buy them and bring them to me. Oh, and I had Lilly clear out the office next door to me for you.''

''Lilly?''

''My receptionist. There's a nice desk and a filing cabinet in that office. Cherry, so it matches the rest of the furniture. I was thinking magenta and hunter green for the decor, what do you think?''

''Magenta?''

''It can be so warm and inviting while at the same time *élégant et d'un goût raffiné.*''

''Oh, yeah, sure.''

''And about that coq au vin recipe—I'll need it by tomorrow. It's for a show we're filming at Mayor Sedgewick's house. All about how they entertain at dinner parties, and Nancy Sedgewick *specifically* requested coq au vin. Something she tried in France, she said. It should be kitchen tested before you give it to me, because it's supposed to be from Nancy's own recipe file. If I know Nancy, she'll test it again herself. You understand, don't you? I told her I'd come up with one. You can test it tonight for dinner.''

''Sure I can.''

Well, at least it's a job, Jane thought, as she made her way to the television station.

The clerk at the station was helpful. She showed Jane where the archives were and how to view them. She was also chatty.

''The whole station's in a state of shock over Miss Davis getting killed,'' she said. ''I just can't believe it. I mean, you see her eating her salad in the lunchroom one day, and the next, she's dead.''

''Yes, I'm sure it was a shock,'' Jane said, hoping the

young woman wouldn't recognize her name, which she
had given her in order to view the tapes. Hers as well as
Hillary's name had been on the television news as the
ones who had found Sylvia's body.

"She used to come in here to the archives all the time,
too. She'd look at her old tapes to see how she could
change her interviewing style or how she could change
her hair to look younger. She was real professional."

"Ummm," Jane said, determined to remain noncom-
mittal. The less she said, the less the young woman would
learn about her.

"I always tried to be nice to her, though, in spite of
everything."

"In spite of everything?"

"Well, yeah, I mean, you know, she wasn't the easiest
to get along with. She was what you'd call a perfectionist.
Dave Malone was the only one who really liked her."

"Dave Malone? That name sounds familiar," Jane
said, in spite of the fact that she had never heard it before.
She was searching for some way to keep the young
woman talking.

"Oh, you must be one of those people who reads the
credits after a show. He used to be one of our producers."

"Oh, *that* Dave Malone."

"He was just crazy about her. She wouldn't give him
the time of day hardly."

"Really?"

"Poor guy. Got so he couldn't hardly work he was so
lovesick. Finally, he just quit. I heard he's selling cars
now. But, you know, it wasn't too long after he quit working here that they started going out together."

"Did you say he's selling cars?"

"Yeah, over in Montgomery? You've seen him. Does
all those commercials for Crazy Dan's Used Cars?
Dresses up like a chicken, takes a bath in Jell-O, all that
stuff."

"Oh, you mean Cyclone Malone."

"Yeah, that's him. Calls himself Cyclone now that he's
a car salesman. You've heard his commercial, haven't

you? 'Cyclone Malone, dealing up a storm.' I hear he's doing real good. Manager of the place now. Gives all of us that works here at the station a good deal on his cars. I heard even Sylvia was fixin' to buy one from him. Can you believe that? After the way she treated him?''

"Hard to believe." Jane was remembering the message on the answering machine tape. It was something about a sweetheart of a deal from someone named Cy.

"Poor thing," the clerk continued. "What happened to her, I mean. Who woulda thought?''

"Not me."

"You work for the cops or something?''

"Who, me?''

"Well, I just thought maybe you were, you know, like, investigating the murder?''

"Oh! No, it's for—for a paper I'm writing for—uh, a college course. It's about women in television.''

"Oh, well, good luck," the young woman said. She gave her a little wave and went back to her desk in the reception area, and Jane got down to the business of viewing the tapes.

It didn't take long to learn that Sarah had been at least partially right about Sylvia Davis's show. There did seem to be a lot of politicians sitting there sweating because they had been accused of misappropriating money or having affairs. There were long discussions about taxes and zoning laws and election returns and other minutiae of local politics. It was late in the day before Jane found that one of the tapes featured Chester Collins, a city alderman, who also happened to be the minister of a local church, and who was suspected of using his government expense account to help pay for a personal vacation in Florida. Sylvia hit him hard with questions about how the money was spent, how he justified such expenditures, and what possible connection the Pelican Bar and Lounge in Miami could have to city government in Prosper, Alabama. There were also some questions about some items he purchased at Naughty Nighty and Paraphernalia while he was there. Particularly a lot about paraphernalia. Sylvia showed herself to be an astute, hard-hitting journalist who showed no fear. Reverend Collins was, indeed, sweating by the time the show ended.

Jane went back the next day to watch the rest of the tapes, but before she did, she stopped by her new office to apprise Hillary of what she had learned so far and to use the telephone to call Crazy Dan's in Montgomery and ask for Cyclone Malone. He apparently knew Sylvia rather well, and she had spurned him. That could be a motive. Weak, perhaps, but people had killed for less. He was not available, the receptionist who answered the phone said, but he would call her back. Jane left her office number since she couldn't get her home telephone reconnected until she got her first paycheck.

There was nothing of interest in the second day's tapes she previewed until the show that aired the day before Sylvia's death. This time, a woman, Regina Conyers, who had announced her candidacy for a congressional seat, was being grilled about another bit of dirt Sylvia had dug up. In this case, it was an unaccounted-for shortfall in the charity Ms. Conyers had formerly directed.

It was four o'clock by the time Jane had watched all of the available tapes of Sylvia's shows. She had three possible leads: the naughty reverend, the would-be congresswoman, and a television producer turned used car salesman. What she did not have, she realized, just as she pulled into her driveway, was a recipe for coq au vin. She had meant to go to the library to search for a recipe, but today was Wednesday, the day the library closed at noon—the result of recent budget cuts. Why was it libraries always got cut before sports stadiums and local ball teams?

No time to ponder the inequities of that now, though; she had to create a recipe. But first she had to drive Sarah to soccer practice. Sarah was waiting for her on the front steps already in her soccer uniform, when Jane pulled into the driveway. Guilt stabbed through her. A good mother would be home when her daughter got there.

"You're late," Sarah said as she slid into the seat next to her.

"Sorry, honey."

"Mrs. Scarborough came by."

"Oh?"

"She said you were supposed to bring her a recipe. Some kind of cocoa or something."

"Coq au vin."

"What's that?"

"I'm not sure. I think it's chicken with vinegar."

"Well, anyway, she wants it. I told her we had soccer practice, so she said bring it over to her house when we're done. She said Mayor Sedgewick and his wife would be there. Here's her address," Sarah said, handing Jane a slip of paper.

"Oh, yes, they're going to be on her show."

"And you'll get to meet them?"

"I suppose."

"Gee, Mom, now that you're in television do you think maybe you'll get to meet someone really important someday? Like Oprah?"

"You never know."

Jane spent the entire hour of soccer practice worrying about a recipe for coq au vin and wondering where she could find one. She decided, finally, to write down her mother's recipe for chicken soup, but to add a little vinegar, and maybe some wine. How much? A whole bottle of wine maybe—the French were big drinkers—and a cup or so of vinegar should do.

That out of the way, she tried to relax and enjoy watching her daughter on the soccer field. She might have been able to do that if she hadn't caught sight of Beau Jackson cruising around the field. He wasn't in a blue-and-white police car, just an ordinary Chevrolet. Was he watching her? Was he really serious about thinking she had killed Sylvia Davis?

The whole idea made her more than a little uncomfortable. She was eager for soccer practice to end so she could drop the recipe off and go home. There was something about the safety of one's own four walls that was comforting.

She tried not to let Sarah's request to go out for pizza with the coach and the rest of the team upset her, in spite of the fact that her instinct was to gather her child up under her wing and protect her from the world right now. There was certainly no point in upsetting Sarah or even in letting her know how uncomfortable she was. In the end, she gave her permission for Sarah to go with the team. The coach, Liz Dobson, would bring her home, she said, so Jane set off for Hillary Scarborough's house.

It was a large house, larger even than Sylvia Davis's, and built in antebellum style. It was old and beautiful, and, Jane supposed, probably full of things like walnut glue-gunned turkeys.

"Jane, thank God you're here," Hillary said, when she met her at the door. She was holding a Pekingese in one arm. The little dog, festooned with pink ribbons, greeted Jane with two high-pitched yips, then growled menacingly.

"Martha, you naughty girl!" Hillary said. She stepped aside for Jane to enter. The house was beautifully furnished in the same old-South monied style as Hillary's office, and with the same sweet smell of potpourri simmering somewhere. "Mayor Sedgewick and his wife are in the drawing room," Hillary said in a half whisper. "I didn't want to keep them waiting any longer. This is my *big* opportunity, Jane."

Jane gave her a weak smile. It was the first time in her life she had ever heard anyone actually use the term *drawing room*.

Hillary was still exuding her excitement. "Just think, the mayor's dinner party planned on my show! Can you imagine! Oh lord, I wish Sylvia was still alive so I could gloat. Just wait until you see what it does for my ratings. Do you have the recipe? But first, tell me what you found today."

"I found a couple of people with a motive. Just need to do a little more investigating."

"I knew you could do it, Jane!"

Jane pulled the hastily scribbled recipe from her hand-bag and handed it to Hillary. "Here's the recipe," she said. "Call me if you have any questions."

"What do you mean, call you? You have to stay. Come and meet Arnold and Nancy."

"Arnold and Nancy?"

"The Sedgewicks. The mayor, honey," Hillary said in her syrupy voice. "I'd like you to meet my husband, too, but he's away on one of his safaris in Georgia."

"Safari? In Georgia?"

"Oh, you know, bird hunting. Billy loves hiding under bushes and making noises like a duck." Hillary was pulling Jane along toward the drawing room as she spoke.

A tall man, who looked to be in his late sixties, with a full head of thick white hair, stood as they entered the room. He was not quite portly, but he had gone to fat around the middle and at the jowls.

A woman, whom Jane assumed was his wife, remained seated on one of the Queen Anne sofas. She appeared younger than her husband by about twenty years. She had, perhaps, once been beautiful, but her face now was a bit too puffy, either from too many collagen injections or from middle-aged water retention. It was hard to tell. Her carefully coiffed blond hair was a bit too dry, as well, but she was impeccably elegant-casual in a coral silk pant suit with nails and lipstick to match.

"Mayor and Mrs. Sedgewick, may I present Jane Fer-guson, my new executive assistant," Hillary said, etiquette-book correct.

"How do you do, Miz Ferguson," the mayor said. His wife gave her a condescending smile and gazed, disap-provingly, at the navy blue dress Sarah had picked out for her to wear that morning.

"Hello, Arny. Hi, Nancy," Jane said. The strain of the day had made her weary enough to forget for a moment that she wasn't in California anymore. The Sedgewicks gave her a look that was part stunned and part disapprov-ing. Martha growled again.

A little nervous laugh came from Hillary. "Jane and I both have had a rather trying day. We're not quite ourselves, are we, Jane? I'm sure you saw the six o'clock news," she said, turning back to the Sedgewicks. "More about us being the ones who discovered Sylvia Davis's body. But I'm not at all worried now that Jane is on the case."

"We were on the news again?" Jane sat down in the chair opposite the Sedgewicks, who were both on the sofa.

"Oh my, yes. They keep doing all these follow-ups. The reporters called me at home, but I wouldn't talk to them. You can't trust reporters, you know. Didn't they call you?"

"I don't know. My phone's been . . . uh, out of order, and anyway, I was at soccer practice all evening."

"Soccer practice?" Mrs. Sedgewick said, as if soccer practice was somehow disgraceful.

Hillary turned back to the mayor and still chattered on, all the while stroking Martha's head. "Jane has been investigating, and she's found the real murderer."

Jane tried to interrupt. "I didn't say—"

Hillary ignored her. "There are things going on in this world you'd never believe, Arnold, and there's even a used car salesman who probably knows the whole story."

"Good lord!" The mayor looked shocked.

Hillary turned to Jane. "I'm surprised some reporter didn't corner you while you were down at the TV station."

"TV station?" the mayor asked.

"Just a little assignment. For Hillary," Jane said before Hillary could explain anything. She thought it best that they not divulge any more details about her snooping than Hillary had already done, lest it get back to Jackson and he saw it as meddling.

"This whole thing will be over before you know it," Hillary gushed. "Jane is so clever. She's practically a lawyer, you know. She knows how to find out these things. And I must say it can't be any too soon. You have no idea." Hillary put a hand to her forehead.

"I'm sure it was tryin' on both of y'all to find the body," the mayor said.

"Oh yes," Hillary agreed.

"And don't you worry your pretty little heads about Beau Jackson puttin' y'all right up there on the list of suspects."

Jane felt a sudden void in her chest and glanced at Hillary, whose face had grown white. She looked as if she might drop Martha. Nevertheless, Hillary managed to speak in her syrupy voice. "Why, mayor, what ever would make you think that we . . . ?"

"I had a conference with Beau, of course. As the mayor, I have to keep abreast of these things."

"We're not *really* suspects," Jane said. "I mean, we haven't been arrested or formally—"

"Well, of course you're not." The mayor gave her a wave of dismissal. "Like I said, don't worry your pretty little heads." He turned to Hillary. "You were smart not to talk to the media, my dear." He pronounced the word *deah*. "I have found the less you have to deal with them, the better off you are."

"And anyway. I told you, Jane has this all figured out," Hillary insisted.

"It's such a terrible thing to happen during our administration," Mrs. Sedgewick said.

"A terrible thing to happen at any time." Jane rubbed her throbbing temples. She was going to have to talk to Hillary, convince her somehow that she did *not* have this all figured out.

Mrs. Sedgewick gave her another of her condescending smiles.

"Oh, now, girls, can't we find somethin' more pleasant to talk about?" Mayor Sedgewick said. "Anyway, I'm sure it was just an accident of some kind." He smiled at Jane.

"The police are calling it homicide," his wife said with some impatience.

The mayor ignored her, nevertheless. "Hillary is very

lucky to have you workin' for her,'' he said, smiling at Jane again.

"Thank you," Jane said.

"I didn't know you were a lawyuh, though."

"I'm not really a lawyer, I just—"

"Lawyer? That rings a bell. Oh, of course. *Now* I know who you are," Mrs. Sedgewick said. "You're Jim Ed's ex-wife. Jim Ed. Now *there's* a lawyer. Fine boy. He's married to my niece now, you know."

"I'm sure your niece deserves him. A fine boy like him, I mean," Jane said with her best smile.

Somewhere in the house, the telephone rang. Jane expected Hillary to hurry off and answer it, but she ignored it and, instead, she said with a show of mild shock, "Oh lord, you married your cousin."

"Shouldn't we discuss this television show?" Jane said, desperate to get the conversation off of both murder and her former marriage. If it weren't for the fact that Jim Ed had written into the divorce settlement that she would lose child support if she left the state, she would go somewhere faraway, Alaska maybe, where nobody ever heard of Jim Ed Ferguson or his ex-wife.

"Oh we have it practically all planned," Hillary said. "I have a special segment on making your own paper for the invitations and the name cards for the place settings. Then there's the segment on fresh flowers from the garden. You know, how to grow them, how to arrange them. And, of course, the menu. We'll be demonstrating how to prepare the main dish as well as how to prepare the edible flowers."

"You're going to eat flowers?"

Martha couldn't keep her eyes off of Jane. She growled and yipped again.

"Excuse me," a voice said, before anyone could answer Jane's question. It was the maid. She actually had on a black dress and a white apron, which Jane found almost as incredible as edible flowers. "Telephone for Mayor Sedgewick," she said.

"Here, take Martha away for me, will you, Millie?

She's being naughty.'' Hillary said, handing the dog to the maid.

''Is the recipe kitchen tested?'' Mrs. Sedgewick asked.

''Many times,'' Jane said. ''It's my mother's recipe.''

''Your mother made coq au vin?'' Mrs. Sedgewick looked down her restructured nose.

''Oh yes, it was a favorite in the trailer park.''

Hillary seemed oblivious to the exchange. ''I think an elegant pant suit would be best for the first segment, don't you, Nancy? Something like the one you're wearing?''

''Oh, I could never wear this old thing anywhere important. I was thinking of something in black,'' Mrs. Sedgewick said.

''Perfect!''

Hillary and Mrs. Sedgewick went on with their planning, leaving Jane to her throbbing head. Nancy was saying she wanted to test the recipe herself, and Hillary was assuring her everything would go well. Jane hoped she could leave soon. She wanted a hot shower and an aspirin, and she wanted to be home by the time Sarah got there.

The mayor bustled into the room, interrupting them. ''I'm afraid we're going to have to leave, Hillary, dear. One of the aldermen wants to go over that new tax proposal with me.''

Mrs. Sedgewick stood. ''Well, of course, darling.'' She glanced at Hillary. ''Being the wife of a statesman, you can never keep a normal schedule.''

''Oh, I'm sure you're right, lamb!'' Hillary gushed.

Hillary saw them to the door, and once they were out, she turned away and click-clacked her way back into the drawing room.

''Where does that woman get her nerve? What did she mean she could never wear that thing she had on anywhere *important*? She thinks coming to my house isn't *important*? I can tell you, it doesn't matter what she wears, she'll still look like white trash.'' She glanced at Jane with a stricken look. ''You didn't mean what you said about the trailer park, did you? I mean if you did, then I don't mean white trash is *bad*. No, what I mean is, even if you did marry your cousin—"

"Relax, Hillary."

"How can I relax? The mayor's wife insults me. The chief of police thinks I'm a murderer . . ."

Jane kicked her shoes off and brought her feet up on the chair. "I think we have a chance of pointing the suspicion somewhere else. But, listen to me, Hillary. That doesn't mean I have this figured out."

"Oh, I know you don't, dear, I just said that to help us all relax. But you're close, aren't you? I mean, you have to be. I can't take this much longer. And where are we going to point suspicion?" Hillary looked and sounded as weary as Jane felt.

"Well, you weren't too far off when you mentioned the used car salesman, although you shouldn't have, Hillary. We shouldn't talk about this to anyone. The mayor might mention all this to Beau."

"Oh dear, getting mixed up with murder is so complicated." She shook her head. "But tell me, what else have you learned?"

"Remember those two messages on Sylvia's answering machine? One said something about her car being ready?"

"Well, I kinda remember."

"Get this. She apparently was going out with that guy. He's the used car salesman with all the dopey television commercials. Cyclone Malone."

"Nooo! Sylvia? Dating a used car salesman!" Hillary laughed, then sobered quickly. "Oh, I know I shouldn't speak ill of the dead, but isn't that just what you would expect of someone who had red drapes?"

"It may just be a blind alley, but I'm going to try to talk to him, nevertheless."

"Of course. And I'll go with you. I need to do some shopping in Montgomery, anyway."

"OK, but I'll drive."

Jane stayed only a few minutes longer—long enough

to drink a soothing cup of tea made from herbs Hillary said she had grown and dried herself.

When she left Hillary's house, she didn't notice the headlights in her rearview mirror at first, not until she made the second turn and saw how closely the car was following. Her route took her from Hillary's old, elegant neighborhood to where she lived in the newer Meadowview Acres on the outskirts of town. When she turned onto the stretch of unlighted rural highway, the sides overgrown with hickory, cypress, and pine, the car was still behind her.

Then, suddenly, the car was too close. Jane accelerated. The car behind her accelerated as well and bumped her small Toyota from behind. Icy fear gripped her and brought cold sweat to her forehead and down her stiffened back. She tried to accelerate again, but the Toyota's small engine was giving her all it could. The headlights behind her were blinding when she looked into the rearview mirror, but she could tell that the car was now trying to pass her.

She slowed, hoping the game would be over once the car had passed, then accelerated again when she realized the driver could possibly have a gun pointed at her. The car continued to move around her, but with very little space between them. She had to swerve to keep the driver from hitting her. She righted her car, only to have the menacing vehicle move in close behind her again.

It was impossible to tell the make of the car because of the unlighted road. She could tell only that it seemed to be a large sedan, dark in color.

As Jane approached a curve, the car behind her moved up beside her again, dangerously close, and forced her to the left side of the road. She looked quickly to the right, hoping to see the driver, but he hid behind dark tinted windows. Suddenly the lights of another vehicle coming from around the darkened curve loomed in front of her, headed straight for her. A scream froze in her throat, and she felt as if her head would burst. At the last instant before an inevitable head-on crash, the vehicle turned with a jerk, and she saw the pickup pass on her right side.

The driver of the dark sedan had apparently seen what was coming and had headed straight for the ditch on the left side of the road. Dirt from the roadside flew into the darkened night as the car's tires ground and spun, trying to move out of the ditch. Jane took advantage of the moment and pressed her accelerator to the floor.

She drove at top speed, watching for the car behind her until she came to the first road, an unpaved path overhung with trees. She turned onto the road and switched off her lights. Her heart was racing and her breath came in short, uneven gasps.

She waited and watched through her rearview mirror.

Finally, a dark sedan drove past the intersection. Her hands, which she realized had been gripping the steering wheel, relaxed. Jane slowly turned her head from the mirror and screamed when she saw a face staring at her through the open window.

4

The eyes staring at Jane widened, then the face came closer to hers. It was a big, grizzled face with heavy jowls and loose, thick lips. She heard a man's voice. She wasn't sure what he said. She was too preoccupied with trying to remember how to start the car. How to make it go forward and away from whoever was about to attack her through her open window.

The man spoke again. "You all right, miss?"

"No, I'm not all right!" she screeched. The Toyota wouldn't start. It did that sometimes—failed when she tried to start the engine too soon after it had been turned off. She turned the ignition again, heard the grinding noise again, heard the man's voice again.

"I seen your car when you come off the highway. Thought you might be in trouble."

She kept up her frantic attempt at starting the car, and turned once again toward the man, realizing he had made no move to open the door, no move to reach inside and grab her.

"I was out settin' some traps, and I seen you, like I say, and I was thinkin', *Well, now that's funny*. The motor died and the lights went out, so I thought I'd just walk over here, and—"

"Everything's OK. Nothing wrong, nothing wrong." Jane, still cautious, was trying to roll up the window, but the stranger's beefy arms were resting on it, prohibiting her. Still, he made no move toward her. He simply watched. Jane's heart pummeled her chest and her breath was coming in short gasps.

"I think you got 'er flooded. Just let 'er set a minute or two, then try again," the man said.

It seemed to Jane now that it would make no difference what she did, the car wasn't going to start. She was trapped.

"What you doin', anyhow? I mean, how come you come flying off the highway like that, then turn your lights out?"

"Oh, well, I—I took a wrong turn, that's all."

The man eyed her suspiciously. "You runnin' from the cops?"

"No, no, I—"

"Ah hell, it don't bother me none if that's what you was a doin'. I got my own problems with the law."

"Oh?" Jane's fear rose again.

"Burglary. Grand theft." There was pride in his voice. "I'm what you call a professional."

"Oh, I'm sure you are."

"Hell, a man's gotta live, you know."

"Oh, yes."

"I tell you what, you just keep your lights out till you get back to the highway, then you kinda blend in with the traffic, you most likely lose 'em. Some a them cops are dumber than a jackass. Didn't look like they follered you off the road nohow."

"I hope not."

"Go ahead, try it."

"What?"

"Try startin' your engine."

"Oh, of course." She tried again and heard the welcome sound of the pistons firing.

"Now, you do like I say; you ease up on the highway," the man said, still leaning on her door.

"I will, I will."

He still hadn't moved his heavy arms from the door. "If the worst happens and you get caught and you need a good lawyer, I know one."

"Thanks, I'll remember that." Jane was trying to decide whether or not she should try to speed away while he still leaned on the window.

"Name's Ferguson, and he's— Say! That's why you look familiar. I knowed I'd seen you before. You're his old lady. I'm Buddy Fletcher, remember me?" He stuck out his beefy hand.

"Buddy? Oh, yes." Jane felt shaky with relief. Buddy was one of a string of petty criminals Jim Ed had defended when the court had appointed him as a public defender for those who couldn't afford to pay a lawyer. She remembered this one's name only because Jim Ed had been so proud of himself for getting him off with his clever defense. He had, in fact, gloated about it for weeks.

"How is ol' Jim Ed, anyhow?"

"I wouldn't know; we're divorced. He moved to Birmingham." Jane immediately regretted saying that. Maybe Buddy wouldn't like it if she was divorced from his hero.

"Well, I'll swan," Buddy said, shaking his head. "Sure sorry to hear that." He brightened a little and straightened his back. "If you ever need anything, you just let me know. Ol' Jim Ed took care of me, so I'll take care of his woman for him."

"I'm not his . . . I'll remember that, Buddy." She slipped the car into drive, gave Buddy a smile, and, with great relief, drove away.

She got back to her house only minutes before Coach Dobson pulled into the driveway and dropped off Sarah. Jane felt another moment of relief when she saw her daughter. She would not have wanted Sarah to be home alone, but she didn't want her out there on the streets, either, not even with Lisa Dobson, whom she trusted implicitly. Trust and reason had lost their logic for Jane now. It made no sense that anyone would want to harm Sarah, but neither did it make sense that anyone would try to run her down on the highway. Or did it? Had she gotten too close to finding a motive in all that digging she'd done at the television station? If that were true, how could any of those people who might have a motive to kill Sylvia know what she had done? But if they did somehow know, couldn't they also know about Sarah?

There were no answers, only fear now, and the instinctive need to gather her young to her bosom.

Sarah was in a talkative mood. "Mom, guess what! Coach Dobson said if I keep improving, I might get to play sweeper when we play the Goldtoes next week."

"That's nice, honey." She didn't want to think of Sarah playing sweeper out on that soccer field, unprotected.

"Did you see me when I dribbled the ball?"

"Yes, of course I did. You were wonderful."

"It needs work, though. That's what Coach Dobson said, so I'm going to practice out on the playground after school, and then Shakura's mom is going to drive us to practice, so you don't have to worry about being home if your new job is—"

"Sarah, sweetie, do you really think you have to go to practice tomorrow?"

"Well, sure I do, because—"

"I mean, I was thinking maybe we could just stay home tomorrow. You know, rent some movies, and—"

"Stay home? You mean not go to school?"

"Well—"

"Mom, what is wrong with you? You're always saying I watch too much television, and now you want me to skip school and watch movies? I don't get it."

"I know, I know, it's just that—"

"And I'm not skipping soccer practice. No way. Not when Coach says I'm almost ready to play sweeper."

"Of course, you're right, honey. I was just thinking . . ."

"What? You were thinking what?"

"Oh, never mind."

"It's that Sylvia Davis thing, isn't it? I told you, you ought to go to a shrink."

"Shrink? Where do you pick up these things?"

"You know what, Mom? You worry too much. Just be cool. The police are taking care of everything."

"Oh yeah? How do you know that?"

"Detective Jackson said that he—"

"You talked to Jackson?" Jane was suddenly alarmed.

"Yeah, sort of."

"What do you mean, sort of?"

"Well, he came to our school today because it's, like career day, you know, where people talk to you about their work and stuff, and this week it was him."

"And he talked about the Sylvia Davis case?"

"Well sure. I mean, people asked."

"Oh," Jane said, feeling relieved. Just career day stuff. Nothing personal.

"But he kind of talked to me separate," Sarah said, and the knot re-formed in Jane's chest. " 'Cause when everybody had to stand up and tell him their name, and I said Sarah Ferguson, he asked me if you were my mom."

Jane did her best to keep her expression calm, not to betray the mixture of anger and fear that came with the knowledge that Jackson obviously was using her daughter to find out more about her, possibly even to trap her some way.

"Uh, Sarah, if Detective Jackson tries to talk to you again, I mean, like on the playground or at soccer practice or anything, I think it would be better if you didn't tell him anything about me. Or about you, either."

"Why not?"

"Well, it's just not any of his business. It borders on violating our civil rights."

"What does that mean?"

"It means—"

"Can I have one of those Twinkies I saw in the cupboard? I only ate two slices of pizza, and I'm still hungry.''

Jane was grateful for the short attention span of a ten-year-old, at least in this case. She didn't want to alarm Sarah unduly by making her afraid or suspicious of Jackson. She only hoped she'd gotten through to her.

Exactly why she was suspicious of Jackson wasn't clear, even to Jane. Maybe what she had done had no significance. Maybe she was just being overly protective of her daughter. But the fact that he had questioned Sarah was one more reason to make her feel uneasy. She couldn't put it all together yet, but it was enough to confirm the fact that she was not going to tell him about the incident on the highway. She would be wary. Very wary. Of everyone.

The uneasy feeling stayed with her the next day. She insisted on giving Sarah a ride to school, rather than allowing her to walk, as she usually did. Jane gave the excuse that she had to go that way, anyway, in spite of the fact that it was actually out of the way to get to her new office. She fabricated a need to speak with a florist on the same street the school was on. For a possible television show about decorating with flowers, she had said.

The uneasiness was still with her when she walked Sarah into the classroom. She could tell the unaccustomed escort embarrassed Sarah. *At least it didn't make her suspicious,* Jane thought, with a measure of gratitude. She didn't want her to become frightened, too.

Jane tried to will away her own irrational fear for her daughter's safety as she drove to the office. She tried to tell herself that it meant nothing that Jackson had spoken to her daughter at school and had asked if she was Sarah's mom. *People in the South did that sort of thing all the time,* she thought. They were always asking if you were so-and-so's cousin or second or third cousin. Or ex-wife. It was nothing more than the Southern sense of family, she told herself. It didn't work.

She could still remember his driving around the soccer field. That was a patrolman's job, not a detective's.

How had she gotten herself into this situation, anyway? Nothing like this ever happened when she was a law student. Her worn tires skidded on the gravel of the parking lot as she drove in and parked her faded Toyota next to Hillary's shiny Cadillac. Maybe she ought to just walk into that office and tell Hillary she was quitting, she thought as she got out of the car. Tell her that she didn't need this. The trouble was, she *did* need this. The job, not the worry.

When she walked into the office, the receptionist, whom Hillary had called Lilly, greeted her with a solemn face, raised eyebrows, and a tilt of her head toward Hillary's office that seemed to say "Watch out!" If that were the case, Jane was *sure* she was going to quit. She couldn't take hassle from a temperamental boss on top of murder. Surely she could find something that would pay the bills. Some place where there was no vanilla potpourri.

"She said for me to tell you she wanted to see you in her office as soon as you came in," Lilly whispered.

"What's wrong?" Jane asked. Her voice sounded tired, even to her own ears.

Lilly shrugged. She was already pushing the intercom button. "Jane's here," she said.

"Send her in," an equally tired-sounding voice on the other end of the intercom said.

Lilly motioned with her head and gave Jane a sympathetic look, but Jane had begun to relax a little now, at least in regards to Hillary. Maybe the poor woman was not going to give her a hassle after all. She probably was just upset about the murder and the investigation, just as Jane was. It was possible she had even had an experience equally as frightening as Jane's wild ride on the highway had been.

That supposition was shattered, however, as soon as Jane walked into the polished cherrywood forest that was Hillary's office.

"Jane Ferguson, what have you done to me?" Hillary's voice had an element of panic to it.

"What—?"

"That recipe!"

"Well, I—"

"That wasn't coq au vin. It was—it was—I don't know *what* it was. The mayor hated it."

"How could he hate it? You haven't even had time to cook it yet."

"No, but Nancy has. She called me early this mornin'. I was going to test it myself, but when I read it, I didn't bother. It was awful, Jane. You said that was your mother's recipe? Were you a victim of child abuse? My lord, Nancy said the mayor took one taste and spat it out. How do you think that would look, if I actually used this recipe on my show? The mayor *spitting out something I've cooked!* That would ruin me, Jane, absolutely ruin me. I may already be ruined! How can I find another recipe and kitchen test it in time for taping? And will Nancy and Arnold even show up for the taping? Jane, if this small dinner party went well, the mayor was going to ask me to cater his charity dinner at the country club. But now? Oh my God! He *hated* your recipe, Jane. *Hated* it. Do you understand?"

"I think I'm beginning to get the idea."

"Oh no. You don't have any idea what this means. It was my big chance. The *mayor* planning a dinner party on *my* show! And then he was going to let me cater the charity dinner!"

"Hillary, I'm sorry. Maybe I'm just not suited for this. Maybe I ought to—"

"Ought to what?" Hillary suddenly looked even more alarmed. "You're not trying to tell me you're fixin' to quit, are you?"

"Well, I just thought—"

"You can't do that on top of what you've already done." Hillary stood up from behind her massive desk and paced back and forth. "What is wrong with you, Jane Ferguson? You need this job. Just what is wrong with you?" Hillary turned back to Jane, looking worried. "Oh

God, I don't know what I'm going to do." She twisted a tissue in her hand.

"I guess we're both a little upset," Jane said, working at being rational. *One of them had to be,* she thought. "I mean finding that body, being questioned by Jackson, his veiled suggestion that we're suspects . . ."

"Oh, yes, and that, too," Hillary said, with a wave of her hand. "I'm counting on you to get me out of that mess, Jane."

"That's something I wanted to talk to you about."

"Don't tell me you can't do it. I won't accept that as an answer."

"That's not what I was going to say," Jane said, although she wasn't at all sure that she should not. "It's that things are getting more and more, well, complicated— and serious. And, to be honest, more scary."

"What do you mean?"

"Someone tried to run me off the road on the way home last night."

"What!" Hillary's hands fluttered to her face in a gesture of shock.

"It was on that dark stretch of highway that leads out to the Meadowview Acres subdivision," Jane said.

"Oh yes, I know. Your house is in that neighborhood. Are you sure it wasn't just some teenager from one of those houses playing tricks?"

"I don't think so. I've driven that stretch after dark too many times, and it hasn't happened before. I think someone was trying to scare me or maybe even kill me."

"But, why, hon? That doesn't make sense." It seemed Hillary's honey-dipped accent intensified when she was upset.

"Of course it makes sense. We were the ones who found Sylvia's body. That was on the news. Everyone knows that now, including whoever killed her. And he— or she—may think we saw too much. Something that could implicate him or her."

"Well, I didn't see a thing." Hillary sounded indignant.

"Maybe you did, and you just don't know it yet.

Maybe someone will try to run you off the road next. Or break in your house, or—''

''Jane! You are scarin' me.'' She said it as if she were scolding a naughty child.

''I hope so. I hope you'll be careful, Hillary.''

Hillary looked worried. ''We have just got to get to the bottom of this.'' Jane did not miss the fact that Hillary had said ''we'' this time. *That,* she thought, *could mean trouble.* Hillary had a kind of focused blindness, a naïveté maybe, that meant she could be more of a hindrance than help.

''I am trying to get to the bottom of this,'' Jane said. ''I started by trying to find people who might have a motive to kill Sylvia.''

''Oh honey, you must have hit a gold mine.''

''There are a couple, at least. There's Crazy Dan, who I told you about, although I'm not sure he had a motive, and then there's someone named Chester Collins.''

''You mean Reverend Collins? From over at the Church of God's Riches?''

''That's the one. He's a city alderman, too, you know. Sylvia had him on her show and brought up some stuff about him spending taxpayers' money in questionable ways. There was something in the paper about it, I remember, but Sylvia was the one who broke the story.''

''I wouldn't know about that,'' Hillary said. ''I don't have time to read the paper, and I certainly didn't watch Sylvia's show.''

''Take my word for it, then. It was a big scandal, and Sylvia was keeping it alive, because she had people calling in to her show from time to time to voice an opinion on it. Kind of like Larry King.''

Hillary gave it a dismissive, ''Hmmph!'' Obviously she was not willing to entertain the idea that Sylvia's show could generate so much attention, but the idea of Reverend Collins being a suspect seemed easier. ''Maybe we ought to go talk to Reverend Collins,'' she said.

The very words Jane was dreading.

''Oh, but Hillary, you've got your TV show to think

about, and your decorating business. You've got to find new recipes. You've got things to plant in your garden. Stuff to do with your glue gun. You're just so busy, Hillary. Why don't you leave this to me?''

"But you're going to be helping me with all that, Jane, dear. That's why I hired you. Well, maybe you won't be helping me with the new recipes. Nevertheless, I'm going to be relying on you. And anyway, the way I look at it, we're in this mess together, and when we go to talk to Chester Collins, two heads are better than one, don't you think?''

"Not always," Jane said, under her breath.

"What?"

"I said, in a lot of ways."

"All right, then, how are we going to do this? Arrange to talk to Reverend Collins, I mean?'' Hillary's eyes were glowing with excitement now, as if she was enjoying the idea of playing detective.

"That shouldn't be too hard," Jane said. "We're tax-payers. He's our representative on the city council. We make an appointment to see him, and we talk about our concerns.''

"Why, you are so wonderfully logical, Jane. You must do that immediately. Set up the appointment, and we'll have this mystery solved in no time. You get right on it, and I'll get busy finding another recipe.''

Chester Collins was not as amenable to talking to his constituents as Jane had hoped. His secretary insisted that he could not possibly see them for another week because he does have a church to run, you know, and the heavy burden of government is resting upon his shoulders as well.

It did no good for Jane to insist that part of the heavy burden of government was taking time to talk to constituents. In the end, she had to resort to a form of blackmail. She told the secretary to tell Reverend Collins that she wanted to talk to him about his latest order from Naughty Nighty and Paraphernalia in Miami. Jane and Hillary got an appointment the following Monday.

Reverend Collins, dressed in a double-breasted beige suit, so light in color it was almost white, stood up from his desk and greeted each of them with a two-handed handshake. His suit contrasted in a startling way with his thinning, shiny black hair, which was a little too dark and purple-cast to be natural. He was a robust man with a barrel chest, giving Jane the impression that he could have pushed part of that chest up there from his stomach with the help of a girdle.

"Sister Ferguson and Sister Scarborough," he said in his full-of-the-holy-spirit voice. "Y'all come in and have a seat. Miss Whitney, bring us a pitcher of iced tea," he said to the secretary who had shown them in and who still lingered in the doorway, as if she was awaiting the order.

Miss Whitney was a shapely young woman with a voluptuous head of hair that was almost the same color as Collins's suit. She looked as if she could be a model for Naughty Nighty and Paraphernalia.

There was much fussing about as Collins tried to make sure they were comfortable, that Hillary's chair was not too high, whether Jane might need a pillow behind her back. Did the light from the window cause too much reflection? Was the temperature comfortable? When Miss Whitney came in with the heavily sweetened tea, which Jane had learned was so popular in the South, and for which she had never developed a taste, Collins finally seated himself behind his desk.

The desk, it seemed to Jane, had become a tool for him. Or a weapon of defense. It established his status and authority, and it also put a heavy and substantial obstacle between him and his visitors.

"I am so glad you ladies dropped by to talk to me," he gushed. "I am always happy to have my constituents express their concerns to me, and you are right to question me. I must be accountable to my God and my constituents. In that order. I want to take ever' opportunity I can to take care of the nasty rumors that have been floatin' around about me. The devil does not spare the righteous, you know. He steps in with ever' opportunity he can to destroy those who preach the word of the Lord.''

"You know, if you got rid of those printed drapes and went with a solid color, it would give the room a softer look. Teal blue, maybe, or—''

"Excuse me, Reverend Collins.'' Jane leaned forward slightly in her seat. "I don't understand. Did you say the devil?''

"Why yes. He is out there, you know. Very real. Trying to worm his way into our hearts. He is using this scandal to try to destroy me.'' He punctuated his words with a pulpit gesture, slamming his hand down hard on his desk, then he leaned forward himself to meet Jane's gaze. "I ask you, Sister Ferguson, who else could be responsible for all that talk going around?'' He raised both arms heavenward. "I say unto you, it is the devil who does these things, and may God send his angels to protect us all!''

"I thought it was Sylvia Davis who first brought it out,'' Jane said. "Are you saying she was the devil?''

"My goodness gracious, Jane,'' said Hillary, aghast.

"Miss Davis was only the devil's instrument, my child.'' Collins sounded smug. "I can see that you are uneducated in the wiles of the devil. I only hope that you are not equally uninformed in the ways of the Lord.''

"I think I'm beginning to understand,'' Jane said. "You're saying the devil put the idea in Sylvia's head to accuse you of these things.''

"That is right, my child.'' He leaned back into his chair, one arm across the back, relaxed.

"I'm sure it must have upset you when she did that.''

"Well, of course it upset him, Jane,'' Hillary said, making Jane wish, as she had feared, that she hadn't brought her along.

"Indeed. The work of the devil always causes me concern,'' Reverend Collins said.

"Was it the devil, then, who put your name on those receipts from Naughty Nighty? Or maybe the devil made *you* do it. And if I remember right, it was a city credit card you used.''

Collins's face turned as red as the flowers in his printed drapes. "I have no idea how my name got on those receipts," he said. "That is what I told Miss Davis, and that is what I am tellin' you. I must warn you, though, once you let old Satan into your heart, you are bound for destruction."

"Is that what happened to Sylvia?"

"Poor soul, I will not judge her," he said in his most pious voice.

"You must not have been surprised when you heard about her death, though," Jane said. "I mean, if you knew she was bound for destruction." She was aware of how leading her question was. She couldn't say she hadn't learned anything from watching Jim Ed in the courtroom.

"Why, I was shocked!" Collins said. "Stacy and I both were when we saw it on TV that night. I said to her, how terrible to think that woman had been murdered that morning when we were only a few blocks away at a meetin' in the mayor's office."

"Stacy?"

Collins looked flustered. "I didn't say Stacy. I said Miss Whitney."

"Miss Whitney?" Jane said. "Your secretary?"

"Yes," Collins said. He somehow managed to give the word two syllables.

"You were with her the morning Sylvia was killed and that night as well?" Jane asked.

A few beads of sweat popped out on Collins's forehead. He stuck a finger in his shirt collar, as if it was choking him. "Of course, I was with her that mornin'. Like I said, at the mayor's office. And as far as that night, what I meant was, we were working late. I take work over to her house sometimes." He cleared his throat. "Out of consideration for my wife. Don't like to disturb her by staying up late working, you know."

"Of course."

Collins took a long drink from his glass of tea, then removed a handkerchief from his pocket and wiped his forehead. "I hope I have been of some help in your understandin' of this situation," he said. His forced smile showed gleaming white teeth and emphasized the sweat on his upper lip.

"One more thing, Reverend Collins," Jane said. "Did you say you were in a meeting at the mayor's office the morning Sylvia was killed?"

"Yes, I was. I'm on the committee for the charity dinner. Some people use that for political fodder, you know. Like that woman running for Congress. Regina Conyers. She's the chairman, and you can bet the only reason is because she thinks it will get her elected. I, on the other hand—"

"Ms. Conyers was at the meeting, too?"

"She's the chairman. Represents the public sector. I represent the government sector, so by all rights, I should be the chairman, but, like I say, some people are only thinking of political gain, not the Lord's work. That's why I'm active in government, you know, because there's an area where witness for the Lord is needed, and I—"

"Thank you, Reverend Collins," Jane said, standing. Two of her suspects had alibis. That meant she had to do some more digging.

"Well, I hope I've been helpful."

Hillary leaned forward and left something on Collins's desk. "My card," she said. "In case you ever want to do something about those drapes."

5

Jane had changed into an old pair of faded denim shorts
and her favorite T-shirt, the one with the Grateful Dead
picture on the front and a tear under her left arm. She was
relaxing, drinking a diet Pepsi from the can, and she held
the remote control in her right hand, aimed with sharp-
shooter precision at the TV. Her feet were propped on the
magazine-strewn coffee table. Each of her toes had a piece
of cotton stuck between them to keep the wet Tiger Lily
Frost polish from smearing.

The evening news was just ending with a recap of the
same story that had opened the program: Sylvia Davis's
death. The anchorwoman was blond, thin, fashionably
dressed, and able to change her expression in the blink of
a well-made-up eye from smiling and chipper when she
bantered with the weatherman to deadly serious when she
talked about Sylvia. Her coanchor, a square-jawed, dark-
haired, nice looking but not too handsome male, pos-
sessed the same ability. Jane thought of them as
cookie-cutter people. There must be someplace in middle
America, Illinois maybe, where television anchors were
stamped out, slight variations in hair color painted on, and
then shipped out when they were needed.

"To recap our top story, the Prosper Police Department is still not releasing the names of suspects in the brutal murder of talk show host Sylvia Davis," the blond female anchor said. "Police Detective Beaumont Jackson says, however, that the investigation is continuing, and an arrest may be made soon. Miss Davis's body was discovered Monday by Hillary Scarborough of Elégance du Sud, who hosts a TV show on another channel, and by her assistant, June Ferguson. WPRS will bring you the latest on this important story as it develops."

"Jane! It's Jane Ferguson, not June," Jane shouted at the TV. "You know, the one who used to be married to Jim Ed."

The blond anchorwoman and her dark-haired coanchor simply smiled at her as the credits rolled.

"Did you call me, Mom?" Sarah yelled from the top of the stairs. Her voice was muffled from the toothbrush she had in her mouth. "Or were you talking to the TV again?"

"I didn't call you," Jane said. "And why aren't you in bed? You've got school tomorrow."

"I'm going! I'm going!" Sarah disappeared from the landing.

Jane massaged her temples. An arrest was going to be made soon, they said. Was that just hype, or was Jackson really on to something? Did that mean she and Hillary were now off the suspect list, or were they about to be arrested? That was ridiculous, of course. He had no reason to arrest them. No proof of anything.

A knock at the door startled her. She stood, hesitated a moment, worried about who might be out there. She willed herself to relax and go to the door. This was Prosper, Alabama, she told herself. Not L.A. But Sylvia Davis had been murdered in Prosper, Alabama. That thought slowed her steps, and she took a precautionary peek through the curtains at the front window.

A police car was parked at the curb, and she could make out the profile of Beaumont Jackson in the porch light. This, she knew, could only mean trouble. She tried to ignore the throbbing in her temples and the heavy churning in the bottom of her stomach as she opened the door.

Jackson looked as if he was about to speak—probably some standard passage such as *Police, madam. May I come in?* But he said nothing. Instead his eyes took in her faded shorts, her tattered T-shirt, her bare feet with the cotton still stuck between each of her toes. The sight seemed to stun him.

Finally Jane broke the silence. "Mr. Jackson, I presume?"

"Uh . . . yes. Hello, Jane. I mean, Mrs. Ferguson."

"Jane's OK, Beau. We may as well be chummy if you're going to keep following me around." She stood aside and gestured for Beau to enter.

Beau stepped inside. "What do you mean, following you around?"

"Oh, I saw you at the soccer field, and I wouldn't be surprised to find out that was you behind me that night on that dark stretch of road coming back from Hillary's place." Jane threw the words over her shoulder as she walked into the living room. "Trying to play a little rough, weren't you? Isn't that illegal?" She plopped herself down on the sofa. Now she was having a hard time keeping her anger from exploding.

"Hey, wait a minute!" Beau held up a hand as if to fend off her anger and sat down cautiously on an easy chair. "I don't know what you're talking about."

"I saw you!" Jane said, pointing an accusing finger at him. "I saw you at that soccer field."

"All right, I'm not denying the soccer field, but I don't know anything about you being followed on a dark stretch of road."

"What were you doing at the soccer field?"

"Why do you think someone was following you on that dark stretch of road?"

"I asked you first."

Beau looked oddly uncomfortable for a moment but recovered quickly. "Police business," he said.

"Police business?" Jane made no attempt to conceal her sarcasm. "I suppose it's important to the safety of Prosper, Alabama, to watch those ten-year-olds when they're out there on the soccer field. Heaven only knows what kind of subversive stuff they could be up to. And why were you talking to my daughter at school?"

"What?"

"Career day. Tombigbee Elementary."

"I talked to all the kids that day."

"You singled my daughter out. Asked if she was related to me."

"I meant no harm. I was just wondering at the coincidence, since I had so recently met you. She's a very pretty little girl."

"Yes, she is. And I want you to leave her alone."

"I can assure you, I am not bothering your daughter. I'm a policeman for Christ's sake."

"That's supposed to comfort me?"

"Look, lady, I'm just trying to do my job, that's all. I'm not into police brutality or fostering a police state or pushing any kind of right-wing agenda some of you people seem to think we do. I'm not into anything except my job. Now, tell me about what happened on the highway."

Jane was still cautious. He may have claimed he had no agenda, but she wasn't convinced. And beyond that, she was still afraid she was considered a suspect in Sylvia's murder. After several long seconds, she spoke. "It was nothing. Probably just some teenagers playing around."

"Playing around how?"

"Oh just—well, someone tried to—to run me off the road, but I'm not sure it—"

"Did you get a good look at the car?"

"No, it was too dark."

"Where did you say you had been?"

"Hillary Scarborough's house. We had to meet the mayor and his wife there to talk about a television show she was doing with them."

"Did you tell Mrs. Scarborough you'd been snooping

around trying to find out more about the Davis case?''

"I didn't have to tell her. She knows I . . . I mean, I don't know what you're talking about.''

"I know you were at the TV station looking at those tapes. Where else have you been?''

"You tell me. It sounds to me like you know my every move.''

"I know what's going on. That's my job.''

He was making her more and more uncomfortable, and once again, she was thinking hard before she spoke, trying to make sure she didn't entrap herself somehow. "Why did you ask me about Hillary?'' she said, finally.

"Did I ask about Hillary?''

"You asked if she knew I was 'snooping around' as you called it.''

"Well, does she?''

"You're implying somehow that she could have followed me because she thought I was getting close to finding out she had something to do with Sylvia Davis's death.''

"You're putting words in my mouth, Mrs. Ferguson.''

"It's Jane, remember?''

"OK, Jane. Don't try to second guess me. The only thing I mean to imply to you, and the reason I came by, is to tell you to stop your snooping. It could get you in trouble.''

"Oh, come on, now, I don't see how—''

"You just told me someone tried to run you off the road. This is police business, Jane. Stay out of it. And whatever you might have dug up, don't say anything about it to anyone. Especially not to Mrs. Scarborough.''

"You're telling me she's still a suspect?''

"At this point, everyone who might have encountered Miss Davis that morning is a suspect.''

"Including me?''

"Including you. So don't complicate your life by interfering with police business. Now, if you'll excuse me . . .''

He started for the door, but Jane sprang from the couch

as if to stop him. "Wait a minute. You're telling me you think I could be a murderer, or the woman I work for could be a murderer, and that she could be trying to kill me because I know too much. You're crazy, Beau Jackson, because nothing I've uncovered points to anyone except—"

"Except Chester Collins and Regina Conyers. I know."

"But how—"

"Because it's my business to know. I researched those tapes, too, and the clerk told me you'd been there. Writing a paper on women in television? Give me a break! You're wasting your time, Jane. The coroner says Sylvia Davis died between eight and ten in the morning on the day you called me. Collins and Ms. Conyers were both in a meeting in the mayor's office during that time."

"So."

"Don't you see, Jane? I don't know where Hillary Scarborough was that morning. And I don't know where you were, either."

Once again, Jane was too stunned to speak for a moment. Finally, she said slowly, "Oh, I'm afraid I do see."

"Don't bother to see me to the door," Beau said, already on his way. "I know what it's like to have foot problems."

"Foot problems?"

Beau opened the door and was gone. Jane stared down at her feet. Part of the cotton was still there, looking like some kind of weird bandage.

He must think she was some nut with bleeding toes who went around murdering people. Or, at best, consorting with murderers. Because the other possible suspects had alibis. The thought galled her. She opened the door and called out to Beau, "It could have been a burglar, you know!" Her words were lost in the darkness as his car pulled away from the curb.

Upstairs, alone in her bed, Jane found sleep elusive. What would happen to Sarah if she actually got arrested for this crime? Even if she weren't arrested and word got around that she was a suspect, it could be embarrassing, maybe even damaging to Sarah. Jane had the protective instincts of a mother lioness. She wouldn't let anything happen to harm her daughter, not in the smallest way.

Even if she was able to clear herself, there was Hillary's predicament, too. She might be flaky, have a perfect house, do her own gardening, make her own paper, lay her own carpet, maybe even lay her own eggs, but Jane wouldn't hold any of that against her. She was providing her with the best employment she would ever be able to find. The pay was certainly better than the starvation wages she knew to expect if she ever got out of law school and got a job as an assistant district attorney anywhere in Alabama.

She'd given up trying to think of ways to leave the South. For one thing, her child support checks would stop if she left the state. For another, Sarah wouldn't want to leave. She'd made friends here and she loved her school. And, in spite of herself, Jane knew there was yet another reason not to leave. She, too, had grown to like it here. In spite of the heat and the rain and the humidity and the bugs. In spite of the fact that the Ku Klux Klan still thrived and fundamentalist religion made some people unreasonable. In spite of the fact that she heard Jim Ed's name everywhere she turned. She'd come to like the perfumed smell of the air when the magnolias were in bloom, the beauty of the woods and meadows of the countryside, the charm of Southern manners. And there were plenty of people who had risen above the racial prejudice that, for decades, had been a part of their culture. Plenty of people who were not unreasonable. Plenty of people whom she liked.

The point was that her life, for better or worse, was here. She had to make the best of it, and, for now, she had to save her reputation and her job and protect her child.

But how?

She tossed some more in the big bed that she had once shared with Jim Ed. Turned over again, and then again, until the sheets were tangled around her ankles.

A noise downstairs got her attention. She listened, hold-ing her breath. A burglar maybe? Or whoever had forced her off the road? She heard the noise again, and then the sound of garbage cans falling, and after that, the screech of a cat. It was only animals prowling in the night. Not a burglar, after all.

She had tried to suggest to Beau Jackson that it could have been a burglar who killed Sylvia Davis. Was he giv-ing that any consideration at all? Maybe it wasn't a bur-glar. Maybe Sylvia's murder had something to do with those messages on her answering machine. Had Beau lis-tened to those messages again? Or was there something in the house, something she or Hillary had inadvertently left there that had made Beau tag them as suspects? Just how thorough had Beau been in his investigation? Maybe there was something he had overlooked.

Jane's mind drifted back to the possibility of a burglar killing Sylvia. But how would he have gotten in? The only way to answer all of the questions that swirled in her mind as she tossed on her bed was to get into the house and see for herself. But that was ridiculous, of course. The house would be locked, and Beau Jackson certainly wasn't going to let her in.

Jane went to work the next morning feeling tired from her restless night, as well as worried about where Beau's investigation might be leading.

Hillary seemed oblivious to all of it, though. Now that she had managed, successfully, to come up with and test a recipe for her show with the mayor, she was intent upon giving Jane a list of all the products she would need.

When Jane mentioned the fact that Beau had been to her house the night before and that she was worried about where his investigation was leading, Hillary's response was a non sequitur.

"Decorative wreaths are so popular now, and you can make a truly beautiful one out of ivy and apples from your own garden."

"I don't trust him, Hillary. The truth is, I'm to the point that I don't trust anyone. I keep thinking about someone trying to run me off the road the other night.''

"I take the apples from my trees early and slice them and dry them, then you can make rose petals out of the preserved fruit. See, here's one I did. Isn't it lovely? I'm going to demonstrate it on my show. Here's a list of things I'll need, and I'm scared, Jane.''

"What?'' Hillary had caught her off guard again.

"I keep trying not to think about it, but it's no good. We're being accused of murder, and now someone's trying to kill you. That's all I can think about.'' Hillary sat down at her desk, looking worried and defeated.

"Neither of those statements is exactly accurate, Hillary, but . . .''

"But you're scared, too.''

Jane gave Hillary a long look, trying to decide what benefit would come from putting on a facade of strength. "Yeah,'' she said, finally, "I'm scared, too.''

"Did you tell the police about what happened on your way home?''

"I told Beau Jackson. He came to my house last night.''

"Oh dear. I suppose he'll be coming to my house next. Should I have a lawyer present? Oh, listen to me! I can't believe I'm even thinking such things. This is all just a bad dream. I know it is. I'll wake up soon, won't I?'' Hillary buried her face in her hands for a moment, then looked up at Jane. "You've got to get us out of this mess.''

"Hillary, I don't know what else I can—''

Jane was interrupted by Lilly opening the door to the office and saying in a hushed tone, "Someone's here to see you, Jane.''

"To see me?''

"Yes, but I'm not sure you want to see this person. He doesn't look exactly—well—presentable. Says his name is Buddy Fletcher. He says it's important, but I'll get rid of him if you want me to.'' She was holding the door closed, hands behind her back.

"Buddy? Yes, yes, of course, I'll see him.'' Jane was

decidedly curious and a little uneasy about why Buddy Fletcher would be asking to see her. She started toward the door, which Lilly held open for her. The door was open wide enough, apparently, for Hillary to get a look at Buddy, who was pacing the floor, his dirty NRA cap pulled down on his head hard and determined, his long greasy hair and grisly beard giving him a fierce look.

"Who is that person, and why would he want to see you?" Hillary sounded more than a little alarmed.

"It's just somebody I know." Jane was still trying to make her way out of the room, but Lilly had closed the door again, apparently to keep Buddy from overhearing the conversation.

"How could you possibly know him?" Hillary's own curiosity mingled with disgust in those words.

"Jim Ed defended him once, and we got to be—well, friends, sort of."

"Defended him? Against what?"

"Burglary."

"Oh my lord! And I suppose he got him off."

"I never said Jim Ed wasn't a good lawyer."

"Jane, I'm sure you know it's not good for business to have people like that in my—"

Jane felt anger rising inside her at Hillary's words. She turned around and said quickly, "Hillary, don't judge people by the way they look." Her voice was firm, the same tone she used on Sarah when she was misbehaving. "And if Buddy says it's important, then it's important." She turned away and moved with such forcefulness that Lilly had to sidestep out of her way.

"Miz Ferguson!" Buddy said as soon as he saw her walk into the waiting area. He looked worried.

"What is it, Buddy?"

"I came, soon as I heard."

"Heard what?" Jane's curiosity and alarm were both intensifying. "And how'd you know where to find me?"

Buddy looked around the room, nervously eyeing Lilly, who had eased into her chair behind her desk, watching the two of them, wide-eyed. "Is there some place we can talk?"

"Sure. Come into my office," she said, wondering how much longer this would be her office. What she had just said to Hillary could get her fired. When she and Buddy were inside, Jane closed the door. "What's this all about?" she asked.

"That Sylvia Davis. The one what got killed. Word's out you and this broad you work for is about to get busted for that."

"What do you mean, word's out? Who told you?"

"Oh, just some people you don't know. But that don't matter. What I come for is to see if you need a place to kinda, you know, like, disappear to for a while."

"That's very thoughtful of you, Buddy, but . . ." She was silent for a moment, thinking. "What else have you heard about this?"

"What you mean?"

"Well, you must have heard something. I mean have any of your friends—acquaintances—said anything about, well, maybe that somebody broke into her place not meaning any harm, maybe, but things got out of hand, and—"

"Now, Miz Ferguson, you know I don't have nothin' to do with any of them kind of people. It would be a violation of my parole."

"I see." She was thinking that it had certainly been a violation of his parole when he broke into the house over on Oak Street, but Jim Ed had been clever enough to get him out of it by convincing a jury that the stolen property found in Buddy's house was put there, unbeknownst to Buddy, by someone else. She was also thinking that those people Buddy had mentioned who told him she and Hillary were about to be arrested were most likely the very people he wasn't supposed to be associating with.

"But I can tell you this: It wasn't nobody I know broke into her house," Buddy added.

"Oh?"

"Yeah. Anybody I know woulda took something. I

mean, in my profession, you don't go breaking into a house like that unless you want something you can fence. We got our principles, you know. And I heard on TV there wasn't nothing missing.''

Jane nodded. ''That's the way it looked to me.''

''Looked like somebody she let in the door?''

''Maybe. I don't know. Maybe he—or she—got in another way and left the door open when they left.''

''There's ways to do that, you know—break in without it showing.'' Buddy dropped his eyes, a surprising show of shyness or humility. ''I don't mean to brag, but I'm the only one I know of around here that can do that. Break in without leaving no signs, I mean, so if that's what happened, it was somebody from out of town.''

''You can do that? Break in without leaving any signs?''

He nodded.

''How?''

''It's kinda hard to explain, but I could show you if you wanted me to. I mean, you have to do it different for ever' house.''

If Buddy could really do it, then it might be worth it to find out how, Jane thought. It could help persuade Beau that she and Hillary had nothing to do with Sylvia's death.

Jane stood up and reached for her coat. ''Could you show me right now?''

Buddy's eyes widened. ''Now? Well—I guess I could, but it's daylight! I mean, this is the kind of thing you don't want people driving by and seeing you do. Know what I mean?''

''Buddy, we're not going to actually break in. You're just going to show me how it's done. Then we're going to try to convince Beau Jackson that it can be done. Maybe we can even suggest that it was someone from out of town.''

Buddy gave her a blank look for a few seconds; then he slowly nodded his head. ''Oh, I get it.''

''We could go right now,'' Jane said. ''I've got to go out anyway to buy some stuff for Hillary's next show.''

If Jane hadn't stopped by Lilly's desk on her way out to tell her where she was going, Hillary would never have overheard her. But as it was, she called from her office.

"You've got all day tomorrow to get the stuff I need, Jane. I need you to stay here and go over next week's script with me."

"Hillary, I, uh . . ."

"We're fixin' to go over to Sylvia Davis's place," Buddy blurted. "We got some business to take care of. She won't be gone long."

Hillary was out of her office and in the waiting area in seconds. "You're going where?"

"Buddy didn't mean that, really, he—"

Hillary was insistent. "What kind of business?"

Buddy still couldn't keep his mouth shut. "I'm just going to show her how to break into the place."

"You're what?"

"He didn't mean that."

"Course I meant it. Didn't you just say—"

"Buddy!"

"Will somebody please tell me what's going on here?"

Hillary stood with her hands on her hips—a demanding stance. The green of her linen dress turned her eyes to emeralds.

Jane felt she had no choice but to tell her the plan she'd devised. Hillary saw her reasoning quickly.

"I'm going with you," she said. "We'll take my car."

"Hillary, I don't think that's a good idea," Jane said.

Hillary was still insistent. "Why not? You're going, aren't you?"

"Well, yes, but it could be dangerous. I mean, returning to the scene of the crime, and—"

"Nonsense. If you're going, I'm going."

Fifteen minutes later, they were in Hillary's car, turning onto the street where Sylvia's house was located.

"You're one hell of a driver," Buddy said, as they careened around the corner on two wheels.

As they approached the house, he spoke again. "Now, if it was night, we'd pull this Caddy up in the driveway with the trunk open so we could throw the VCR, TV, whatever, in there quick, but daylight jobs is trickier.'' He turned to Hillary. ''You let me and Jane out, see, and you park the car about a block away, then we carry the TV and VCR down to it. You'd be surprised at the folks that will see us and not think twice about it. They'll think we're repairmen or something.''

''Buddy,'' Jane said, ''we're not actually going to burglarize the place, remember? You're just going to show us how someone could get in if they wanted to without being seen or without breaking the door down.''

''Oh, yeah. I guess when you enjoy your work you just get carried away,'' he said by way of apology.

''I think I ought to park a block or so away anyway,'' Hillary said. ''It just won't look good for me to have my car in Sylvia's driveway, under the circumstances.''

Jane couldn't argue that point, so they walked the block together, Buddy in front, Jane and Hillary following behind with Hillary's high heels tapping out her excitement on the sidewalk.

''Now, most of these old houses got old-fashioned locks,'' Buddy said, leading them around to the backyard. ''So it ain't no trick to pick the lock.'' He pulled a locksmith's tool from his pocket, bent down, and began working on the door. He tried for several minutes before the lock released, only to find that the door was secured by a dead bolt.

''Damn! She's gone and had that extra lock installed,'' he said. ''Odds are, she's got one in the front, too.'' He was right. The front door proved equally formidable, but at least it was shrouded by enough bushes that it couldn't be seen from the street. Buddy stood up from his crouched position in front of the door and scratched his head. ''Have to try a window,'' he said. ''Upstairs is usually best.'' He walked around the house, looking at all the windows. ''That one,'' he said, finally, pointing to an upstairs window at the side of the house. ''We can climb up that tree, see?''

Buddy made a jump for one of the limbs and swung

himself up, then wove his way through the tree, arms alternating rhythmically, reaching and grasping, legs following in the same rhythm. Jane could see him reach for the window and do something with his hands and a tool at the base. Suddenly, the window was open and Buddy was inside.

"Buddy!" she called. But she was afraid to call too loudly lest the neighbors be alerted.

"Oh my lord!" Hillary said, a hand clasped over her mouth.

"Buddy, you get down here this minute!" Jane called again.

Still no response.

Jane kicked off her shoes, hiked her skirt, and reached for the lowest tree limb.

"What are you doing?" Hillary called to her.

"I'm going after Buddy to get him out of that house."

Jane was at the top of the tree, leaning toward the open window when she heard Hillary again.

"Oh my lord!"

Jane looked down and saw what Hillary had seen. It was Beau Jackson in his police car.

6

She tried calling to Buddy in a hushed tone, as if Beau, two stories down and inside his car, might hear. "Buddy!" Then a little louder. "Buddy! You've got to get out of there, the cops are out in front."

Buddy appeared in shadowy form across the room. "Huh? What you say?"

She pointed to the street. "I said the cops are—"

"Get your butt in here!" Suddenly he had crossed the room and grabbed her arm. She had no choice but to let him pull her inside or risk falling out of the tree. She could see Hillary, out of the corner of her eye, moving toward a large lilac bush.

"Are you crazy? We can't do this!" She spoke in a hoarse, squeaky whisper as she tumbled and fell awkwardly through the window and into the room. It was meant to be a bedroom but obviously was used mostly for storage. Boxes were stacked around the walls. An old exercise bicycle sat in one corner, and there were two chairs covered with cloths in another corner.

"Cain't do what?" Buddy was helping her to her feet.

"We can't be in here like this. It's breaking and entering. I told you we weren't going to actually come inside.

Now, Beau Jackson is down there, and we're up here, and—"

"Relax, Miz Ferguson. Ever'thang's going to be all right."

"What do you mean, relax? I just told you . . ."

He was moving away from her, bending down, pressing his ear against something. She noticed for the first time that he had put on a pair of gloves.

"What are you doing?" She was still half whispering, but her tone was full of anxiety. "He could be downstairs."

"What am I doing? I'm just going to open this here safe."

"You're what? Oh, my God!" Jane went to the window. "You stop that! Come on, we've got to get out of here." She leaned out, sucked in her breath at what she saw, and moved away from the windowsill as if it were hot to the touch. Her hand was over her mouth, her eyes wide.

"You sure are a nervous woman," Buddy said, raising his ear from the safe for a moment. "Now, you got to be quiet so I can hear them tumblers."

"He's down there! Parked on the side street. Just a little ways up from this very window."

"What's he doing?"

"Sitting in his car. Like he's working on something."

"Paperwork. Probably filling out a report." Buddy's ear was back on the safe again. "Don't worry."

Jane rushed toward the bedroom door. "Maybe we can get out the front door before he comes in." She opened the door.

"Close that door!" Buddy barked at her.

"But—"

"You want to meet him coming in? Just wait a minute. We'll leave the way we came. Soon as I finish."

"You're not going to finish anything, Buddy Fletcher. Do you understand? You are not going to break into that safe."

It was too late. Buddy moved away slightly with a big

smile. "Got it," he said, opening the heavy door.

In spite of it all, Jane could not help moving a step closer to peer inside the metal cavity.

"Damn!" Buddy said, sounding disappointed. "Nothing but a bunch of papers." He picked up a handful.

"Put them back, Buddy. Put thcm back right now." She hurried to the window again. "Oh no! He's getting out of the car. He's walking toward the house."

"Hmm. What's this?" Buddy was giving all of his attention to one particular piece of paper on the top of the stack. "You might want to have a look at this, Miz Ferguson."

"No, I do not!" There was a sound downstairs. The front door opening.

"This here looks to me like it might be a blackmail note."

"Come on. We've got to get out of—a what?"

"A blackmail note. Looky here." He walked to the window to give it to Jane. She reached for it but retracted her hand, remembering fingerprints, and read it as Buddy held it. The note was printed in block letters. It read:

CONSIDER OUR MEETING YOUR FIRST WARNING. THIS IS THE SECOND. THERE WON'T BE A THIRD. $500,000 OR YOUR REPUTATION AND THEREFORE YOUR CAREER ARE RUINED. WAVE IS DEAD NOW AND CAN'T TALK, BUT I CAN. NOON, DAY AFTER TOMORROW. SAME PLACE.

Jane took her eyes from the note and looked at Buddy. "Oh my lord," she whispered. Then there was the sound of footsteps on the stairs. A door opening, then closing down the hall. Jane once again sucked in her breath, saw Buddy's eyes widen. He turned quickly, placed the stack of papers back into the safe, closed the door, spun the knob, and raced toward the window.

"I'll go first," he said, leaning out and reaching for the tree limb. "Then I'll help you." He slipped out the window with an amazing agility, but it seemed to take an eternity for him to position himself on the limb and then to reach his hands toward her. She could hear the sound of footsteps in the hall again, just outside the door.

She turned away from the window, her eyes wide with fright. She saw the doorknob turn. Quickly, she dropped to her knees, lifted the voluminous cover of one of the chairs, and ducked under it. She heard the door open, footsteps in the room, then silence. She held her breath and prayed that he would not look under the cover. Seconds ticked by. She tried not to breathe lest he hear her. Minutes. An eternity. Finally, she heard the door open and close again. Cautiously, she lifted the chair covering and peeked out. The room was clear. But for how long?

Standing, she hurried to the window and opened it again. She leaned forward, feet on the windowsill. It was a long way down. She had to close her eyes. Neither Buddy nor Hillary were anywhere in sight. She leaned forward, fell toward the tree.

One of the large branches caught her, but she scraped her knee and tore her stockings on the rough bark, then felt one of the branches jab her in the ribs. She managed to right herself and tried to move downward with the same quick, greased, hand-over-hand, foot-over-foot motion that had taken Buddy up the tree, but Jane had grown up in the city. Her experience with trees was limited, and she felt herself falling again, taking some of the leaves and branches with her until she landed with a thud on the spongy grass beneath the tree. She stood up. Her arm hurt, her hair was in her face, her hose were little more than shreds, but at least she was alive.

There was the screeching sound of tires on the pavement and the roar of a motor. The gold Cadillac, with Hillary at the wheel and Buddy in the front seat, was just rounding the corner from the next block. It stopped at the curb, motor still running. Hillary motioned for her to hurry. Jane opened a back door and slid inside. Before the door was closed again, the tires screeched once more, the motor roared, their heads were thrown back, and they had made their getaway.

"I was watching for you from the next block," Hillary said, as she careened around a corner. "Saw you fall out of the tree, Jane. Saw Buddy come down first. Good thing he found me. Before y'all came down, I was hiding in that lilac bush, but I couldn't stay there. It was such a mess. Lilac bushes should be trimmed after blooming, and then treated for mildew and leaf spot. Doesn't hurt to add a little lime to the soil, either. What were y'all doing up there all that time? I thought you'd never come out."

"Nothing," Jane said. "Breaking into the safe," Buddy said at the same time.

Hillary's eyes widened as she took them off the road to stare at Buddy. "Breaking into the . . . ? Oh this is fun!"

"Watch that truck!" Buddy yelled.

"There is nothing fun about this!" Jane screeched.

Hillary swerved around the truck. "You have to tell me what you found. Tacky costume jewelry, I'll bet."

"Nothing much," Jane said. "A blackmail note," Buddy said at the same time.

"A blackmail note?" Hillary took her eyes from the road again. "Oh I love it! What did it say?"

"Somebody wanted half a million bucks or they'd ruin her career," Buddy said.

"How?" Hillary was taking it all in hungrily. "What juicy information did they have on her?"

"Didn't say," Buddy said. "Just said somethin' about somebody named Wave being dead." Jane could barely hear his words above the sound of horns blaring as Hillary swerved into a lane of oncoming traffic. When, at last, Hillary pulled into the parking lot next to her office, Jane sank back against the seat, exhausted.

Lilly looked surprised, or maybe alarmed, when the three of them walked in. Jane assumed it was her appearance—torn hose, disheveled hair, scratched face and hands—that caused the stare. Lilly's eyes followed her all the way to her office door, but she seemed too shocked to speak.

"Both of you, come into my office," Jane said over

her shoulder to Buddy and Hillary. "We've got to talk."

When they were all inside, Jane collapsed into the chair behind her desk. Then, mustering all the energy she could, she leaned forward, pointed a finger at Buddy.

"Don't ever do anything like that again."

He took on an innocent look and shrugged his shoulders. "What? I was just trying to help."

"Breaking the law. Getting *me* involved in breaking the law. Almost getting me killed in that tree. None of that is helping."

Buddy looked hurt. "Well, shit. I showed you how easy it is to break in, just like you wanted me to. And how about the blackmail note? I found that, didn't I? Maybe that'll take the heat off of y'all. Now the cops will be looking for whoever was blackmailing her. Or whoever killed Wave."

"Who's Wave?" Hillary asked.

"Look, Buddy," Jane said, ignoring her, "if I'm going to assume Beau eventually is going to open the safe and find the note, I have to assume he would have found it whether or not you broke into the house. Which I told you specifically not to do."

"How long do you think it's going to take Beau to figure out how to open that safe? And who's Wave?" Hillary asked, glancing from Buddy to Jane.

"It shouldn't take too long. It's a crime scene. He doesn't need a court order," Jane said. She rubbed her temples. "And I don't know who or what Wave is."

"Weird name," Buddy said.

"It sounds vaguely familiar," Hillary said.

"I don't think Beau has opened that safe yet," Jane said, thinking aloud. "But he will, and he'll find that note. Maybe he'll know what it's all about."

"Well then, we can stop worrying. And Buddy's right. It'll probably take the heat off us." Hillary was all smiles now. "I'm going back to work."

"There's just one problem," Buddy said.

Jane felt a twinge of nervous fear. "Problem?" The

sheepish expression on Buddy's face made her even more fearful.

"Well . . ."

"What is it, Buddy?"

"I, uh, I'm gonna, you know, have to put the note back in the safe before he can find it."

"What do you mean?" Hillary and Jane asked in unison.

"Well, you was rushing me to get out of there, and . . ."

"And what?" Jane was definitely nervous now.

Buddy didn't speak. He pulled his gloves out of his hip pocket, put them on, then reached into his breast pocket and pulled out a crumpled paper and smoothed it with his hands as he laid it flat on Jane's desk. She recognized the blackmail note immediately. "I put them other papers back, but we was in such a hurry, I—well, I thought it might be important. But, course I can see now that I . . . There ain't nothing to worry about, really. I can put it back." Buddy sounded part defensive, part boastful.

It was Jane who was speechless now. So, apparently, was Hillary. They both stared at Buddy, until finally Jane said simply, "Oh shit!" and dropped her head into her hands.

"What?" Buddy said. "It ain't no big deal."

"It means you'll have to break into the house again," Hillary said, sparing Jane the necessity of speaking the words she didn't want to speak.

"Oh, that's OK," Buddy said cheerfully. "I can do that on my own time."

"No, Buddy, you are not going back in the house. Don't you see? You're already in enough trouble. You have just committed a felony. *We* have committed a felony by breaking into that house, and you have compounded it by taking something, compounded it doubly because it was a crime scene." Jane's voice was squeaky with anxiety again.

"What are you saying?" Hillary sounded worried.

"I am saying we are in deep shit."

"Well, I never meant no harm," Buddy said. Buddy's frown made his face look crumpled.

"We've got to think of some way to get that note back in the house without Beau knowing it," Hillary said. "Maybe one more little break-in won't hurt."

"No! We can't break into that house again." Jane paced nervously across the thick Persian rug.

"Then what do we do?" Hillary asked. "Turn the note over to the police? Get us all arrested? Not just Buddy, Jane, all of us."

"Hell, no," Buddy said.

"Well?" Hillary asked, impatient.

"I don't know," Jane said, running her hands through her disheveled hair. "I've got to think."

"Well, I don't never have to think," Buddy said. "All I got to do is get this damn paper back in that damn safe." He started for the door.

"Wait!" The urgent tone of Jane's voice halted him. He turned toward her, a question in his eyes. Jane felt a moment of disconcerting indecision. "I'll—I'll go with you," she said finally. She felt that knot in her stomach again.

Hillary wanted to come along, too. To drive the "getaway car," she said. Jane didn't think she could take another bout of Hillary's driving, however, and it took some time to convince her that there wouldn't be any getaway this time. "It will be quick and dirty," Jane said. An unfortunate choice of words. They only served to pique Hillary's sense of excitement. In the end, though, a telephone call from a client who wanted help planning a rather elaborate and expensive wedding kept her in the office.

Jane took the time to rearrange her disheveled hair, to wash her face, and to remove her tattered hose before she and Buddy drove to Sylvia's neighborhood in her old Toyota. First, they drove by the house to make sure Beau's car was gone, and then they parked several blocks away, since, as Jane explained to Buddy, there was a chance Beau would recognize her Toyota if he was still in the area.

"You wait in the car, so's nobody will see you walkin' down the street," Buddy said. "And I'll go put this stuff back and be right back."

"Buddy, maybe I should go." She was wondering if she could trust him. Would he really just put it back and not take anything else?

"No, it's gotta be me," he insisted. "If anybody seen you walkin' around down here, they might get, you know, suspicious."

"What about you? Won't they get suspicious if they see you in the neighborhood?"

"Naw, they'll just think I come to check out the neighborhood for a heist is all. No big deal."

"Buddy, that's just the point. If . . ." It was too late. Buddy had already started down the block, his large, graceful movements eating up the distance rapidly. Jane thought of calling to him again, but she knew it would do no good. It might only attract attention.

Instead, she sat in the car and waited. She watched him disappear around the corner, and then kept her eyes glued to that spot where he would eventually reemerge. The minutes seemed like hours as she waited, feeling sweat, born of anxiety as well as the heavy, humid air, trickle down her back and between her breasts. She had left the Toyota's motor running, along with the air conditioner, which was making a clacking and squeaking sound but doing very little cooling.

"You got car trouble or something?"

The muffled voice heard through the closed window and over the sound of the air conditioner startled Jane, and a little cry emitted from her throat. Her heart pounded wildly and the pounding grew even wilder when she saw the face of the person speaking: Beau Jackson. He had come up from behind her. In her rearview mirror she could see his car. It was the noise of the air conditioner, she supposed, that had kept her from hearing him drive up.

She rolled down her window. "What?" Her nervousness made her feel disoriented.

"I thought maybe you parked here because you were having engine trouble." He motioned toward the hood of the car. "Sounds like something's not right in there."

"Oh! Uh—yes, it does, doesn't it?"

"Want me to have a look?"

"Oh—well, I—"

"Pop the hood."

She hesitated only a moment, then pulled the lever to open the hood, thinking it best to do as little as possible to arouse suspicion. Beau bent over, peered at the engine, reached in, and pulled at something. "Shut off the air conditioner," he said. She did. He pulled at something again, raised his head again. "Turn it on now." She did. The rattling and squeaking continued.

Beau closed the hood with a practiced finality, dusted off his hands, and walked to her window again. "It's your air conditioner, all right. I wouldn't run it anymore, if I were you. Not before you have it looked at. Could be the compressor."

"Is that expensive?"

"Couple hundred to replace it, maybe more."

Jane felt sick. "Damn!" she said, under her breath, but she managed a weak smile and thanked Beau.

"I said I wouldn't use the air conditioner till you get it checked," he said, pointing to the air conditioner switch as a signal for her to turn it off.

"Sure. OK." She switched the air conditioner off. In front of her, she saw Buddy, rounding the corner, walking toward the car. Beau was positioned at a right angle to Buddy's approach and apparently had not seen him.

"And don't try fixing it on your own. I can see how you've scratched your hands trying."

"What? Oh, yes! Yes, I did."

"What are you doing in this neighborhood, anyway?" Beau asked.

Jane didn't answer immediately. She glanced at Buddy and knew by the way he hesitated that he had seen Beau. "I uh . . ." Buddy turned around, headed back the way he had come. "I was—looking at the chinaberry trees."

"Looking at the chinaberries?"

"Beautiful, aren't they?"

Beau looked around at them, as if he'd never noticed the tall, thick-trunked trees lining the street, heavy with their delicate, lilac-colored flowers.

"I had to check them out for one of Hillary's TV shows. On, uh, on chinaberry trees. You know, how to make tea out of the berries. How you can coat the blossoms with sugar and serve them for dessert."

"Uh huh." He wore a puzzled frown.

"She's into edible flowers big time."

"OK. Just get that air conditioner fixed."

"Oh, I will."

"Want me to follow you back to your office, just to make sure you make it? Could be something else wrong, too."

"No! I mean, no, thank you. I'll be fine. I'll go by the garage first and see if I can get the car repaired." She gave him her best smile.

Beau hesitated only a moment, then gave her a little salute and went back to his car. Jane had no choice but to drive away, as if she were going to a repair shop, leaving Buddy, she presumed, to wander around the neighborhood and get into God only knew what.

7

Since repairing the air conditioner was a luxury Jane could not afford, she drove home, rather than to the repair shop. She changed her clothes quickly, then found Buddy Fletcher's name in the telephone book and called him. No answer. Where was he? Back at Sylvia's? That possibility filled her with more than simple anxiety.

She thought of driving by Sylvia's house again to check if he was there, but that thought made her even more anxious. Beau might see her there again, and how would she explain her presence a second time? Instead, she went back to work and called Buddy several times from there. Still no answer.

There was plenty of work at Elégance du Sud to keep her busy, in spite of her worry about what Buddy might be doing. Hillary had apparently forgotten her disapproval of Buddy as well as Jane's defense of him. She was busy with her own work. Another television show was shaping up to be a real headache. It was to be filmed partly in Hillary's own garden, featuring her expertise with roses grown from cuttings, and partly in the studio, featuring flower arrangements using the roses she'd grown. There were always endless details to deal with, and now Hillary was having a particularly difficult time concentrating on those details because she was excited about the charity dinner the mayor had hired her to plan, in spite of the coq au vin recipe. Concentration, Jane had learned, was not Hillary's strong suit, anyway.

"Jane!" she said, drawing the name out. "This is not just any party, you know. It's the mayor's charity dinner. At the country club. He's fixin' to announce that he will run for governor, and he's going to do it then. At *my* party. Told me that himself. And I thought I was ruined after that coq au vin incident." Hillary had called Jane into her office to give her this information.

"That's wonderful, Hillary." Though she tried, Jane couldn't keep her remark from sounding halfhearted. She still had other things on her mind. Buddy, for one thing; not to mention someone with the unlikely name of Wave, who was dead; blackmail notes; and Cyclone Malone, who had never returned her call. The more she thought about it, the more she thought it was possible he hadn't forgiven Sylvia for snubbing him. And if those insane television commercials were any indication, it was also possible he was crazy enough to want the ultimate revenge. But how did that tie in with the blackmail note? The whole thing was infinitely more complicated than Jane even wanted to think about.

"We'll both be attending, of course. Not just as caterers, but as guests," Hillary was saying. "I hope you have something to wear, Jane." Jane glanced down at her five-year-old burgundy knit dress as Hillary emphasized, "This is important. And you'll need an escort, of course."

"An escort? I'll be working."

"Well, of course you will, but honey, a lady doesn't go unescorted to a function like this."

"Why not?"

"Jane! This is the South, not Los Angeles. We're much more . . . well, mindful of appearances. Maybe that policeman. You know, Beau Jackson."

"Are you crazy?"

"Well—"

"He's trying to pin a murder rap on you. Maybe both of us."

"Oh, all right, but think about it. There must be *somebody*." Hillary gave her a worried look, then dismissed her with a flutter of her perfectly manicured hand and began rifling through the papers on her desk.

"Hillary," Jane said, deciding on the spur of the moment that this was as good a time as any to say what she had to say. Hillary took her eyes from the papers on her desk to glance at Jane. "I was thinking that I ought to, well, instead of coming in to work tomorrow, that maybe I should go to—"

"I need you here, Jane. Why do you need to go anywhere?"

"Well, to see Cy Malone. In Montgomery. Since he was seeing Sylvia, maybe he knows something about that blackmail note. Maybe he even knows who Wave is."

"Oh!" Hillary seemed to be considering what Jane said for a moment then a familiar light came on in her eyes. "Maybe I should go with you."

"But what about the dinner? The TV show?"

"We can finish up the work on the show today, and the dinner's a week away."

"But I thought—"

"I wouldn't miss talking to Cy Malone about this for the world. We're good at this, you know. We were a great team making that getaway from Sylvia's place. I haven't had so much fun since I learned how to macrame!"

Jane was silent a moment, trying to think of some excuse not to have Hillary come along, but none presented itself. "All right," she said, finally, "but I'll drive."

"Your car?" Hillary looked genuinely appalled. "No offense, Jane, but—"

"That way no one will recognize you when we leave town," Jane said, congratulating herself on her fast thinking. There was really no reason to believe it would matter if Hillary was seen leaving town, but she'd try anything to keep from having to ride thirty miles with Hillary at the wheel.

"Oh, I see. We'll be undercover." Hillary touched a mauve wine fingertip to her lips and sounded as excited as a child. "Oh, Jane, you are obviously a complete disaster as a cook, and I suspect you don't know a rose from a rhododendron, but you are so wickedly clever and devious."

The next morning, after Jane got Sarah off to school, she drove to Hillary's house. Hillary met her at the door, wearing dark glasses, jeans, sneakers, a billed cap with Atlanta Braves stenciled on the crown, and an incongruously expensive linen shirt. Jane was dressed in her brown suit, thinking the information she needed might be more forthcoming if she had a professional look.

Surprised, Jane scrutinized her from head to toe. "Hillary? Is that you?"

"It's great, isn't it? And that car of yours is perfect. Who would ever expect to see *me* in this?"

"You're right, Hillary. It's perfect." Jane felt she had to humor her, lest she change her mind and insist on driving herself.

The drive to Montgomery, although hot with no air conditioner, was uneventful, a fact for which Jane was thankful. She didn't wish even to consider what the trip might have been like with Hillary at the wheel.

The car dealership where Cy Malone worked was located in a relatively new section of Montgomery, surrounded by other dealerships and a sprawling shopping mall that had the look of all shopping malls from California to Maine.

Cyclone Malone was not available, the pretty receptionist informed them. The nameplate on her desk identified her as Tiffany.

"Not available? Does that mean he's busy with a customer and will be available in a little while? Or does it mean he's gone for the day, or what?" Jane knew she was being California pushy rather than acting the part of the Southern lady, but the long drive in ninety degree temperature and ninety percent plus humidity with no air conditioner had put her in no mood to be pleasant.

"I'm sorry, but I just don't know," Tiffany said, being courteous and apologetic. "You see, he just lost somebody who was real close to him? And he's really not doing too good? Just keeps himself closed up in his office there. I mean, he won't even return telephone calls or talk to customers or anything. I guess you could say he was in mournin'."

Jane edged a little closer to the young woman's desk. "Was the person who was real close to him named Sylvia, by any chance?"

"You know, I think she was. Sylvia somebody, from over at Prosper. Some kind of a TV star."

Hillary suddenly came alive behind her dark glasses. "Star? She was no star, she was just a—"

"That's right," Jane interrupted. "She had the *Sylvia Davis Show*. Why don't you tell Mr. Malone we're friends of Miss Davis, and we'd like to see him."

"Friends?" Tiffany looked uncertain.

"That's right," Jane said. Hillary adjusted her dark glasses and pulled her cap down further on her head.

"Well, I don't know . . ."

"Just tell him." Jane moved closer, placed both hands on Tiffany's desk, and leaned toward her. She'd seen Jim Ed use the same subtly intimidating tactic on a witness.

Tiffany wasn't ready to give in just yet, however. "If y'all are friends of Miss Davis, then you know that her death was, well, you know, not what you'd call a regular way of dying?"

"Yes, we know," Hillary said before Jane had a chance to speak. Hillary moved toward Tiffany's desk. "That's why we're here. We thought we might lend some comfort to Mr. Malone in his time of grief," she said in her most overly dramatic voice. "You see, we were with her near the end, and we thought if we could just share some of our feelings, it would help lift the dark velvet curtain of despair for all of us and allow us some glimmer of the morning light shining through the gauzy sheers of hope."

"Oh my," Tiffany said, her eyes wide. "Well, in that case . . . Maybe I could at least ask if he would see you."

"God bless you, child," Hillary said, and she extended a hand in a dramatic gesture toward Tiffany, who was moving toward the closed door behind her desk.

As soon as Tiffany opened the door to the office, Hillary took off her glasses and smiled broadly at Jane.

Jane shook her head in disbelief. "Dark velvet curtain of despair? Gauzy sheers of hope?"

Hillary put her dark glasses on again and looked, with confidence, at the door to Cyclone Malone's office. "In the South, Jane, mourning is an art."

Within seconds Cyclone Malone himself was filling the doorway of his office, beckoning with large hands and calling out in a booming voice, "Ladies, ladies, please come in."

The office walls were lined with photographs of a smiling Cyclone standing beside various people who appeared to be important, all taken, apparently, during his television days. Most of the people Jane didn't recognize, except for Wayne Newton and Garth Brooks. Wayne and Cyclone stood side by side, dressed in white tuxedos. In the picture with Garth, Cyclone's ten-gallon hat was pushed back on his head and his jeans were tucked into a pair of elaborately hand-tooled cowboy boots. There were also photographs of Cyclone in the various wild costumes he donned for his used car television ads. One big placard boasted his motto, which he repeated ad nauseam in his commercials: Cyclone Malone, dealing up a storm!

"Hi, I'm Cy Malone," he said, offering first Jane and then Hillary his big hand. They each introduced themselves. Hillary told him her name was Fanny Cook. He was wearing a gaudy gold watch and a diamond ring as well as designer jeans and a shirt that was unmistakably Ralph Lauren. The used car business was obviously profitable. He ushered them into his office and indicated two plush chairs across from his desk. Then, going back to his own chair behind his desk, he said, "Y'all were both Sylvie's friends?" He had an eager expression on his face, as if their friendship might somehow restore her to life.

"Everyone in Prosper knew her," Jane said evasively.

"Oh, I know they did. I lived there myself, you know. Used to be in television. But I don't want to talk about me. Tell me about Sylvie. They say she was murdered." The expression on his face was one of genuine grief.

"That's what they're saying," Jane said.

"It's hard to believe," Hillary said, as if the Academy Award judges were seated in the room. "I just can't think of any reason why anybody would want to do that, can you?"

Cyclone first shook his head, then, with a worried squint, said, "Well . . ."

"Yes, Mr. Malone?" Jane's voice sounded eager.

"Cy. Call me Cy."

"Cy. You were saying . . ."

"What? Oh, well, there was this one person, down there in Prosper that was Sylvie's rival. Had some kind of a cooking show or something on another channel."

Hillary sat up straighter. "Cooking show? It's more than that, it's—"

"But that was just a friendly rivalry, wasn't it, Cy?" Jane said, interrupting. "I mean, one would hardly think that kind of thing would lead to murder. I was wondering about some of those investigative reports she did. She must have made a few enemies that way."

Cy shook his head. "She never talked about that. All she could talk about was that dame with the cooking show. Mostly she just kept worrying about that crazy cooking show beating her on the ratings. Said the woman that was on it was up to cheap tricks. You know, hinting that she was going to have famous people on her show like Martha Stewart and Julia Child when there wasn't any truth to it. Sylvie said that woman was even trying to sour the advertisers on her."

"What! I never—"

"Still, is that enough to suspect murder?" Jane gave Hillary a quick warning glance.

Cy shook his head again and rubbed his face with his hands in a gesture of weariness. "No," he said, "not really. It's just that this cooking dame was somebody she

talked about. Can't remember her name. Rosland maybe.
Or Nancy? Barbara? I don't know. Had the same name
as a president's wife. The truth is, I don't know why anybody would want to hurt my Sylvie. She was the sweetest
thing. Oh, I know she sounded tough on that TV show of
hers. All those politicians. All that muckraking. But that
was her show business personality. Like me when I stick
myself in a tub of Jell-O or dress up like a clown. That's
not the real me. And that tough gal ever'body saw on TV
wasn't really Sylvie. But then y'all know that, don't you?
Bein' friends of hers.'' Cy shook his head again and
dropped it into his hands.

Jane, who was temporarily moved by his obvious grief,
let Hillary gain the advantage.

"You know, Cy, Sylvia used to love to talk about her
competition. The cooking woman, I mean? Do you remember what she said?'' Hillary smiled sweetly.

Cy glanced up, brightened a little, even chuckled.
"Her? Well, she had this plan to get her over to her house,
see. Told her she wanted it decorated. Seems this woman
owns one of them redecorating stores as well as havin'
that TV show. Anyhow, Sylvie was going to see if she
couldn't get some kind of an investigative piece out of it.
You know, she figured the woman would promise something she couldn't deliver, decorating wise, or give her
shoddy fabric or something, then she'd have her story.''
Cy chuckled again. "Sylvie was smart as they come. And
sweet, too, just as sweet as she could be.''

"Shoddy fabric! Of all the nerve! I'll have you know
I never—''

"You're right, Cy,'' Jane said, still trying to keep Hillary under control. "Sylvia was both smart and sweet.''
Jane leaned closer and said in almost a whisper, "Did she
ever say anything to you about, well, about needing
money?'' Jane was fishing, looking for some way to find
out who or why anyone might be blackmailing Sylvia.

"Sylvie?'' Cy chuckled. "You know how she was,
bein' friends with her and all.''

"Oh, well, yes, of course we know. But—she wasn't well off, of course," Jane said.

"Spent money like it was going out of style. Good thing her daddy was rich." Cy shook his head and smiled, as if he was entertaining a fond memory. "Well, now, I've done all the talking," Cyclone said. "Now it's y'all's turn. Tell me what you know about Sylvie. It helps just to talk about it, you know."

Jane and Hillary looked at each other, both speechless for the moment. "Well . . ." Hillary said, uncertainly.

"Did she suffer?" Cy looked once again as if he might cry.

"I—I'm not sure," Jane said. Cy's obvious pain, along with her own charade, was making her uncomfortable.

"There was a sofa pillow that—" Hillary stopped speaking when Jane gave her a threatening look. "What I mean is," Hillary began again, "well, what I mean is she had new sofa pillows, which she had purchased from the woman who was going to redecorate her house, who, incidentally, is marvelous at what she does. So all I'm saying is that even with the few touches that Mrs. Scarborough had already added to the poor woman's house, there was this added element of elegance to her house, and—"

"You're tellin' me she died an elegant death," Cy said. He gave Hillary a warm smile, as if that somehow comforted him.

Jane wanted to ask him if Sylvia knew someone known as Wave, but she didn't dare stay any longer. She knew she had to get Hillary out of there before she got worse.

Later, in the car as they were driving back to Prosper, Hillary finally removed her Atlanta Braves cap and pushed her sunglasses up to rest in her thick, chestnut-colored hair, which she had loosened from its ponytail.

"I just can't believe anybody could be so tacky!" Hillary said in that breathless, restrained way Jane had come to think of as Southern Belle Indignant. "Can you imagine? Planning an investigative piece on me? Why, my family has lived in Alabama since *before* the War Between the States"—old Southern-speak for the Civil War, Jane had learned—"and we have always been upstanding and honest, well mostly at least, in our business dealings, and that woman was nothing but—"

"Don't speak ill of the dead," Jane said.

"Well—" Hillary sputtered a moment. "She was a Yankee. What can you expect?" Another point Jane had learned: Anyone who was disliked or different and who had the misfortune of hailing from someplace else, sometimes even northern Mississippi, was given the despicable designation of *Yankee.* "What good was this trip here to Montgomery, anyway?" Hillary continued. "We didn't learn anything we didn't already know, did we? Except that Sylvia was even more devious and underhanded than we could imagine."

"I don't know," Jane said, musing. "Maybe it was a wasted trip. But maybe it wasn't. I just don't know yet. It does seem to me, though, that about all we learned that we didn't already know is that Sylvia's daddy was rich."

"Money doesn't count for everything," Hillary said. "There's such a thing as breeding and good taste, you know."

When, after a while, Hillary grew tired of venting her anger about Sylvia, she launched once again on the importance of the mayor's party she was to plan.

"We are going to make this live up to our name of Elégance du Sud, Jane. The hors d'oeuvres must be just that, *élégante,* the French pronunciation. I was thinking roast tarragon chicken with grilled figs and grilled asparagus and for dessert, my favorite genoise with a marzipan icing. You and I, of course, will dress in basic black. Simple without being plain. And definitely not shoddy. *Élégante,* Jane. Think *élégante.* Oh, and Jane, you *must* have an escort."

"Hillary, I still don't see why that's necessary. I don't care if this is the South, we're the caterers, not regular guests."

"We are ladies, Jane. We don't go to functions like this unescorted."

"Oh, come on, this is not the nineteenth century."

"No, it is Prosper, Alabama. If you like, I can arrange for someone for you. Billy's cousin is available, I think, and—"

"Never mind, I'll find my own escort."

"Good. And don't forget the black dress. It must be—"

"I know. Simple and *élégante*."

By the time Jane dropped off Hillary and finally got home, she was very glad to change into her simple, if not-so-*élégante* shorts and T-shirt. She had only a few minutes to relax before Sarah came home from school, bringing her friend Shakura with her.

"Hi, Mom," Sarah said. "How was Montgomery?"

"Hot. I've got to get that air conditioner fixed. Just can't fit it into the budget yet."

"My brother can fix it for you," Shakura offered. She was an attractive child with very dark skin and large, melted-chocolate eyes and a fine-boned, waifish look. "He's real good at stuff like that."

"Thanks, Shakura, but I wouldn't want to trouble—"

"Oh, it wouldn't be trouble, Miz Ferguson. Dushawn works on folks' cars all the time. It brings in extra money for him and helps him out with his schoolin'. He's goin' to school, too, you know, just like you did. Over at Prosper Junior College? He wants to be a lawyer, too, someday."

"Well, if he would let me pay him—"

"You ask him, Miz Ferguson. He won't charge too much."

"Thanks, Shakura. I'll do that," Jane said.

"Want a snack, Mom?" Sarah called from the kitchen, where she was already digging into the ice cream carton.

When the three of them were seated at the kitchen table devouring the pecan praline ice cream, Sarah asked, "So, did you solve the mystery?"

"Mystery? You mean about the used car I was looking

for?'' Jane asked, trying to give Sarah a warning look.

"No, the murder.''

"Sarah!'' Jane cut her eyes discreetly toward Shakura.

"It's OK, Mom. Shakura's cool.''

"Oh, yes,'' Shakura assured her. "I know all about Miss Sylvia Davis. Sarah says you're snooping around investigating all about her gettin' killed. You're real smart, Sarah says. Just like a real lawyer.''

"Just like a . . . ? Look, girls, I don't think this is something we should be talking about.''

"Dushawn says he's not surprised.''

"Not surprised? About me?''

"No, about Miz Davis.''

"Oh?'' Jane's interest was definitely piqued.

"I don't think he liked her much. 'Cause he tried to get her to look into Rashaud's accident, and she wouldn't do it.''

"Rashaud's accident?''

"My brother. He was killed in a car wreck last year in June. June twenty-fifth.'' Shakura's eyes grew murky.

"Yes, I know, but why would Dushawn want her to look into it?''

"For Mama's sake. Mama always did say Rashaud was a good boy, and he wouldn't get drunk and run off the road like that and get himself killed. She thinks somebody else run him off the road. It happened over in the next county, you know. But Dushawn says the sheriff over there's not gonna investigate anything for black folks. Mama says she wishes Beau Jackson could do the investigatin'. Mr. Jackson's a fair man, she says.''

"Oh?''

"Dushawn says don't count on it. But since Rashaud died, Dushawn, he doesn't count on much. It's like he's mad all the time. At everybody. 'Cept Mama, maybe. He was sure mad at Miss Davis, I can tell you that.''

"I think a lot of people were mad at her, Shakura.''

"Do you think someone was mad enough to kill her, Mom?'' Sarah asked.

"I don't know, honey.''

"Is it true Hillary is one of the suspects?"

"Sarah! Where did you get such an idea?"

"Mom, really, I'm not dumb. I've heard you on the phone with her. I know that's why you're doing all this investigating. To help her out, I mean. You don't think she did it, do you?"

"Of course not. But this is not the sort of thing children should be talking about. I want you to forget it, Sarah. Think about something else."

"Mom! You treat me like a child."

"You're ten years old, my precocious darling. You *are* a child."

The argument would have gone on if the doorbell hadn't rung. Sarah and Shakura, expecting another friend to join them, ran to answer it, but it was not another ten-year-old who stood at the door to greet them. It was, instead, Beau Jackson.

Jane recognized his voice. "Sarah! Hi!" she heard him say while she was still in the kitchen putting the ice cream dishes in the sink. "And you're Thelma Young's daughter, aren't you? Xena?"

"Xena is my sister. She's away at college. I'm Shakura."

"No! You can't be little Shakura."

There was a giggle from both of the girls, and Shakura's voice again. "You're Mr. Jackson, aren't you? The man with the horses?"

"Horses!" Sarah said with the usual ten-year-old's passion for the creatures.

"That's right," Jane heard Beau say, just as she came into the living room, drying her hands on a dish towel. "Xena used to come out and ride them sometimes." Jackson glanced at Jane, gave her a smile before he turned his attention back to the girls. "Maybe you and Sarah would like to come out."

This time, a unison squeal, and Sarah turned to Jane. "Oh, Mom, could I? Please, could I?"

"We'll see, dear. Is there something I can do for you, Mr. Jackson?"

"Beau. Remember?"

"OK, Beau."

"A glass of ice tea would be nice."

Jane hesitated a moment, staring at him, wondering just what was going on. "OK," she said, finally. "I'll just be a minute."

"You don't have to bother bringing it to me," Beau said, taking a step further into the living room. "I could just have it in the kitchen."

Another moment of hesitation before Jane said, "Sure." Then she pulled a pitcher of tea from the refrigerator and poured some in a glass. She had learned the Southern habit of keeping ice tea available at all times. She set the glass in front of him and asked, "So, how's the investigation going?"

Beau took a long drink of the tea before he answered. "You tell me."

"What?"

"Still doing a little investigating of your own, I hear."

"I don't know what you're talking about."

"Cy Malone? In Montgomery? I already knew about you asking questions at the TV station. Did I tell you that?"

"You told me."

"And talking to Reverend Collins?"

Jane managed to cover her shock with a cool, "My, my, word does get around, doesn't it?"

Beau shrugged. "It's my job."

"Obviously, you do it very well. And by the way, that thing with the horses was very clever of you. All ten-year-old girls are crazy about them. You could probably get any kind of information you want with a bribe like that."

"Hey! Come on, that's hitting below the belt."

"Is it?"

"I'd never do that. Bribe a kid like that, I mean."

"Yeah? Well it sounded awfully close. And that's my daughter you were talking to. I don't take kindly to—"

"I'm sorry, Jane, OK? I swear, I didn't mean a thing

by it. I know how you feel about your daughter. Lordy!''

''You do?''

''Well, sure. I mean, I never had a kid of my own, but I love kids. I always wanted them. That was one of the problems with my marriage. I wanted them; she didn't.''

A gray look came over Beau's face, taking Jane aback. All she could manage was a weak, ''Oh.'' Then, guardedly, ''I'm sorry—that you didn't have kids, I mean. They're great. I mean, Sarah's great. A pain in the ass, sometimes, but really she's . . . Look, I'm babbling. It's just that she's very important to me. She's all I've got, and I love her like you wouldn't believe, and I don't want you or anyone else—''

''I understand,'' Beau said. He stood up and gave her a smile. ''It's been a long day for me, and it's not over yet. Thanks for the tea.'' He turned and was on his way back to the living room.

''But—'' Jane stammered, disconcerted.

Beau turned back to her with a questioning look.

''Why did you—I mean, what did you come here for? Not just for tea, I know.''

''No,'' he said. ''Not just for the tea. I just wanted to see you. I mean to check on you,'' he added quickly. ''See if you were all right.'' He was actually blushing as he turned away again. He was just about to let himself out the door when it opened, seemingly on its own. There, in the doorway, stood Buddy Fletcher.

8

"Hey there, Jackson!" Buddy said.

Beau gave Jane a quick glance that might have been questioning, then he said, "How's it going, Buddy?"

"Can't complain, I guess," Buddy said. But he was saying it to Beau's back. Beau had already moved past him and was walking away.

Buddy stepped inside and closed the door. "Got any tea?" he asked as he made his way to the sofa.

"Geez, what am I running here? The Tea House of the August Moon?"

"This ain't August. It's September already."

Jane breathed a weary sigh, then shrugged. "I can't argue with that, Buddy." She turned away to fetch another glass of tea.

"Whatsa matter?" Buddy asked when Jane handed him his glass. "You look kinda worried or something."

"I am worried. I think Beau knows something."

"About who done that woman in, you mean?"

"No, about us being in her house."

"Why you think that? He say something?"

"Not exactly. I mean, well, sort of. What he did was let me know that he knows just about everything else that

I've done, and I think he was just kind of feeling around to see if I would say something about being in the house.''

Buddy shook his head. ''The trouble with you, Miz Ferguson, is that you think too much. Way too much.''

''Buddy, listen to me, he's—''

''No, I mean it. You see, your trouble is, you get to thinking, and then, the next thing you know, you're imagining all kinds of things. Thinking don't do you no good. Now, you take me, I do what you call use my head,'' he said, tapping at his skull with his forefinger, ''but I don't never think too much.''

''Oh, yeah, I see how that works. You spent a year in the can. I guess that was because you were using your head.''

Buddy took on a hurt expression. ''Hey, that was before I met Jim Ed. I was using my head when I hired him, and I ain't never been back in jail since.''

''You didn't hire him, the court appointed him, but what's that got to do with Beau knowing about us in that house?''

''I was gettin' to that. In fact, that's what I come to tell you. Ever'thing's took care of. We ain't got nothing to worry about.''

''Does that mean you put the paper back?''

''Well, not exactly.''

''Not exactly?''

''I was fixin' to climb up that tree, you know, but I decided I oughta have a look around first, and that's when I seen Jackson out there talkin' to you, and I thought, man oh man, I got to git outta here.''

''You didn't put the paper back in the safe, and you say I've got nothing to worry about?'' Jane's head was pounding.

''Well, the thing is, I'm fixin' to put the paper back in the safe.''

''What do you mean you're 'fixin' to'?'' By now, Jane assumed her blood pressure had to be off the chart. Sylvia Davis's murder should have absolutely nothing to do with her, but by some crazy twist of fate, she had gotten herself undeniably tangled up in it and with an ex-con as well, who, it seemed, had a way of making things go from bad to worse.

"See, it was like this. After I seen Jackson, there I am kinda hangin' out, you know, waitin' for him to get outta there so I can go in."

"He didn't see you, did he?"

"I'm gettin' to that. So, I'm over on the next block, walkin', you know, 'cause you drove off and left me, which was OK, 'cause it woulda look suspicious if you hadn't. So, anyway, here comes Jackson cruisin' by. He seen me."

"Oh, lord!"

"No, now, wait a minute. So he stops his car, see."

"There is an end to this story, isn't there?"

"He stops his car, and he hollers at me. 'Buddy,' he says. Well, it scared the shit out of me. I thought, *This is it.* But anyhow, I turn around, bein' the good citizen that I am, I turn around, and I say, 'Hey.' "

"I don't think I want to hear the rest of this."

"I'm wonderin' what in hell does he want with me. I ain't done nothin'."

"Except commit a felony or two."

"If you don't quit interruptin', I ain't never gonna get to the good part."

"Forgive me. By all means, get to the good part."

"Like I say, I was wondering what I done wrong, and he just says, 'Hey, Buddy, what's new?' And then, the next thing I know, he's askin' me—get this—he's askin' me if I will open Sylvia Davis's safe for him."

"What?"

"Open her safe. That's what he said. 'Buddy,' he says, 'you're just the man I need. A professional,' he says, 'so we won't have to blow it up and do any damage,' he says. So I say, 'Yeah, sure, glad to help out.' So that's how I'm gonna get that paper back in there. When I open the safe, I'll just slip it in. He won't know the difference."

Jane found that she was unable to speak for a moment. She could only stare at Buddy, wide-eyed and mouth agape. Finally, she said, "It won't work, Buddy."

"Sure it will, I'll just—"

"Beau will be right there, looking over your shoulder, I'm sure. He'll have you open the safe, then he'll have you move out of the way while he retrieves what's inside. There'll be no chance at all to put anything back."

"Now, there you go again, thinking too much. It'll work out. Just wait. You'll see."

Jane was pacing the floor now, worrying. "That's why he gave you that look when he was leaving here. That's why he was so uncomfortable about telling me why he was here. He must think I've asked you to do the same thing for me. Open that safe. He's been investigating me, you know. Knows just about every move I've made. I can't afford any trouble, Buddy. I've got a daughter. If any of this hurts Sarah in any way . . ."

"Wait a minute, back up," Buddy said. "You say Beau Jackson's been investigatin' you? Knows ever' move you make? Listen, if you want me to, I can fix it so's he won't never bother you no more. Then you won't have to worry 'bout your kid or nothin'."

"I don't even want to ask what you mean by that, Buddy. Just don't fix anything, OK?"

"You sure?"

"I'm sure."

"Well, you just tell me when you want something. It's yours. I can't never repay Jim Ed for what he done for me, but I can take care of his woman."

"I'm not Jim Ed's woman, Buddy, but thank you, anyway." Jane rubbed her temples and collapsed into a chair.

"Hey, you don't look so good," Buddy said. "Want me to get you a aspirin or something?"

"No thanks. I'll be all right."

"Look, Miz Ferguson, if all this is botherin' you too much, I'll just go back to the first plan we had. I'll go in there some night, and I'll put that paper back. I'll get around all them cops somehow."

"All what cops?"

"I guess I forgot to tell you. Beau said he was going

to have the house under twenty-four-hour surveillance.''

"He *does* suspect something. I knew it.''

"Tell you what. There's gonna be a big wingding at the country club Friday night. All the big shots will be there. Including Jackson. That would be a good time for me to break in. You know, when ever'body's busy doing other things.''

"What about the surveillance?''

"I'll figure out something. At least it won't be Jackson that's there. He'll be at the wingding. Just give me the word.''

Jane shook her head. "No, Buddy, I'm not going to tell you to break into the house again. I never should have brought you into this in the first place.''

"Well, OK,'' Buddy said with an elaborate shrug.

"When are you meeting with Beau to open the safe?''

"Monday mornin'.''

"Monday? Oh, God, why can't it be tomorrow? Why can't we get this over with?''

Buddy shrugged again. "It's their schedule, not mine. Hey, look at you. You got that worried frown. Don't worry, OK? And if there's anything I can do for you, anything at all . . .''

Jane sat up straighter, and her head seemed to clear ever so slightly. "You know, there is one thing.''

"Just name it.'' Buddy gave her an eager smile.

"You could be my escort at that wingding.''

"Me?''

"Why not?'' She was thinking, *Why not, indeed?* Not only would he be the escort Hillary insisted she needed, but it would be one way to make sure he stayed out of trouble.

"I ain't got the clothes.''

"Neither do I, but it's not stopping me.''

"What will Jim Ed think?''

"Jim Ed is *married*, Buddy. To someone else. I don't *care* what he thinks. Besides, this isn't a date. I just need an escort, that's all. Hillary says I can't go without one.''

"Well, in that case . . . I just don't want Jim Ed to think I'm out of line."

"You'll be protecting me, remember? The car that tried to run me off the road? You said to let you know if I needed you, didn't you? Well, you just never know who might be looking for me at that wingding." She was being manipulative, she knew, making up things as she went along. Anything to convince Buddy. And it seemed to be working.

"Well, OK. If you really need me, then I guess you can count on me."

"Thanks, Buddy. It's nice to have someone I can count on. And don't let that note from Sylvia out of your sight."

A golden genoise, which Hillary had made using six eggs, a cup of sugar, a teaspoon of vanilla extract, a cup of sifted cake flour, and a quarter cup of clarified butter, was cooling on a rack in her kitchen. It was a miracle the cake had turned out at all, considering the disaster Jane had created when Hillary asked her to clarify the butter. Jane, not having the slightest idea what clarified butter was, had put it in the saucepan Hillary had handed her, and then had proceeded to scorch it until a minor grease fire erupted in Hillary's spotless, gleaming porcelain kitchen.

Hillary had screeched, thrown a towel over the fire, and then, with amazing efficiency, had gone about cleaning up the mess.

"My lord, Jane," she said. "You just wait for the froth on the top, that's all, then strain it and throw away the sediment. You don't have to *burn* it, for heaven's sake. Here," she said, handing her a mixing bowl with one hand while she wiped up spilled burned butter with the other. "Make the marzipan. That's easy enough. The secret is to add a little confectioners' sugar to the almond paste along with the egg white and food coloring if it seems too oily."

Jane had tried, but the rose petals she attempted to shape from the rolled balls of marzipan looked like blobs of something suspicious rather than roses, in spite of the fact that she followed Hillary's instructions exactly.

In the end, Hillary sent her home. She was never going to get the food ready for the mayor's big party at this rate, and she'd just as soon do it herself. Jane could work on the accounting for Elégance du Sud, which Hillary never had time to do and didn't understand anyway, and she could fill out some of those endless government forms that are the curse of small-business owners.

Jane was glad for the assignment and glad to be able to go home to work on it. She had flour on her face, her fingers were stained with red, green, and yellow food coloring, and her hair smelled of scorched butter. In her opinion, accounting books and asinine government forms were a welcome respite.

"Did you find something to wear to the party?" Sarah asked when she got home from school.

"No," Jane said. "Hillary says it has to be something black and understated. The only thing I own that's black is a pair of sweats."

"What's Buddy wearing?" Sarah asked while she looked for the TV remote. "Can you trust him not to wear his NRA cap?"

"It would go with my sweats," Jane said. She got up to give Sarah a welcome-home hug. "I don't know what Buddy's wearing. And I can't trust him for anything, except maybe to do something completely unpredictable and possibly dangerous to the welfare of us all."

"Then let's start with you," Sarah said. She gave up looking for the remote, went to her mother, and took her hand, pulling her toward the bedroom and her closet. "Let's see," she said, hand on her chin while she studied the row of T-shirts, jeans, cotton shorts, and a reasonable collection of slightly out-of-date clothes suitable for work, all hanging side by side on the closet rack, carelessly, like soldiers at rest in formation.

Sarah shook her head, discouraged, then whirled suddenly, snapping her fingers. "I have an idea!" she said and raced off to her own bedroom. In a few seconds she came back with a silky black dress hanging by two thin straps to a wire hanger.

"That?" Jane recognized the slinky little number. "I gave that to you to play dress up."

"It's still in perfect shape. Shakura and I only played with it a few times."

"But I can't wear that. It's from nineteen-seventy-nine. It's a disco dress."

"It's so retro, Mom. So perfect! Here, try it on." Jane took the dress, shed her other clothes, and slipped it over her head. "Terrific!" Sarah said as the soft material fell over Jane's hips.

"I feel almost naked," Jane said, fingering the thin spaghetti straps. She turned around to get a view of her back in the mirror. "But I guess it's not too bad. Considering it came out of the rag bag, so to speak."

Jane had to let the accounting go for the rest of the day, because Sarah insisted, once Jane's dress problem was solved, that she help her pack for the overnight she was planning at Shakura's house. They got out the sleeping bag, Sarah's favorite pajamas, her teddy bear, and Jane's video of an old Elvis Presley film, which recently had become Sarah's favorite movie.

The next day, Jane had the dress cleaned and pressed, dug out her grandmother's little gold earrings, washed her hair and curled it loosely, then brushed it into a shining gold-flecked cascade almost to her shoulders.

"You look stunning, Mom," Sarah said.

Jane gave her a quick kiss, then loaded the sleeping bag and baggage into the car and drove her to the Youngs' house. Even though the house was a short distance away, Jane was concerned that the old Toyota wasn't going to make it. The car was smoking and smelled of exhaust fumes. Apparently, there was more than just the air conditioner that needed repairs. But Jane's paycheck was still ten days away. She'd have to wait for that.

When they arrived at the Youngs' home, Thelma Young met her at the door. "Hi there, we've been waitin' for y'all," she said. "Please come in." Thelma was a few years older than Jane. She'd been widowed since Shakura, her youngest, was two months old. She'd made a living for her four children even before her husband's death, relying on her mother, who lived with her, to help care for the children while she worked her way up from stock clerk to manager of the local JC Penney department store. "I'm grateful I had the opportunity," she had once confided to Jane. "It's something my mother would have been denied."

Jane had remained friends with Thelma Young ever since they'd met through their daughters, but Thelma's need to make a living and, recently, Jane's law school, had kept them from having time to grow close. On the occasions that Jane saw Thelma now, it seemed that she always looked even more tired than she used to—a change that had come about since the accident that took the life of her oldest son, Rashaud.

"That you, Sarah?" a voice called from the kitchen. It was Thelma's mother, Truly Newell. She was a short, rounded woman with eyes that shone with a devilish twinkle. Arthritis had forced her to walk with a cane. "Oh, Miss Jane," she said when she stuck her head into the living room. "My, my, ain't you dressed up. If that no-count ex of yours could see you now, wouldn't he be sorry?"

Jane laughed, a tired sound. "Wouldn't faze him, Mrs. Newell. He's got Miss Alabama now, you know."

"Hmmph," Truly said, "wait till she's your age. She'll go to saggin' in the butt and the boobs, you mark my word."

"Mama!" Thelma said.

Truly turned back to the kitchen, hobbling on her cane and ignoring her daughter. "You give 'em hell tonight, Miss Jane," she said over her shoulder. "You ain't hardly saggin' too much nowheres yet."

"Well, you do look pretty," Thelma said, as Shakura and Sarah ran off, giggling, to Shakura's room. "You didn't buy that at Penney's," she added with a wry expression.

"Actually, I did. Back in seventy-nine."

Thelma laughed. "You know what they say about quality. It never goes out of style." She moved aside for Jane to enter, and Jane couldn't resist. She wasn't anxious to go to the party. She took a seat in the chair Thelma offered her.

"Thanks for watching Sarah for me tonight," Jane said. "I think she's actually excited about being away from me. I don't go out much, so she's always with me."

"Shakura's the same way. Lord knows, I'd be too tired to go out, even if I got the opportunity," Thelma said. "I hear this is supposed to be some fancy party you're going to."

"So I'm told. And I'm just part of the hired help. One of the caterers. Do you think I'm a little overdressed for that?"

Thelma dismissed the idea with a wave of her hand. "Of course not. At that kind of party *everybody's* supposed to be dressed up. Besides," she said, cocking her head, studying Jane's appearance, "the dress is what you'd call understated. Basic black. No jewelry except for small gold earrings. It's perfect."

Jane breathed a heavy sigh. "I guess you can tell I don't really want to go. I'm not good at this pretentious kind of thing. Maybe I can spend most of the time in the kitchen, since I'm the hired help."

Thelma shook her head. "Oh, I hear Mrs. Scarborough has a whole staff to watch over the kitchen when she does one of those parties, so she can just mingle with the crowd. Probably expects you to do the same thing."

"Just my luck," Jane said. "I hear the mayor is going to make some kind of political announcement about running for governor. I'm not crazy about politics, either."

"Oh now, you'll have a good time," Thelma said. "And the mayor's OK. Just a little pompous, that's all. He was real nice to me after Rashaud died. Even helped my daughter get a scholarship to State. It was in all the papers—that accident—because Rashaud was such a football player. You should have seen him run, Jane, you should have seen that boy run.''

"I'm sorry I never did. I just wasn't into high school football, I guess.''

Thelma smiled, remembering her son. ''I didn't expect anybody, especially not a white man, to take such an interest in my problems. I guess it was because Rashaud was such a football player that he did. But I'm grateful, whatever the reason. I don't know how I would have managed to send Xena to college without that scholarship. It's good to have friends in high places, as they say.''

Jane stood and gave Thelma a smile. ''OK, for your sake, then, I'll try to remember that and behave myself.'' Before she got to the door, Dushawn, a tall, gangly seventeen-year-old, stepped inside. He was wiping his hands on an oil-stained cloth.

"Hi, Dushawn,'' Jane said. It always made her heart ache to see Dushawn. He'd changed since his brother's death. Grown sullen at times.

"Shakura, she tell me you got air conditioner trouble,'' Dushawn said. He'd taken on the habit of speaking in Ebonics dialect at times, in spite of the fact that Thelma insisted upon standard English.

"That's right.''

"Ain't nothin' but a wore-out belt. You want me fix it, jus' bring yo' car over.''

"Really? Just a belt? You're sure? Not a new compressor? Not two hundred dollars' worth?''

"Just a belt. You Sarah's mama, I won't charge you nothin'.'' At least he was being congenial tonight. He pulled another rag from his hip pocket. ''You know 'bout this? Stuck in yo' tailpipe, and the muffler, it be full of holes. Not regular holes like when it wear out. Look like somebody be pokin' 'em in.''

"What?'' Jane remembered the smoking and the smell of exhaust. Could someone have sabotaged her car? Thelma looked shocked, too, so that she'd apparently forgotten to correct Dushawn's speech as she usually did.

"Dis be dangerous,'' Dushawn said. ''Dis rag be causin' a fire and yo' car blow up. Even if it don't blow up, it's for sure you drive all the way to the country club with yo' windows up, you gonna die! Good thing your air conditioner ain't workin' so you keep yo' windows down.''

"Oh my lord, son, what are you saying?" Thelma looked stricken.

"What I say is, look like somebody want Miz Ferguson dead.''

9

Jane's first inclination was to take Sarah and leave. Go someplace where they could hide out and be safe.

"Where would you go?" Thelma's voice was hushed, so the children wouldn't hear, and urgent. "Where would you go that they wouldn't follow you?"

"I don't know!" Jane spoke in hushed tones also, but her voice broke with the frightened tears she was trying to hold back. "I don't even know who *they* are."

"You wouldn't get far in that car of yours, anyway," Dushawn said. He had finally dropped his dialect, perhaps as a result of the seriousness of the moment.

"Why don't you just stay here, with us," Thelma said.

"What's going on?" Truly asked, coming out of the kitchen.

"I'd probably just be putting you in danger," Jane said. "I—oh, I don't know what to do. I don't want Sarah hurt." Tears were streaming down her cheeks, ruining her makeup.

"It's OK," Thelma said, reaching for her hand. "Stay here with us. Nobody knows you're here."

"What's going on?" Truly asked again.

"No, no, I can't," Jane said in response to Thelma.

"They'll find me. They always do. Always know."

"Who? Who will find you?" Truly frowned, looking from Jane to Thelma and back to Jane again.

"I'm calling the police." Thelma turned around and headed for the telephone.

"No! Wait!" Jane was thinking of Beau. He was the one person she knew of who seemed to know her every move, who kept showing up in unexpected places. She didn't know why, but she was afraid to trust him. "I mean. Not yet," she said. "Let me think. I—I'll call later. I'll— Thelma, promise me you'll take care of Sarah."

"You know I will, Jane, but—"

"Maybe they won't find her if I leave her here. Maybe they'll just follow me to the—Beau will be at the dinner. That way, I can watch and see if he—if Sarah's not with me, she'll be safe, won't she?"

"Jane, you're not making sense."

"Nobody make no sense," Truly said. "Who be after you, Jane? The Klan?"

"I don't know. I don't know who it is," Jane said, "but Dushawn just told me someone tried to sabotage my car, and a few nights ago, someone ran me off the road."

"Lordy! It could be the Klan," Truly insisted. "They don't like white folks bein' friends with black folks."

"I'm afraid it's not that simple," Jane said. "I think it has to do with Sylvia Davis's murder."

"Lordy mercy!" Truly said. "Thelma's right. You stay here with us, child. Don't you be goin' home by yo'self. Don't you be goin' out to no party."

"Hillary's expecting me," Jane said. "There'll be plenty of people there, and anyway, it might be better for Sarah, for all of you, if I'm not around. I'm leaving her here with you, Thelma, at least for the night. Just like she planned. Don't scare her by telling her about the—about what Dushawn found."

"Of course I won't."

"Do you have a gun?"

"Lord no. I've got a ten-year-old in my house. And

teenagers in and out. Dushawn's friends. I won't allow it.''

"I know, I know. Neither will I. I don't know why I asked. This whole thing is driving me crazy. Just keep her safe, Thelma. Promise me that.''

"You know I will.''

Jane gave her a quick hug. "I'm scared,'' she said. "But I'm going to try to lead whoever it is following me away from here.''

"I'll go with you,'' Dushawn said.

Thelma put a hand on his shoulder, and Jane saw fear in her eyes and the haunted expression of a woman to whom the worst has happened. "No, son, I couldn't bear it if you . . .''

"Stay here, please, Dushawn,'' Jane said. "Stay with Sarah. That's the best possible thing you could do for me.''

"At least, take my car,'' Dushawn said. "Leave yours here so I can fix that muffler and tailpipe. It's not safe for you to drive.''

"But if whoever sabotaged it sees it here in your driveway, how safe will that be?'' Jane shook her head. "No, Dushawn, I won't do that. I won't make sitting ducks out of everyone in this house. I'll drive the car. I'll just make sure the windows are down.''

"But, Mrs. Ferguson, you could still be in danger, if—''

"Hold on, son,'' Truly said. "You ain't goin' to win this one. Cain't hold down a woman tryin' to protect her chil'. She be like a mama wildcat. You go on, Jane. We be takin' good care a Sarah for you. But you take care yo'self, hear?''

"I'll do my best,'' Jane said. She gave Truly and Thelma an appreciative hug and offered her hand to Dushawn. "Thanks for your help,'' she said.

As she drove away, she kept a constant watch in her rearview mirror for headlights that might indicate she was being followed. She saw nothing to make her suspicious, not even when she turned off the main route into a residential section that took her the long way about to the country club. When she drove up to the stately building with its white columns, wide verandas, and gleaming crystal fires that were the chandeliers showing through high-arched windows, there were already a few cars parked along the driveway that was bordered with a dark and heavy green velvet forest of oak and pine. She spotted Hillary's gold Cadillac among them. It was a shining gem in a string of more sedate sedans. Buddy's pickup, looking like a mud-covered crustacean, was parked just beyond Hillary's car.

Buddy waved to her from inside the pickup. The fact that he had shown up was a good sign. At least he wouldn't be getting into trouble. Jane parked her faded Toyota and got out to meet Buddy, who was now walking toward her.

"You're late," he said and shifted a wad of tobacco farther back against the inside of his cheek. "And you smell like exhaust. You look pretty good, though."

"Let's get inside, Buddy." Jane took his arm and dragged him along with her as she walked with long, quick strides toward the club building. She stopped just as they got to the veranda, took a deep breath, and turned to Buddy again. "Get rid of that disgusting wad, Buddy."

Buddy complied, spitting into a rose bush and wiping his mouth with the back of his hand. "You a little testy, ain't you, gal? What's wrong with you? Thought you'd say something about my duds." He made a vain attempt at straightening his tie, which featured a lurid and realistic rendering of a full-size bass fish. He was also wearing black jeans and a brown tweed coat.

"I'm sorry, Buddy. You look nice. The coat is very— retro," she said, using Sarah's word. "Those wide lapels. And the tie is . . . Oh, Buddy, someone tried to kill me. Let's get inside before they see me out here." She turned and started up the steps to the country club's veranda.

Buddy's big hand came down gently but heavily on her shoulder, stopping her. "Whoa there! What's that you say?"

Jane took a quick, anxious look all around. At least they were standing in the floodlights. Maybe that was some protection. "Someone sabotaged my car. Messed with the exhaust system. It could have killed me and Sarah both if my friend's son hadn't found what was wrong."

"What? Just tell me who it was. I'll take care of the son of a—"

"I don't know who it was, Buddy, but I have a feeling it's the same person who killed Sylvia Davis and the same person who was trying to run me down that night I saw you in the woods. I think whoever it is thinks I know something I don't know."

The door swung open, and Hillary, in butterfly-yellow silk, fluttered out. "Jane, I was wondering where you— Oh!" Her eyes fell upon Buddy and moved up and down the full length of him.

"Hello, Hillary," Jane said. "You remember Buddy, don't you?"

"Yes, but what's he—?"

"He's my escort."

Hillary's mouth fell open as she glanced back at Jane. "Oh . . . I see. Well . . ." Her eyes went back to Buddy again, and she managed a smile. "I was just about to get some things out of my car. I hired a delivery van for most of it, but there is a pâté in the car I wanted to keep my eye on. Would you mind getting it for me, Buddy? Here are the keys. Just make sure you lock it when you get the platters out."

Buddy glanced at Jane, as if he was seeking permission.

"It's all right, Buddy. Go ahead," Jane said. He nodded and started for the car. "Just don't take anything *except* the pâté," Jane called to him.

He turned around, quickly, as if he'd forgotten something. "What's a pâté?"

"It's in the front seat of the car," Hillary said. "The only thing in the front seat."

"It smells like liver," Jane called to him.

"Unusual choice for an escort," Hillary said when Buddy had started for the car again.

Jane shrugged. "It's the best I can do."

"Oh, I doubt that," Hillary said, giving Jane's dress a quick glance before she turned to go inside. The yellow silk of her skirt billowed and whispered as she moved.

"I thought you were wearing basic black," Jane said, following her.

"I was, but then I thought, *This goes so well with the genoise.*" Hillary fluttered away.

"Do I get to meet your husband tonight?" Jane asked, trying to keep up with Hillary.

"Billy? Of course. He'll be here a little later. He called me and told me he'd be home by six-thirty. He said he'd change quick and be here by seven."

They were inside the reception hall of the club building, which was sumptuously furnished in burnished mahogany, brocade upholstery, and heavy swag drapes. Large bouquets of flowers, each spanning almost three feet, were arranged in cut crystal bowls and sat on the tables. Silk masquerading as life. The chandeliers shone like dancing, sunlight-drenched droplets of water. Jane had been inside the building only once before when she had attended a bar association function with Jim Ed shortly after they moved to Prosper. She had been struck by the look and feel of old money then, as she was now.

"I'm glad you're here before most of the guests," Hillary said, as they walked through the entry hall and the dining room and ballroom toward the kitchen. "I want you to see the food display. Beautiful, if I do say so myself. And it would be good for you to hear me instruct the kitchen staff so you'll get a feel for it in case you ever have to do it. I'll be relying upon you more and more to—"

"Hillary, there's something I have to tell you."

"We'll start with hors d'oeuvres, of course, the pâté and a nice caviar that I found in Birmingham the last time I was there. Along with that there'll be—"

"Hillary—"

"Sherry, of course. I thought of champagne, which is always appropriate for an aperitif, so there'll be a fountain for that, but sherry is so much more, well, tasteful, in my opinion.''

"Someone tried to kill me again. This time Sarah was with me, and the reason I'm telling you this is . . .'' She had Hillary's full attention now. In fact, Hillary was staring at her, speechless at last, and with such a frightened expression, it was unnerving to Jane. ''. . . is because I'm afraid whoever it is may try to get at you, too.''

"Me? But why . . .''

"Because you're in this, too, Hillary. Whoever it is thinks I know something I don't know, and it's reasonable to assume they think the same thing about you.''

"Know something?''

"About Sylvia's murder, of course.''

"But I don't know a thing. Not a thing.''

"Neither do I. But that's beside the point. Listen to me. Someone thinks I know something, and they're trying to kill me. They may try to get at you, too.''

Hillary grabbed Jane's arm and pulled her into the kitchen. Behind them, the staff was a dissonant symphony of clinking dishes and conversation. "What are we going to do?'' Hillary whispered. The look on her face was that of genuine fright.

"I don't know. Be very careful, I guess. Are you sure your husband's coming home tonight? I don't think you should stay in that house alone.''

"Oh dear. I hope so. I mean, I told him how important this dinner is. Do you think we should tell the police?''

"I—no, I don't,'' Jane said.

"But why not? They're supposed to be investigating.''

"I'm not sure we can trust anyone at this point. I don't know what to do, Hillary, except tell you to be careful. Be very careful. Especially when you're driving alone. And we'll have Buddy check your car before you leave here tonight.''

"Jane, you're scaring me again.''

"Just watch out, Hillary.''

Hillary nodded and turned, with some reluctance, back to the kitchen staff. Before long, she was immersed in her duties, and she was, Jane found, very good at handling a staff. She knew exactly how she wanted things done, and she knew how to convey it with authority peppered with a sprinkling of good humor and absentminded enthusiasm.

"Now," Hillary said, when she had finished with her instructions, "let's go out and enjoy the party. Let's try to forget this dreadful stuff about murder."

"All right. Just remember what I told you," Jane said.

"Oh, everyone here is perfectly trustworthy, I'm sure," Hillary said as she floated away on her yellow wings.

Jane looked around for Buddy and spied him in the opposite corner of the room, holding a drink and watching the two women near him. One was a young woman in gold lamé and the other, fiftyish, in a sequined gown of royal purple that fit her stout figure like the scales on a fish. While Jane watched, a man in a tuxedo walked up to Buddy and tapped him on the shoulder. He said something to Buddy, pointing toward the door, and Buddy seemed to be arguing with him.

Jane moved across the room as quickly as she could. "Is something wrong?" she asked.

"Don't trouble yourself, ma'am," the tuxedo man said. The pinched look of his face made him appear as if he smelled something unpleasant. "Just a gate crasher. I'll take care of it. This dinner party is for invited guests only," he said, grasping Buddy's arm.

"He's with me."

"I beg your pardon."

"I said, he's with me. We *are* invited guests."

The tuxedo man looked stunned. "Oh, I see," he said finally, "and who might you be?"

"I might be Jane Ferguson, and this might be Buddy Fletcher." She gave a little wave to the mayor, who had caught her eye. Tuxedo man saw the wave, saw the mayor give a wave of his own in recognition.

"Very well then," he said, and turned away, but not before he gave Buddy another disapproving, I-smell-something look.

Buddy straightened his fish tie. "Thanks, Miz Ferguson. I coulda took care of him myself, but I didn't want to raise no ruckus and embarrass you.''

"Thoughtful of you, Buddy, and go easy on that champagne," she said, pointing to his glass.

"Oh, sure. Want me to bring you some? How 'bout some of that liver patty?''

"No, thank you, but you go ahead," Jane said. Buddy drifted away toward the hors d'oeuvres, and Jane spied Hillary standing next to the mayor. They were deeply engaged in an animated conversation. She glanced around the room for someone else she knew. There was Nancy Sedgewick, with a flock of individuals bobbing around her, political birds pecking for position. There were a few other people whom she'd met through Jim Ed, and there was Reverend Collins with a heavy, mousey-haired woman she assumed was his wife. The voluptuous Stacy was nowhere around. Jane was in no mood for small talk with anyone, however, and she couldn't help looking at everyone there with a measure of suspicion, as if each might be the one who tampered with her car and tried to run her off the road.

"Hello," a voice said from somewhere over Jane's left shoulder. She turned around to see a thin woman, her dark hair pulled back severely from her angular face. She was dressed in a black suit, made formal with a touch of velvet and a long skirt. The woman was smiling at her, holding out her hand. "I'm Regina Conyers, and I'm so glad you could come. I'd appreciate your vote in November.''

"You're Regina Conyers?''

"Why, yes, I am. I take it you've heard of me. And my campaign, I assume. I'm running for Congress.''

"Sure, I've heard of you. You're the one Sylvia Davis had on her show a few weeks ago. Something about money missing from some charity.'' Jane surprised even herself by launching into the matter so suddenly. A part of her regretted it. She wasn't at all sure she wanted to know any more about Sylvia Davis's relationships with anyone. It was proving too dangerous. On the other hand, knowledge could also protect her.

"Oh my," Regina said with a confident little laugh. "There was nothing to that. Just a misinterpretation of the accounting books. It was cleared up immediately. I don't suppose you saw the story in the paper explaining that?"

"No, I'm afraid I didn't."

"I didn't think so. It was on the inside, buried beneath the Kmart ad. Small story. Easy to miss."

"That's unfortunate."

"I'm still doing damage control. Even thought of suing Ms. Davis at one time. But that would have been ridiculous. Instead, I tried to get back on her show to explain things, but she wouldn't have me. Claimed she was booked until after the election. It's too late for any of that now, of course, God rest her soul."

"You were in a meeting with Reverend Collins when it happened, I heard. Sylvia's death, I mean." In spite of herself, Jane was still probing.

"A committee meeting, yes. Chester and I met with the organizers for this event. But how did you know that?"

"Small town. Word gets around."

"Obviously. Have we met?"

"I doubt it. I'm just the hired help. I work for Hillary Scarborough. You know, Elégance du Sud."

"And your name?"

"Jane Ferguson."

"Ferguson. Oh yes." She had obviously made the Jim Ed connection, but at least she had the grace and good manners not to mention it. "You know, the odd thing, Jane, is that Reverend Collins and I discussed Sylvia and her, well, shall we say, aggressiveness, while we were at that meeting. Truth of the matter is, you might say we both had a motive."

"Oh?" Jane was genuinely surprised at Regina's candor.

"Well, of course we did. She had damaged us both. I tell you, it's a very odd and disconcerting feeling when someone who has hurt you dies. There's the feel of unfinished business and the nagging questions about how it could have been different if maybe one or both of you had tried harder.''

"Yes, I see," Jane said. She was finding herself liking this woman and also finding it difficult to think of her as a murder suspect.

"Regina! There you are!" a youngish man said, rushing up to her. "Come with me. There's someone you have to meet.''

"I'll be right there," Regina said and turned back to Jane. "My campaign manager," she said, sounding apologetic. "There are some disadvantages to running for office,'' she added with a little laugh. "It was very nice to meet you, Jane." She sounded as if she meant it.

Jane spied Beau at the same moment he saw her. She hardly recognized him in his tux. He did a double take and looked surprised, as if he hadn't expected to see her there. Jane gave him a little wave, since there was no way to pretend she hadn't seen him. He didn't seem to be able to move. He simply stared at her for a moment until she felt self-conscious, as if maybe something was wrong with the way she looked. She started to move away, to take refuge in the kitchen, perhaps, but now he had started toward her. He picked up two glasses from a waiter's tray as he walked by.

"Hello, Jane." He still had that little worried frown. "You look—really good. Nice! I mean, nice. You look nice.''

"Thank you." She was puzzled that he was so uncomfortable. He seemed perfectly comfortable with her when she had cotton stuck between her toes or when she had on her old brown suit.

He thrust one of the glasses toward her. "Would you like some champagne? Or would you rather have the sherry?''

"I'm on duty, you know.''

"Oh. Sure. I'm sorry.''

She had meant it as a mild joke, but the crestfallen look he now had meant he was taking everything seriously. *Typical of a policeman,* she thought. But she couldn't have him standing there looking so uncomfortable, so she reached for the glass. "But one little glass won't hurt." Why was she doing that? she wondered. Why was she worrying about how other people felt when she was so immensely worried about her own safety and that of her daughter? *Nice-girl reaction,* she thought. *Be polite. Keep everybody happy.* She must be crazy! This was the man who was watching her every move. She should continue to be suspicious of him, not nice to him.

She drank the champagne in one gulp.

"Are you all right?"

"Sure," she said. Too quick. Too crisp. Her eyes swept the room without her knowing who or what she was looking for, and all the while she was thinking that she should be with Sarah. She should have taken the car somewhere as a decoy and then sneaked back to the Youngs' to be with her, to make sure she was safe. But would it have worked? Whoever was trying to kill her seemed to know where she was at all times. And how did he get to her car like that? In the middle of the night while it was parked in her driveway? The thought made her blood run cold.

"Jane?"

"What!"

"I said, do you need to sit down?" Beau now had a concerned frown. "Can I get you something?"

"Get me something? Like what?"

"I don't know. An aspirin maybe. You look like you don't feel well."

"I'm fine." She scanned the room again. "Where's Hillary?"

Beau gave the room a casual sweep with his eyes. "I don't know. In the kitchen, probably, or—"

"She was right there a minute ago. Talking to the mayor."

Beau's perpetual worried frown was replaced for the moment with a puzzled expression. "I can look in the kitchen if it'll make you feel better."

"No, I'll look in the kitchen." She set her glass down

and walked away, aware that Beau was following her.

The atmosphere in the kitchen was like backstage in a theater just before a big production. Indeed, that was what was about to happen: a big production. The guests would be seated and the dinner served within minutes. The staff had been given its instructions by the production's director: Hillary. Now there was a mood of anticipation, much last-minute scurrying about, everyone taut as guitar strings. But Hillary was nowhere around.

"Could she have stepped outside?" Beau asked. "Or maybe she went to the rest room. I'm sure she's all right."

"You can't be sure!" Jane said, knowing she sounded every bit as testy as Buddy had accused her of being.

"Look," Beau said with exaggerated calmness. "You check the rest room. I'll have a look around outside."

Jane nodded. She didn't want to argue. Didn't want to have to talk to him, didn't want to talk to anyone, in fact. She just wanted to go home.

Jane checked all the stalls in the ladies' room and looked at the feet showing beneath the door of the two locked ones. Neither set belonged to Hillary. There were two women in the powder room section comparing the merits of Jenny Craig and Weight Watchers. But there was no Hillary.

She met Beau in the hallway just as he came in from outdoors. "Didn't see her," he said, "but her car's still out there, so she's here somewhere. Wasn't in the rest room?"

Jane shook her head.

"This is a big crowd. It's easy to overlook someone."

"Yeah, I'm sure you're right." Jane tried to sound calm, but she didn't feel that way at all. They walked together into the reception hall. The mayor was about to make his announcement that he would run for governor. In the spacious dining room next door, Jane could see that the salad was already on the table. But Hillary was still nowhere in sight.

In the short time that Jane had known Hillary, she'd

sensed that she liked to control her projects. It wasn't like her to not be here now, overseeing everything.

"Ladies and gentlemen," the mayor said from the position he'd taken on the podium. "I am so pleased to see all of y'all out tonight. You know that part of the cost of your ticket goes to support our project for the homeless; and I want to thank Ms. Regina Conyers and her staff for helpin' us organize this. I have been very busy with my duties as mayor of this fair city, and I had no time to attend any of her committee meetings or even to meet with her, but I trust her implicitly," he said, putting the accent on the first syllable. There was a moment of applause before the mayor launched into his political speech about the honor he'd had of serving as mayor of the town and of his desire to serve the public in greater depth by running for governor.

Jane tried to listen, but she was finding it difficult. Her eyes wandered around the room, looking at the crowd. Beau had moved away from her. Or she had moved away from him. Buddy was nowhere in sight, either. She hoped he was just invisible in the sea of bodies and wasn't out breaking in somewhere. She should have kept a closer eye on him.

"I pledge to bring to state government the same clear judgment and fiscal responsibility that I have exhibited in my capacity . . ." Jane was beginning to feel tired. She wasn't used to late nights. She wondered if Sarah was in bed. She'd missed reading to her or having Sarah read to her: their special ritual. Was Sarah missing her, too? Or was she giggling with Shakura right now with Jane the farthest thing from her mind? She'd go to Thelma's early tomorrow to get her. Maybe even go by and check on her tonight.

Suddenly, a flash of yellow in the window stopped her random thoughts. Hillary? What was she doing out there? She appeared to be running, but why?

"Excuse me," Jane whispered, as she moved through the crowd. "Excuse me," over and over again, until she made her way to the door. She stepped out into the light-

flooded space and looked around her, but she saw nothing.
The window she'd been standing near and through which
she'd thought she'd seen Hillary was around the corner
of the building. She hurried to that spot. There was less
light and more shadows.

"Hillary," she called again, softly. No answer. She
called again, and moved cautiously toward the shrubs
around the window. There was a movement in the shrubs,
and a screech. Jane's heart seemed to stop, and she sucked
in her breath, thinking she should run but seeming unable
to. In the same instant, she saw a cat run from the shrubbery, crying out with its screeching meow, followed
closely by another cat.

Jane took a step back and looked all around her. There
was another movement in the distance, back where the
light did not reach at all, in the trees just beyond the
swimming pool and tennis court. Behind her she could
hear the faint sound of applause coming from the clubhouse.

"Hillary," Jane called again, directing her voice toward
the movement.

She heard something—ever so faint a sound. Was it
someone calling her name? Was it Hillary? Jane's high
heels made an eerie sound in the darkness as she ran
across the tennis courts. She called Hillary's name again
as she moved beyond the pool area, headed toward the
dark forest of trees.

Jane slowed as she reached the forest. The darkness it
held in its midst was thick and heavy, and she could feel
its dampness seeping out toward her.

"Are you in there, Hillary?"

There was no answer. Nothing except the heavy, dark
silence, and then the flutter of wings.

"Come out, Hillary, please come out." Jane took a
cautious step into the forest, and then another and another,
until she was surrounded by the blackness. She could feel
her high heels sinking into the marshy ground. Something
ran across her foot, and she screamed. Then she heard
what sounded like someone calling her name. A male

voice. She turned around to look behind her, trying to determine the direction from which the sound had come, but she couldn't be certain.

"Who's there?" she called. She turned around again, searching. She heard a sound then. Someone behind her, moving through the trees. She tried to run, but it was too dark to know where she was going. Then, suddenly, her feet were entangled in something that wrapped around her ankles, her thighs, trying to pull her down. She'd stepped into a tangled vine. She shook herself free and tried to keep running, but something stopped her again. This time it was an arm, encircling her neck from behind.

10

Jane tried to scream, but the arm, heavy and solid, constricted her throat. Her lungs felt like lethal carbon dioxide–filled balloons in her chest. She grasped the soft wool of a sleeve and tried to move the arm from her throat.

It did no good. The man tightened his grip. It was a man, she was sure of that, not only because of his strength, but because of the feel of the fabric on the sleeve under her neck; the wool of a suit or a tuxedo. A kind of numbness seeped into her head, spread to her chest, her arms, warm and liquid at first and then wooden and dark.

Suddenly the arm was gone, and her freedom startled her. She coughed, gagged, felt as if she would vomit. She was still dazed, but she could sense a struggle. Her assailant and someone else? A few grunts, a male voice uttering a curse: "Who the hell . . . ?" Then, when she turned around and tried to run, hands grabbed her again, arms encircled her, this time around the waist—a bear hug squeezing the breath out of her. She struggled again and kicked at the shins of the assailant.

"Whoa, there. I ain't gonna hurt you. Whatza matter wit choo? You ain't got no biness bein' out here. You gonna git youself . . . Ouch! Damnit, you kicked me!"

"Buddy?" It was too dark to see, but she sensed him hopping around on one foot. "Buddy, was that you who— No, it couldn't have been. Did you see who it was?"

"I didn't git a good look, but listen, you ain't got no biness bein' out here." Buddy still sounded as if he was in pain, but he held her arm firmly, leading her out of the woods. "You just plum crazy. You know that? If it wasn't for me follerin' you out here, you coulda been kilt. I tried to holler at you and stop you, but you just kept on."

"That was your voice I heard, then. But who could that have been attacking me? You sure you didn't get a look?"

Buddy shook his head. "Too dark."

"Listen, Buddy, we've got to find Hillary."

"Well she ain't in the woods, that's for sure. I seen her. Over yonder."

"Over where?"

"Out yonder at the far edge of the parking lot. Runnin' to beat all hell."

"You mean she wasn't— Are you sure you didn't see who attacked me?"

"See? Hell no. It's too dark to see anything. Just some bum lookin' to mug somebody, and you give him the perfect opportunity. I bet there's plenty of 'em hangs around here lookin' for the chance to hit some rich dude that wanders out to his car. Or maybe some rich bitch. Only women usually ain't like that. Too smart to wander out in the dark. You ain't too smart, Miz Ferguson. I seen you come out here and go into them woods, and I thought, *that damn woman, what the hell is she a-doin'? Don't even know how to take care of herself.* And considerin' all the dangerous stuff that keeps happenin' to you, you ought to learn to use your head or else—"

"It wasn't some bum looking to mug me."

"Oh, yeah? I know what you're thinkin'. You're thinkin' it coulda been whoever messed with your car. But don't you see? It don't matter who it was, you just got to be careful."

"It was someone from the party."

"Aw, come on. It was dark. You couldn't see who it

was, and besides, why would one a them swells want to mug you?''

"I couldn't see, Buddy, but I know. He had on a nice suit, a tux maybe, and he didn't want to rob me, he wanted to kill me. And maybe Hillary, too.''

Buddy stopped, still holding her arm. They were in the flood of lights around the swimming pool now. "No shit? About the tux, I mean?''

"No shit.''

"Then we walked right into it, didn't we?''

"What do you mean?''

"If it's one a them rich dudes in there that's been messin' with your car, tryin' to hurt you or whatever, then we give 'em the perfect opportunity by coming here. Good thing you got me with you. You was using your head for once when you asked me to come.''

"I'm glad you're here, Buddy, and you've still got to help me.''

"You name it. After what Jim Ed done for me, I—''

"Help me find Hillary. Show me where she was the last time you saw her.''

"Right over yonder,'' Buddy said. He pointed to the far end of the parking lot that bordered the forest. "But the way she was a runnin', there ain't no way she'd still be there.''

"We'll look,'' Jane said. "The whole length and breadth of the parking lot.'' She felt sick with worry. Maybe now was the time to tell Beau about all that had happened. Time to stop being suspicious of him and put some faith in the police department. Maybe she should let the police handle everything and just go home to her daughter. But even if she could convince herself to stop being suspicious of Beau, she couldn't take the time to go looking for him now. She had to find Hillary. If she was injured, then every second would count. Jane wouldn't allow herself to think that Hillary was dead, that whoever was stalking them had been successful in his mission.

"Wonder if her car's still here," Buddy said. "It was, when I come out looking for you."

"She wouldn't leave in her car—unless someone forced her."

Buddy shrugged. "Wouldn't hurt to look. See if it's still there."

Jane glanced toward the street where Hillary had parked her car at the curb across from the country club. "OK, Buddy," she said, leading the way to the curb that ran along the west side of the building where she and Hillary had both parked their cars. "We'll check there first." The area, lined with tall trees, was not as well lighted as the front of the building, and the light that might have filtered in from the pool area was curtained by the massive foliage of the trees. Still, even in the semidarkness, Jane could see that both her Toyota and Hillary's Cadillac still sat where they each had originally parked them.

Buddy, apparently, had seen both cars as well. "You wait here. I'll go check it out," he said, reaching slightly behind him to place a momentary restraining arm across the front of her torso.

"Check it out? Why? It's plain to see her car's still here, and she's not in it."

"You stay here where there's light." Buddy's voice was a command, and he had already started toward the Cadillac. Jane didn't heed his command. In spite of his urging her not to, she followed him toward the parked car, but she was having a hard time keeping up with his long strides. He reached the car well before she did and bent down to inspect the interior. Jane was still a few feet away when she heard the shot ring out and saw Buddy fall to the ground.

She screamed and then stood momentarily frozen in place, not knowing whether to go to him or hit the ground herself. In the next instant she heard an angry voice crying out, "Stay away from my car, you bastard, or I'll—"

"Hillary!"

Hillary, who had run out from the shadow of the trees, turned suddenly toward Jane when she heard her call her name. "Stay back, Jane. This could be dangerous." She was approaching Buddy, the gun now aimed at his head.

"Hillary!" Jane called again as she ran toward her. "Don't shoot! It's just Buddy." She could see Buddy trembling as he raised his arms to protect his head. Apparently, he had hit the ground as a protective measure, not because a bullet had found him.

"Buddy?" Hillary relaxed her aim and then turned to glance at Jane. Buddy, with his amazing agility, took the opportunity to come to his feet and within what seemed to be only a second, had Hillary's wrist in his big hand, forcing her arm up so that the gun she held posed no danger. Hillary kicked Buddy in the shin.

"Ooh!" Buddy said, letting go of her hand to hold his leg and to hop around on one foot. Once again, Hillary had the gun leveled at him, but by this time, Jane was at her side.

"Put the gun away, Hillary. Don't you see? It's Buddy!"

"Yes, I see that, but he was trying to break into my car."

"He wasn't trying to break into your car. He was just checking to see if you were in there. We've both been looking for you."

Buddy was still moaning, still hopping around on one foot, oblivious to the gun, which was still pointed at him.

"Someone tried to break into my car. I saw them tampering with the door when I came out to get that extra platter of hors d'oeuvres Buddy forgot. He ran off down the street when I saw him. Would have shot him, if I could have gotten close enough."

"Well, it wasn't Buddy trying to break into your car. It was someone else. Probably the same guy who attacked me."

"Attacked you?"

"I ran into the woods looking for you, Hillary. I was afraid someone was after you. I had no idea it was you who was doing the chasing, but someone grabbed me and tried to choke me."

"Oh, my lord, Jane."

"Did you get a good look at the guy?"

"Oh yes, dirty hair, jeans, T-shirt, skinny arms."

"Skinny arms?" Jane asked. "Bare arms?"

"Yes, why?"

"Then it wasn't the same one who . . . Where did you get that gun?"

Buddy, who had finally stopped howling and was now bending over to rub his sore leg, looked up at Hillary with interest, as if he, too, had been wondering where she'd gotten the gun.

"Why, I always carry a gun, hon. And I'm not afraid to use it, either," she said, with an eye toward Buddy. "My Billy taught me all about guns." She gave Buddy a menacing look. "That was just a warning shot I fired, you know. If I really want to hit something, I don't miss."

"Yes, ma'am," Buddy said. He was standing upright now, looking pale in the shadowy moonlight.

"What's going on out here? I thought I heard a gunshot." The three of them turned in unison to see Beau approaching from the direction of the clubhouse.

"It was nothing," Jane said. "It was just me," Hillary said at the same time, holding her gun up and waving it to draw Beau's attention to it.

Beau kept a cautious eye on Hillary. "You have a permit to carry that thing?"

"Course I do. I have been through the required training. And Billy has taught me even more."

"You know it's illegal to discharge a firearm within the city limits."

"Yes, I know that, but this isn't technically within the city limits, you know, and besides, I was protecting myself and my property."

"Against who?"

"This man." Hillary used the gun to point toward Buddy.

"What were you up to, Buddy?" Beau asked with caution and suspicion both in his voice. He was standing next to Hillary now and was holding his hand out as if he expected her to hand him the gun. To Jane's surprise, Hillary handed it to him.

"I was looking for Miz Scarborough," he said. "Just checking her car to see if she was inside."

"Umhum." Beau had opened the chamber of the pistol Hillary had handed him. "And why did you think she would be in her car when there's a party going on inside the building?"

"Well, I—"

"It was my idea," Jane said. "I was worried when neither you nor I could find her. Then I saw her out in the back there when I was glancing out a window. She was running, and it alarmed me. I mean, I thought she was running away from someone, so Buddy and I came out here to check on her, and when we couldn't find her anywhere else, we decided to check out her car."

"That's right," Hillary said. "I was running, just like she said. Chasing someone who was trying to get into my car. I saw him when I came out to get a platter of food, but I lost him. Then, when I came back, I saw Buddy."

"And mistook him for whoever was breaking into your car to begin with," Beau said.

"I don't know whether it was a mistake or not. Maybe they're in this together," Hillary said.

"Hillary!" Jane said, "Buddy was with me."

"Hey, lady, you give me the keys to your car once." Buddy sounded angry. "If I'd wanted to steal it, I coulda done it then. Cadillacs ain't my style, though. I like four-by-fours."

Beau, who had been glancing from first one to the other of the three of them, now settled his eyes on Hillary. "That right, Mrs. Scarborough? You gave him the keys to your car at some point?"

"I did. You can't let pâté just sit in a closed-up car, you know. Think of the smell! That's why I came out here, because I know he missed one platterful. It's a good thing I had those other hors d'oeuvres as a backup, because—"

"I'm going to give this back to you because I have no

other reason to charge you. You're right about this being out of the city limits,'' Beau said, placing the gun in Hillary's hand. "But I advise you not to be firing it indiscriminately. In fact, I advise you not to fire it at all except at inanimate targets out of the city limits.''

"She won't.'' Jane spoke quickly, for fear that Hillary might put up some kind of argument. She didn't want any more trouble than they had already.

"Billy bought it for me for protection, so I can't promise—''

"She won't fire the gun,'' Jane said again, interrupting her.

Hillary, thankfully, seemed to have gotten the message at last. She didn't say a word. Beau was silent, studying their faces for a few seconds. "Good,'' he said, finally. "Now, did you get a good look at whoever was trying to break into your car?''

Hillary told him that she had, and she gave him the same description she'd given Jane.

"Why don't you go back in and enjoy the party,'' Beau said. "I'll have a look around, see if I can find him. Oh, and I think you can leave the gun in the glove compartment for now.''

"But—''

Jane gave Hillary's arm a squeeze, stopping her protest. For a moment, Hillary glanced back and forth from Jane to Beau, wearing a troubled and uncertain expression. Finally, though, she unlocked the car and put the gun inside the glove compartment.

"What's going on? I heard a gunshot.'' Jane saw the mayor hurrying across the parking lot.

"Ms. Scarborough took aim at a burglar,'' Beau said.

"Good lord, did he get away?'' the mayor asked.

"I'm going to have a look,'' Beau said.

"I'll help,'' the mayor said, in spite of the fact that he was puffing from his sprint across the parking lot.

"All right,'' Beau said, "but the rest of you go back inside the building.'' Beau held out an arm, as if to guide the women inside. His sleeve brushed Jane's arm as he did so, and she felt the soft weave of his suit—the same softness she had felt earlier when the arm was around her neck, choking her.

"Roast tarragon chicken is a perfect entrée when you're serving a crowd." Hillary was beaming as she watched the guests enjoy the meal she had planned and prepared. She was seated next to Jane at one of the tables as the meal was being served. "And the grilled figs give it an elegant touch. Grilled asparagus for a splash of green. You see, Jane, elegance is so simple. The genoise iced with a liqueur marzipan and served with a lovely gelato, of course, is the pièce de résistance. Perfect after a simple meal. That's my rule, Jane. If you serve a heavy meal, keep the dessert light and simple. Or, if the meal is light and simple, an elaborate dessert. As for leftovers, you can mix the chicken with apple and carrot slaw, add a creamy yogurt dressing, and—"

"Hillary, I've got to talk to you." Jane had been wanting a chance to speak to her privately ever since they'd returned to the clubhouse. So far, it had been impossible, since both had been busy making sure the meal was served properly. She and Hillary were seated at the end of the table, near the kitchen, so one or both of them could move in and out easily and unobtrusively, in case a problem arose. No problem was likely, however. Hillary loved entertaining and loved being in charge, so all possible problems had been foreseen and eliminated, and she put the matter of someone tampering with her car at least temporarily out of her mind, especially since Beau had told her he'd radioed in the description she'd given him, and a patrolman had radioed back that a man fitting that description had been picked up trying to break into another Cadillac parked at the country club.

Buddy was seated next to Jane, not only so she could keep an eye on him, but now, since she knew the car burglar obviously wasn't the same person who had attacked, she wanted Buddy near for protection, because that meant the attacker was probably in the dining room somewhere. Beau had somehow managed to get himself seated on the other side of her.

In a little while, Beau excused himself and left the table. Assuming he'd gone to the rest room, Jane saw it as her opportunity to speak privately to Hillary. By now, though, Hillary was leaning across the empty chair next to her, which had been reserved for her husband, Billy, to speak to an older woman with hair as pale and fine as moonlight, perfectly done up in a permed style—the look of a matronly yet well-off dowager. Billy had called to tell Hillary he'd run into bad weather on his way back from Georgia and wouldn't make it home in time for the dinner.

"Stirring speech the mayor gave, wasn't it?" the matronly woman said. "I wanted to tell him so, but poor Arnold looked absolutely *pallid* afterwards and then he just ups and disappears into the men's room."

"Oh, dear," Hillary said, "I hope it wasn't my hors d'oeuvres. But, of course, it couldn't have been. Everyone else ate them and seemed just fine. And Arnold looked fine when we saw him out in the—"

Jane kicked her gently under the table before she said more. Hillary got the hint and said no more. However, her remark had seemed to alarm the woman.

"Look at him." The woman pointed to the opposite end of the table. "He still looks sickly." Jane and Hillary both glanced at the mayor, who, Jane thought, looked perfectly healthy. "And young Beaumont didn't look well when he got up, either. I just hope *all* of us don't come down with something. I've got my garden club meeting next Tuesday."

"You have nothing to worry about," Hillary said, sounding worried herself.

The woman turned away, dabbed her napkin at her mouth, then felt her worry-creased forehead with her open palm. She turned away from Hillary and asked the woman next to her if she thought the hors d'oeuvres had tasted funny.

"Did you hear that?" Hillary whispered to Jane.

"She's going to talk herself into being sick. If she does, I'm ruined. No more catering jobs, and my ratings will fall. Where's Beaumont? He hasn't gone off somewhere to throw up, has he?"

"Stop worrying about that, Hillary. We've got worse things to worry about."

"What's worse than a drop in your ratings and your pâté going bad?"

"Dying."

"What are you talking about? Even if it is food poisoning, it probably won't cause anything more than an upset stomach."

"I'm talking about dying at the hands of someone who wants you dead."

"You mean somebody *purposely* poisoned my pâté?"

"Hillary, forget your pâté. Your hors d'ocuvres have got nothing to do with any of this. I'm talking about the fact that whoever is after us is getting more and more desperate, and that makes him more and more dangerous." Jane was leaning across the table, speaking to Hillary in an agitated whisper.

"Why don't you just let Beau take care of it? You should just tell him everything," Hillary said in an equally desperate whisper.

"I can't tell Beau anything."

"But why not? He's—"

"Because I think he was the one who tried to attack me."

"Oh, my lord, are you sure?" Hillary had a look of disbelief on her face. Buddy, at the same moment, stopped his awkward attempt to cut chicken off of the bone and stared in surprise at Jane.

"I'm not absolutely sure," Jane said, "but I've got good reason to suspect him."

"But how did he—I mean, what did he do?"

"Tried to choke me. He would have, too, if Buddy hadn't shown up. And Hillary, listen to me, please. You've got to understand that whoever keeps doing all these things to me will be after you, too."

"But why would that cop want to do that?" Buddy asked.

"Yes, Jane, why?" Hillary asked. "It doesn't make sense that a policeman would try to kill us."

"I know it doesn't make sense. Nothing makes sense to me. I just have this feeling, that's all. And it scares me."

"I can take care of him for you," Buddy offered.

"No, Buddy. I told you, I don't want you to take care of anything."

"Then maybe I ought not to put that paper back in the safe Monday."

"No, you have to do that, Buddy. We don't want to get in this any deeper than we already are."

"Wait, let me get this straight," Hillary said, "if Beau Jackson is trying to kill you and, heaven forbid, me as well, do you think he's the one who killed Sylvia?"

Jane never got the chance to respond to Hillary's question. She saw Beau approaching the table. She gave him a weak smile and went back to moving her food around in her plate with her fork.

Buddy gave up on his knife and fork and picked up the chicken leg and tore off a long strip with his teeth. Hillary turned once again with an anxious look toward the mayor.

When Beau sat down next to her, Jane noticed that his coat, as well as his hair, was slightly damp.

"Raining a little," Beau said when he saw her looking at him.

"You've been outside?"

Beau was trying to cut one of the grilled figs. "Just went out to have a look around the parking lot. Just in case there was more than one burglar out there."

"We appreciate your vigilance."

"There's something going on you're not telling me about, Jane. Why don't you tell me what it is?"

"What makes you think there's something going on?" Jane buttered her already-buttered bread. She glanced furtively at Beau's arm, visualizing it around her neck, choking her.

"Well, for one thing, you've been three jumps away from a nervous fit ever since you got here, and for another, when I saw all of you out there by Mrs. Scarborough's car, your hair looked like hell."

Some uncontrollable reflex made her hand fly to her head. "What's that supposed to mean?"

Beau took a leisurely sip of his wine. "I don't know. But it looked like you'd been in some kind of a tussle or like you'd been running from somebody or something. Either one is not exactly what a lady usually does when she comes to a party."

"A tussle?"

"What do they call it in California?"

Jane ignored the question. "I was just out looking for Hillary. I got worried and thought she might be in the woods. I guess it messed my hair up when I ran in there looking for her."

"Uh huh." He sounded unconvinced. "You don't lie very well, you know that?"

"What makes you think I'm lying?"

"You get these little beads of sweat right across the top of your nose." He touched the top of her nose gently. "Just like the time you told me you were over there near Sylvia Davis's house just to look at the chinaberries because you were going to fry up those blossoms and eat 'em, or make tea out of 'em or something."

"I'll admit Hillary comes up with some far-out recipes, but, hey, it's my job."

"Jane, you've got those little sweat beads again." He leaned closer and whispered in a surprisingly playful manner. "And chinaberries are poisonous to humans."

Jane felt the sweat grow heavy on the top of her nose. "Well, maybe I, uh, got the wrong tree or something," she said and tried to smile. "Excuse me." She laid her napkin aside, then stood up. "I've got to go make a telephone call." She started to walk away but turned back to look at Beau. "I'm just going to check on my daughter. Nothing sinister."

"Except that's the third time you've called her." He

was right. She'd excused herself to use the telephone right after they sat down, then again during the salad course. "If you'd like, I can call one of the patrolmen to drive by your house, maybe even knock on the door. She's with a baby-sitter, right?"

"No, she's over at . . ." Jane stopped herself, unsure about whether or not she should tell Beau or anyone else where Sarah was.

"Oh, of course. She's probably staying with Shakura tonight, isn't she?"

Jane gave him no response. All she could think of was getting back to Sarah. She turned around, headed for the telephone, which was located in the foyer between the ladies' room and the men's room. Chester Collins had just hung up the telephone as she approached. When he turned around, she saw that he wore a troubled expression, but he managed to mask it quickly with a smile.

"Good evenin', Miz Ferguson."

Jane nodded her response and murmured, "Reverend Collins."

She expected more small talk, but the reverend seemed in a hurry to leave. He rubbed his fingers through his tinted hair in a nervous gesture, smiled weakly, and hurried away. As he left, Jane noticed the mud clinging to his shoes. It was the same that now clung to hers after she'd stepped into the woods.

11

Jane drove as fast as she dared, knowing there was a high probability she was being followed by someone. She didn't want to drive fast enough to get a traffic ticket, though. Not that such a mundane occurrence could upset her now, after all that had happened to her recently. It was just that she didn't want anything to slow her down.

As she drove, she thought of how Thelma continued to insist that Rashaud would not have been drinking and run his car off the road. Jane had always assumed it was nothing more than a grieving mother's denial. But what if Thelma was right? Did that mean someone had deliberately killed Rashaud and tried to cover it up by making it look like an accident? If that was true, if someone was killing children as well as television personalities, was Sarah in danger?

The night spat out its darkness in clumps as Jane drove, passing from poorly lit areas that were almost rural in their atmosphere to the glaring halogen lights of parking areas. By the time she got to the Youngs' neighborhood, the darkness surrounded her again, as heavy as the fear and worry that roiled within her.

She waited a few moments before she got out of the

car, taking some deep breaths and trying to calm herself. She'd had too much of murder and suspicion and stalkings. She was beginning to see danger everywhere. Until recently, she had always thought of the town of Prosper, with its fifty thousand or so residents, as quaint and Southern. And that, in Jane's mind, translated to safe. It was not a town where people were murdered.

Thelma met her at the door wearing a bathrobe and a look of surprise on her face.

"Jane! Is something wrong?" Jane now felt quite numb and, at the same time, exhausted with fear. "Lordy, you look terrible. Come in. Let me get you some tea." Thelma opened the door wider for Jane to come in, then started for the kitchen.

"I don't want any tea, Thelma." Jane sat down wearily on the sofa. Thelma turned around and gave Jane a worried look. "I'm just scared," Jane said. "And worried about Sarah. I know it's completely irrational, but—"

"You don't have to apologize to me for wanting to protect your child. But what brought this on?"

"I don't know. Things just keep happening that don't make sense. Like that rag in the tailpipe, and . . . and someone at the party attacked me, and—"

"What?" Thelma's eyes widened in alarm. "But why?"

"That's just it. I don't know why. It doesn't make sense."

Thelma dropped her eyes. "I know how it feels when things don't make sense."

"Tell me about Rashaud," Jane said suddenly, blurting it out. "Tell me why you think it wasn't an accident, why anyone would want to kill him. It never made sense to me, either, Thelma, because this is Prosper, Alabama, where things like that don't happen. But I'm beginning to see that senseless things happen. I just want to know if there's a connection."

Thelma looked suddenly weary, and there was a long silence, except for the muffled giggles of the two girls coming in occasional cotton candy puffs from somewhere upstairs. Thelma sat down carefully on the sofa, her hands in her lap, not looking at Jane at first. Finally, she turned to her and said quietly but with a trembling voice, "I don't know why anyone would do it. Rashaud wasn't mixed up in any trouble. I've told you all. Maybe it was one of those hit-and-run accidents. The police told me there was that possibility. That whoever ran him off of that embankment got scared and left."

"But you never believed that, Thelma, and you never believed he caused the accident himself, even though there was liquor in his bloodstream."

The look in Thelma's eyes was a mixture of fierce anger and pain. "He didn't drink. I know my boy. He didn't drink. Somehow, they made it look like he did."

"They? Who is they?"

Thelma buried her face in her hands. "I don't know. Whoever killed my boy."

"If you think someone killed your son, then I want to know why. I want to know if there is something going on that would put my daughter in danger." Jane's voice was like hot ice.

"There was nothing going on," Thelma said. Her voice grew stronger as if her agony infused her with strength. "Nothing. Rashaud was a good boy. I told you that. A good athlete and good at his schoolwork when he wanted to be. Never in trouble. And I guarantee you, that boy never had a thing to do with alcohol. When he saw what it did to his daddy, he swore he'd never touch it. So I know he wouldn't get drunk and drive off that embankment like they said. Somebody made him do it. Either accidently or deliberately, somebody killed my boy."

"But who, Thelma, and why, if it was deliberate?" The expression on Thelma's face made Jane regret that she'd been forcing the issue.

Thelma shook her head and spoke through new hot tears. "I wish I knew. I wish to God I knew."

Jane got up and put her arms around her friend. "Oh Thelma, I'm sorry I brought this up. I guess I'm being irrational, worrying about Sarah."

"No, no, I told you, don't apologize for that. And anyway, sometimes it helps to talk about it," Thelma said. "As far as the police are concerned, the case is closed, but there's never been closure for me. That test that showed his blood alcohol was over the legal limit was all the police needed." Thelma dried her eyes and looked at Jane. "I need more than that, Jane. I need to know the truth. And I know what you must be thinking: that I'm just a mother who can't believe her child would be drinking like that. And I know why you came back here in such a state. You think my kids are into something that could make it dangerous for your own little girl. Well, that's not true. They're just like any other kids. I'm trying to get over always thinking something is going to happen to my other babies. I tell myself Rashaud was just in the wrong place at the wrong time. I don't know, maybe he saw something he wasn't supposed to see or something like that. I just don't know."

"You've told other people—the police—how you feel about this?" Jane was thinking of all the things that had happened to her and her own feeling that someone thought she had seen something she wasn't supposed to see and of her own reluctance to go to the police.

"Sure, I told 'em. I even thought maybe the mayor and Beau Jackson were going to help me push for more of an investigation. I told you how Mayor Sedgewick helped me out with the burial and how the whole town came together to support me. But they believed the report, Jane. The mayor. Everybody. Except maybe Beaumont Jackson."

"Beau?"

"He listened. More than anybody else. Told me it was out of his jurisdiction, but he was looking into it, anyway. But nothing has ever come of it, Jane. It's been nearly a year now, and nothing has come of it. I think maybe he's forgotten, too, or decided the police report was right, that Rashaud was drunk." Thelma shook her head and sobbed softly. Jane reached a hand to cover hers.

"I'm so sorry I did this to you, Thelma," Jane said.

"I know I'm being irrational. I guess I'm just scared. For Sarah. For myself. For all of us. It just never seems to stop."

"Oh, honey, I know you're so upset and scared. Why don't you stay here with us tonight?"

"If I do that, Thelma, I may be bringing danger to you."

Thelma gave her a wave of dismissal. "Don't worry about that, hon. Just stay here if it'll make you feel safe."

"Safe? Ain't nowhere safe," Dushawn said with a derisive laugh as he suddenly appeared in the doorway leading from the kitchen.

"Son! What you doin' up? You're supposed to be in bed," Thelma said.

Dushawn ignored her. "Ain't no reason you be scared just 'cause Rashaud died," he said, looking at Jane. "Whatever happen to my big brother happen 'cause he be black."

"Dushawn, you don't know that. And I wish you'd use standard English. Why do you insist on talking that way?"

" 'Cause I'm one of the bros, Mama, and I be proud of it."

"Well, there's no use in stirring up race trouble about Rashaud's death when you don't know the truth."

"I know this much, Mama, if Rashaud had been a white boy, they would have had this solved. But nobody cares about a black boy."

"Son—"

"No, Mama, don't try any of your sugarcoating. People still hate us for the color of our skin. You go on about how much better we have it than your mama did and than you did. But we're still black, Mama, and some of them white bastards don't want us to forget it. They still think we're not as good as they are. I don't know why you can't see that." Dushawn's dialect had disappeared as soon as he got the attention he wanted.

"Dushawn! I won't have you talking that way," Thelma said. "And that hatred you have in your heart, young man! What good does it do? It makes you no better than the worst of them who hate us just because of the color of our skin. I will not allow such hatred. Do you hear me, Dushawn Young? I will not allow it.''

Dushawn ducked his head and mumbled, ''Yes, ma'am.'' His mother's wrath encircled him like a sticky cocoon and humbled his adolescent masculine bravado. Then, suddenly, Thelma threw her arms around her son, and they both wept. It was a moment in which Jane felt she did not belong. She stood, picked up her handbag, and started to leave.

''No, wait,'' Thelma called to her, breaking away from Dushawn. ''I meant what I said about you staying here tonight. I can make you a bed here, on the sofa.''

Jane shook her head. ''Thank you, Thelma, but no. It would spoil it for Sarah if she got up in the morning to find I'd been here all along. I think she needs these little moments of independence. And anyway, I meant what I said about bringing danger to you. I still think someone is after me. If they knew I was here, it could bring harm to all of you.''

''Then maybe Dushawn could follow you home at least. Make sure you get there safe.''

''I'll be fine,'' Jane said, not wanting to disturb the boy any further. ''And Thelma,'' she added hesitantly, not certain how to proceed. ''I want to say again that I'm sorry. I'm sorry about Rashaud. About what it's done to you and to Dushawn. About storming in here and forcing you to talk about something that's painful for you.''

''Now, now,'' Thelma said, giving her a quick hug. ''Don't go taking the weight of the world on your shoulders.''

Jane left, feeling even more disturbed than she had when she arrived. She drove home cautiously, glancing frequently into her rearview mirror for some sign that a car might be following her, watching for parked cars that might pull out from darkened streets. She saw very few cars on the streets at such a late hour, and nothing to make her suspicious. It was not until she reached her house that she saw the police car parked at least two blocks away, in the opposite direction from which she had come. It was something she would have given only a passing thought under ordinary circumstances, no more than a moment's curiosity about why it might be there. Now it aroused her suspicion. She wondered if it could be Beau.

She tried to push her apprehension aside as she prepared for bed. The presence of a police car in the neighborhood should have the opposite effect on her, she told herself. It should make her feel safe.

When she was dressed in her nightgown and robe, she stepped out onto the front porch to look down the street, and she saw that the police car was gone. She was about to turn around to go inside again when she saw it rounding the corner at the end of the block, two houses down. When the car passed in front of her house, she got a good look at who was inside. In spite of the darkness, she was reasonably sure it was Beau.

Jane spent a restless night alone in the house but finally fell asleep in the early-morning hours. She was still asleep at nine o'clock the next morning when she was awakened by a knock at her door.

Startled, she got up quickly and put her robe on, glancing at the clock and thinking she should be at the Youngs' house now to pick up Sarah. More irrational thoughts about what could have happened to Sarah while they were apart flooded her mind as she hurried downstairs. When she opened the door and saw Beau standing there, she was even more alarmed. He stood in her doorway looking almost boyish in an open-collared sport shirt, faded jeans, and tennis shoes.

A smile crept across his face when he saw her, and she knew he must be looking at her hair, which she was sure was sticking out in a dozen different directions.

"What do you want?" She knew she sounded harsh, but she was apprehensive as well as disgruntled, and she made no attempt to hide either fact.

"I was in the neighborhood, and I thought I'd drop by to see if you're all right."

"Why wouldn't I be all right? And why were you in the neighborhood?" Jane didn't know whether to feel relieved that he hadn't come to tell her something dreadful had happened to Sarah or to be annoyed that he had not given her more warning that he was coming.

He shrugged. "It's my job to patrol all the streets of this town."

"You were working last night, it seems to me. Aren't you ever off duty?"

"A policeman is never off duty."

"Of course." She sounded sarcastic. "Well, as you can see," she added, looking down at her bathrobe and her bare feet, "I wasn't exactly expecting company."

"You look great."

She nodded her head, a gesture of suspicion rather than agreement. "Uh huh. You're a terrible liar, you know. But you're after something you think you can probe out of me. You may as well come in and have some coffee while I try to figure out what it is." She moved aside to allow him to enter.

"How'd you get to be such a suspicious person?" he asked, stepping inside.

"I don't know; maybe it's just my nature. But twelve years with Jim Ed Ferguson sharpened my skills." She turned aside and said over her shoulder, "Make yourself comfortable for a few minutes while I get dressed."

"Don't get dressed up just for me," he called.

"Don't flatter yourself," she said, without looking at him as she hurried up the stairs. Once in her bedroom, she threw off her robe and pulled on a pair of jeans and a shirt, then smoothed her hair. She didn't bother with makeup. She was surprised at herself at how calm she felt now. Beau Jackson had been at the top of her list of suspects for stalking her until she had seen Chester Collins's muddy shoes. Of course, Beau's shoes as well as the mayor's had been muddy, but they'd both been out chasing a burglar. Maybe that meant she could trust Beau.

Maybe he was just a careful policeman after all. Still, she couldn't be sure.

He certainly looked safe enough, standing there in her doorway, boyish and a little shy. Even if he wasn't harmless, Hillary would likely be calling her before long, and if she didn't answer, she'd come check on her. In the short time she'd worked for Hillary, she'd learned, now that her phone was working, that Hillary would not hesitate to call her at any time, even on the weekend, usually about something regarding her TV show. Now she could be thankful for it. Just as a precaution, though, she took a small can of mace from the bureau drawer. She'd bought it shortly after Jim Ed left.

When she got downstairs, Beau was not in the living room where she had left him. Instead, she heard him rattling around in the kitchen while he whistled to himself. She found him making coffee. He glanced at her, then proceeded to butter the toast that had just popped out of the toaster.

"Thought you might want some breakfast, and remember, you did say to make myself at home."

"I said, make yourself comfortable, but it doesn't matter, I'll eat the toast."

"Good," he said, setting the plate on the table and wiping his hands on the back of his jeans. "Coffee'll be ready in a minute."

Jane sat down and took a bite of the toast. "OK," she said, wiping crumbs from her mouth, "tell me why you thought you had to stop by to see if I was all right."

"I told you, it's my job."

"Cut the bullshit, Beau."

He grinned. "OK, I just wanted an excuse to stop by." He opened a cupboard, looking for cups for the coffee.

"What's that supposed to mean?"

He shrugged. "I like you." He had met her gaze briefly as he said that.

"Uh huh." She studied his face, still suspicious.

"What?" He had taken on his innocent look.

"You like me well enough to stalk me. And my daughter. And to try to sabotage my car." She was surprised at her own gall at testing him like that. She reached in her pocket, fingering the can of mace.

"What the hell are you talking about?" He stared at her in what seemed to be genuine shock and surprise.

"You tell me."

He threw the second piece of toast onto a plate. "Cut the bullshit, Jane. What's this about somebody stalking you and sabotaging your car?"

"I've seen you, Beaumont Jackson, driving around my daughter's soccer field, which you never explained to my satisfaction. Then I saw you in your police car last night, parked just a block down the street. And then I saw you drive by. And you always seem to show up soon after something happens. Like those holes in my muffler and the rag stuffed in the tailpipe. And last night in the woods when you tried to attack me . . ." She pulled the canister all the way out of her pocket. Her hand was still under the table, but she was poised, ready. "I know that was you."

"Goddamn it, Jane, why haven't you told me about this before?"

She was tense, her hand gripping the mace raised almost to the level of the tabletop. She had expected him to do something dangerous once she confronted him. Instead, he sat down heavily across from her, wearing a troubled frown, both arms on the table, fists clenched. She tried to speak, but he interrupted her.

"You're right about me being at your daughter's soccer field, but it was you I was looking for, not her. I had to check you out. You and Mrs. Scarborough both, after you found Sylvia Davis. So, yeah, I watched you for a little while. And you're right, I was parked down the street, and I drove by your house, but that was for your protection. Something scared you last night. I don't know what. And since you wouldn't tell me, I just took the precaution of driving by. And I'll admit, I made up excuses to drop by. I guess I just wanted to get to know you a little better. I didn't mean to scare you."

Jane stared at him, unable to speak. She felt herself falling for his line. But how could she help but believe him when he looked so innocent? And so troubled by what she had told him?

"But you better goddamn well tell me about somebody messing with your car and attacking you in the woods," he said, his troubled expression changing almost to anger.

If he was going to attack her, wouldn't he have done it already? And why would he want her to go through all the details of what had happened to her if he already knew them? She found that she wanted desperately to tell someone. Someone other than Hillary and Buddy, who were as powerless as she was in this case. She slipped the mace can back into her pocket and took a deep breath.

"The first incident happened one night when I was driving home from Hillary's," she began. "I told you it was a teenager playing a prank, but it wasn't." She told him everything, from being run off the road to Dushawn finding the rags stuffed in her tailpipe and the holes in her muffler, and about the attack in the woods near the country club.

When he asked again about the car, she again told him, no, that she hadn't gotten a good look at the car that had pursued her and then run her off the road, except that she knew it was a dark sedan. And no, she hadn't seen the attacker in the woods, but she had felt the soft wool of the sleeve of his suit and then seen mud on Chester Collins's shoes.

"Everyone there had on a wool suit, and the mud on the shoes doesn't mean anything in and of itself." He stood, pacing the floor with his toast getting cold on the plate. "You've already established that Chester has a motive, but . . ." Finally, he placed both hands on the table and leaned toward her. "OK," he said, "tell me why you think Chester Collins, or anyone for that matter, would want to kill you."

"I can only guess. Maybe I saw something I shouldn't have. Something to do with Sylvia's murder, I mean. But if I did, I don't know what it was."

Beau straightened again, turned around toward the coffeepot to pour a mug full. "Doesn't it strike you as strange that there've been no such threats toward Mrs. Scarborough?"

"Hey, wait a minute. You're not still thinking of her as a suspect, are you?"

"At this point, everyone's still a suspect." He put the coffee mug in front of her and sat down across from her.

"Oh, well, that makes this little rendezvous cozy, doesn't it? Since I assume 'everyone' includes me."

Beau shrugged slightly. "Like I said when I first questioned you, there's not enough evidence to warrant an arrest."

"That's supposed to be comforting to me?" Jane pushed her plate of toast away, unable to eat more. "And, anyway, you're wrong about Hillary. Someone *did* try to break into her car, you know."

"Means nothing. Lots of cars get broken into. Especially Cadillacs. And, anyway, we found the guy."

Jane leaned forward, with her hands on the table. "She didn't do it, Beau. Why are you wasting your time investigating innocent people when there are plenty of other people out there with motives?"

"Oh, there are motives, all right," Beau said. "But opportunity is another matter."

"Well, you're being ridiculous to suspect Hillary. Why are you so intent on implicating her?" Jane got up in a huff and went to the refrigerator. She felt a little overheated arguing with Beau. A glass of orange juice might cool her off.

"Why are you so intent on defending her?"

"Because she's innocent," Jane said, her head stuck in the depths of the refrigerator. "And you didn't answer my question." She straightened, with the orange juice in her hand.

"I'm not intent on implicating her," Beau said. "I'm just looking into all possibilities. Look, I'm one of the good guys. I'm not out to try to arrest anyone falsely or ruin anyone's reputation. I'm just trying to do my job."

"At least one person in this town thinks you're one of the good guys. Oh, besides you, I mean."

"And who might that be?" The look on his face seemed to suggest that he was surprised she would know anyone who would think that.

"Thelma Young." She held a filled glass toward him. "Orange juice?"

He accepted the orange juice absently. Something had come up behind his eyes. A question, maybe, but wariness, too.

"She said you're the only one willing to listen to her theory that her son's death was no accident."

"That case is officially closed," he said.

Jane was intrigued by the way his eyes had grown cold, as if he were willing them not to reveal anything. "Do you think his death and Sylvia's are in any way connected?" she asked. He jerked a glance toward her, and for a moment, there was surprise or maybe alarm in his face, then the wariness again before he willed the blank look back.

"That's a little far-fetched. Why would you think that?"

Jane tried an innocent shrug. "Well, murder isn't very common in Prosper. And I just thought if both Sylvia and Rashaud were actually murdered, then maybe—"

"The MO was different. Sylvia was suffocated in her home. Rashaud died in an automobile accident with liquor on his breath and in his blood. I don't see how you could say the two were related."

"OK, you're the cop. I have to assume you know what you're doing." She glanced at the clock on the stove. "Oh lord, look at the time! I've got to go pick up Sarah."

"I've got work to do, too," Beau said. He stood and picked up some of the dishes from the table and took them to the sink.

"Work? On the weekend? You really do work all the time, don't you?"

He shrugged. "This won't take long. I'm meeting Buddy Fletcher."

"Meeting Buddy? To get him to open the safe?"

"He told you about that, huh?"

"I thought it was Monday he was going to do that."

"I changed it to today. Got other things to do on Monday."

Jane picked up the butter knife and orange juice glasses from the table. "Well, maybe you'll find something in there that will help your investigation."

"Like what?"

"Oh, I don't know. Just something," Jane said, with her back to him as she put the dishes in the sink, wishing she could take back that last provocative remark.

"Buddy's really good at breaking into things, isn't he?" Beau said, speaking to her back.

"Is he? Jim Ed convinced a jury he wasn't." She turned toward him to put the orange juice back in the refrigerator.

Beau grinned. "He did that for sure, didn't he?" He dried his hands on the kitchen towel. "Can I put those things in the dishwasher for you?" he asked, pointing to the dishes in the sink.

"What? Oh no. No, I'll do it, thank you," she said. There was an awkward moment of silence between them.

"Then I'll just let myself out," Beau said finally. "Thanks for the breakfast."

"Sure," she said, watching him go. He had just reached the door leading to the living room when she called to him. "Wait!" He turned around. "I, uh—I was wondering if—well, if I could maybe, you know, come along when Buddy does the safe."

A little laugh, slightly condescending. "I don't think so."

"Why not?"

"This is part of the investigation. We don't invite the public."

"I'm not the public, and you know it."

"Oh, yes, you are. If the press got hold of it, they'd want to know what right you had to be there. It would look suspicious."

"Not if I came as Buddy's legal representative."

"What are you talking about? You're no lawyer."

"All I lack is one more year and the bar exam."

Beau shook his head and laughed again, then turned to leave without saying a word.

"No, wait!"

He turned back to look at her once more.

"Buddy has asked me to be there as his representative."

"You're making this up as we go, aren't you?"

"Well, maybe, but really, I just think that as a concerned citizen, I should—"

"OK."

"—well, should be able to go, and especially since I was one of the ones who found the body. Doesn't that make me—"

"I said OK."

"What?"

"You can come. Meet me at the police station at one-thirty. I have a feeling I need to keep an eye on you, anyway."

12

Jane closed the door and sank down onto the couch. Beau's last remark haunted her. Did it mean he suspected something? She ran her fingers through her hair and tried to think. If he found out she'd been a party to breaking into that house and arrested her, what would happen to Sarah? Maybe she should just stay away this afternoon. Maybe Buddy didn't need watching. Even if he got caught trying to get the note back in the safe, there was no reason to believe he'd implicate her. He'd be loyal. Because she was Jim Ed's woman in his eyes.

But she had to be loyal, as well. In spite of the fact that Buddy had compounded their problems, it was she who had gotten him into the mess in the first place. She had to be there, not only to make sure he didn't bungle something worse, but in case he did. She had to be there to give him support and, if need be, rescue him. She had no idea how she might do that, though.

Before she met with Buddy and Beau, however, she still had to pick up Sarah. She raced upstairs for her keys and driver's license and was just about to leave for the Youngs' when the telephone rang. Jane stopped on her way to the door, considering whether or not to answer it.

It was getting late. Sarah would be expecting her. She took another step toward the door. The phone rang for the third time, and the answering machine picked up the call. She waited, hearing her own voice asking the caller to leave a number, and then, "This is Cy Malone. We gotta talk. Give me a call. It's about Wave."

Jane raced for the telephone, but her "Hello" was answered only by a dial tone. She would have to call him back. But where was his number? She'd written it down somewhere when she'd gotten it from the Montgomery telephone book Hillary had in her office. But it wasn't on the pad next to the telephone. She rifled through her purse, trying to find it, but it was nowhere. She picked up the telephone to dial directory assistance, but as she did so, she glanced at the clock. She should have left ten minutes ago in order to be sure Shakura and Sarah got to the soccer game on time.

She slammed down the telephone and raced out the door. Once she got the girls to the soccer game, she'd look around for a pay phone, call directory assistance to get the number, and make the call.

When she pulled up in front of the Youngs' place, she saw Dushawn with his head under the hood of a car. When he heard her approach, he raised his head and looked at her, but he said nothing. The fact that he had heard her at all surprised Jane because of the rap music on his radio, jerking and pulsating at alarmingly high decibels.

Jane smiled and nodded. She had almost reached the door when he called to her, "Miz Ferguson." She turned, slowly, to face him from across the distance of the front yard. "About last night," he said, "I'm sorry."

Jane saw the look on his face. Was it anguish or anger? The incomprehensible words to the song bounced out of the radio, bumping and pumping into every fiber of her body. "Did your mother tell you that you had to say that?" she asked evenly, hoping she could make it easier for him. Hoping they could get this over with. Hoping he could hear her over the noise.

Dushawn reached an arm inside the window of the car and turned down the radio. "What I wanted to say is . . ." There was a pause, as if he was searching for the right word.

"You don't have to say it," she said. "Let's just forget it, OK?" She was about to turn away from him again when he stopped her.

"No, what I want to say is, she did tell me I had to do it, and I didn't want to at first, but now . . ."

"I accept your apology, Dushawn," Jane said, all the while wondering what was going on in his mind.

"None of what happened to Rashaud is your fault, and I really didn't mean to take out my anger on you."

He had her attention now. Her eyes held his, waiting, because he looked as if he had more to say.

He looked down at the greasy rag he held in his hands, then back at Jane. "Shakura, she likes you and your little girl. I don't want to cause any misery for Shakura."

"Nobody wants to cause any misery for you, Dushawn. I think you're miserable enough."

Dushawn shrugged. "You're OK, I guess."

"You're OK, too." Jane started, once again, toward the door, and once again Dushawn stopped her.

"Is it true what Shakura and Sarah say about you? You really gonna be a lawyer?"

"I hope so. Someday. When I can save enough money to go back to law school."

"Me, too. I'm going to be a lawyer, I mean."

"I know."

"Shakura tell you that? That girl, she talks too much." Dushawn seemed to be trying to suppress the tiny smile that kept playing at the corners of his mouth.

Jane gave him a friendly nod and walked to the Youngs' front door. She could see Shakura and Sarah through the screen, in their soccer uniforms. As soon as they saw her, they rushed toward her, making the noise of a multicolored horde.

"Mom! Where have you been?"

"Mama, she's here."

"What took you so long?"

"We're leaving, Mama!"

"Where's my backpack?"

"Wait a minute, I forgot my shoes."

"We're late, come on!"

"Thelma, I've got the girls," Jane called into the house. Thelma appeared in the kitchen doorway, holding a dish towel and waving her OK.

Truly peered around Thelma. "You act nice, Shakura, you hear?"

"Yes, Grandma," Shakura called.

The girls kept up their tumult of chatter and giggles all the way to the park where the soccer field had been marked off. The game had not yet started, but the team was assembled around the coach, getting last-minute instructions. The portable bleachers were filling rapidly. As the two girls ran to join their teammates, Jane looked around for a pay phone from which she could call Cy, but the park was surrounded by homes. The nearest public telephone would most likely be at the gas station on the corner, two blocks away.

The two teams were moving out to the field now. Sarah was among the players taking positions. Her first game as a starter. She would be bitterly disappointed if Jane didn't see her play. Jane found a seat in the bleachers and tried to concentrate on the game. In the past, she had vowed not to succumb to what she considered a yuppie affectation of owning a cellular phone. Right now, though, she would give her Grateful Dead record collection for one and throw in her Stones albums as well.

She tried to concentrate on the game, telling herself there was no emergency and that there would be plenty of time to talk to Cyclone later. It seemed an eternity before halftime rolled around and Jane raced to her car to drive the two blocks to the pay phone. Sarah's team was a point behind. They would be returning to the field with aggression and resolve to catch up and pass the other team, and Jane felt an obligation to cheer them on. She'd have to hurry to make the call and get back before the game started again.

Jane started her car and roared away, leaving a little rubber on the street where she'd pulled out of her parallel parking spot. She sped to the station in a manner that outdid Hillary's driving style. There, just as she had hoped, was a public phone in front of the station, near the street. A teenage girl wearing a Crimson Tide T-shirt and baggy jeans had the receiver to her ear while she leaned against the telephone stand, giggling and chatting.

Jane swore under her breath. The next closest phone would probably be blocks away. She had no idea which direction to drive to find one, though, and she hadn't the time, anyway. Perhaps if she walked up to the telephone, the girl would get the hint that she needed to use it and would cut her conversation short.

Fat chance. The girl seemed not to notice she was there. She chewed her gum, fidgeted a little and said, "Really!" and "I am so sure!" and "He is like, totally cool." Valley Girl with a Southern accent.

Jane tried to calm herself by counting the earrings the girl wore along the outer rim of her ear, but she lost count when the girl turned toward her and gave her a dirty look while she relayed a story into the receiver about a dude, a hunk, and a motorcycle. In the distance, Jane heard noises coming from the soccer field.

"Excuse me," she said. "This is sort of an emergency. Could I please use the phone for just one minute?"

"Fuck off!" the girl said.

There was a roar from the soccer field in the distance. Jane turned away, frustrated and angry. When she got back to the field, her parking place was gone, and she had to park a block and a half away. She ran to the bleachers and squeezed into the spot where she'd sat before.

"What's the score?" she asked the woman next to her, an overweight blond in plaid shorts.

"Tied, two and two. That little girl made a goal." She seemed to be pointing to Sarah.

"That one?" Jane asked. "The little blond-haired girl

with skinny legs?'' Disappointment was prickling at her.

"Yeah, that's her," the woman said. "You know, Jim Ed's little girl."

Jane didn't know what happened during the rest of the game, but she didn't dare leave again. Sarah would probably be inducted into the Sports Hall of Fame if she did. All she could think about as she tried to watch what was going on out on the field was Cyclone Malone, his cryptic message about Wave, and how she was going to get to a telephone to call him.

She would just have to wait until it was over, of course, and then rush home with Sarah and call Cy. She had never known a soccer game to take so long. It seemed an eternity before it finally ended and the players came rushing off the field. She had no idea of the score.

Jane moved down the bleachers to the field to meet Sarah and Shakura. "Did you see me, Mom? Did you see me make the goal?" Sarah asked as she came running to her side. She was pink and sweaty from excitement and exertion.

"Of course I did. You were great, honey." She could feel the sweat on the bridge of her nose.

"Can you believe what that goalie did?"

"No, I can't. That was really terrific."

"Terrific? Mom, it was awful. It almost made me lose my chance. Didn't you see that?"

"Sure. What I meant was *you're* terrific, Sarah."

"Thanks, Mom." Sarah was beaming, apparently satisfied.

Jane, for her part, was developing a headache and a queasy feeling in her stomach. She didn't like lying to Sarah. It made her feel guilty and inadequate.

"She was our hero. She helped us win the game." Shakura's words came out breathless because she was almost running.

"Gee, Mom, why are we walking so fast?" Sarah asked, as she, too, struggled to keep up with her.

"What?" Jane hadn't realized she'd been almost sprinting to the car. "Oh, I have to get home to make a phone call, Sarah. And then I have to meet Buddy down at the police station at one-thirty.''

"Police station? Is he in trouble again?''

"I hope not.''

"If he is, does that mean Daddy will be coming back to defend him?''

"No, your father doesn't practice that kind of law anymore, Sarah. He represents big insurance companies and huge corporations now.'' Jane glanced at Sarah, sitting beside her as they drove Shakura home. Did her inquiry mean she *wanted* her daddy to come back? The divorce was something else to feel guilty about. She saw no sign of anything on her daughter's face, however.

"Poor Buddy,'' Sarah said, finally. "Guess he'll just have to stay out of trouble. At least until you get your law degree.''

Jane laughed. "Don't forget, I plan to be on the other side of the fence. I'll be a prosecuting attorney.''

"I'm not going to be any of those things,'' Sarah said. "I'm going to be a veterinarian.''

"Me, too,'' Shakura said.

"You'll both be terrific veterinarians.''

"We're going to go to the University of Alabama just like Leslie Ann did,'' Sarah continued. "Maybe we'll both be Miss Alabama and we'll be on the soccer team there, too. Do they have a soccer team?''

"I don't know. I suppose so.'' It bothered her that Jim Ed's bimbo of a wife could be Sarah's role model.

"We should find out.''

"There's plenty of time. There's high school to get through, first, you know.''

"Do they call it the Crimson Tide? The soccer team, I mean, just like the football team?'' Shakura asked.

"I don't know,'' Jane said, distracted. She was wondering how late Cy Malone stayed at work. Maybe he went home at noon on Saturdays. If that was the case, then it was already too late to reach him. They dropped Shakura off at her home, and Jane drove away with no more than a quick wave to Thelma.

Sarah was still enthusiastic about the game. "Do you think I'll be on the sports page?"

"Hmmm?"

"Like Shakura's brother. Rashaud was always on the sports page."

"That's nice."

"They called him a funny name. Something like a ripple running into the Crimson Tide. Maybe they'll call me that, too, huh Mom?"

"That's nice."

"Mom! You're not listening to me."

"Of course I'm listening," she said as she pulled into the driveway. She got out of the car and opened the front door. Sarah ran in ahead of her and went straight to her room to change out of her soccer uniform. She was miffed about something. Could it be she was moving into moody adolescence early? Jane couldn't worry about that at the moment. For now, she had a telephone call to make.

When Cyclone Malone answered the telephone himself, Jane was stunned that her luck had turned around so abruptly after the disastrous morning.

"Ms. Ferguson, thank God you called me back. I was just about to leave," he said.

"What's this about the Wave you wanted to tell me?" she asked.

"Not on the phone," Cy said. His voice sounded strained and worried. "Come to my office."

"All right. I can arrange to leave work early Monday and be there by—"

"No, today. We're open all weekend, and this can't wait. Can you leave now? It'll take you, what? An hour tops?"

"I can't leave until after three o'clock," Jane said, remembering that she wanted to be present when Buddy met with Beau to open the safe at Sylvia's house.

"Four o'clock then? My office. I'll be here."

Before Jane had time to either agree or disagree to the time, he had cut the connection. Jane hung up as well and glanced upstairs, toward Sarah's room. She still felt enormous guilt at missing her big play at the game. Maybe she could make it up to her with dinner and an early movie in Montgomery. She could take her to the police station with her, and they'd leave for Montgomery from there.

"You mean a *real* movie. Not videos from Block-buster?" Sarah said when Jane gave her the plan she'd devised.

"Sure, and you get to choose. You can choose the restaurant, too. We're celebrating the goal you made at the game today."

"Cool!" Sarah said, all smiles again. "I'll ride my bike down to the grocery store and get a Montgomery paper so we can see what's on."

"No need for that, Sarah. We'll pick one up on the way to the police station." Jane was pulling the bread and peanut butter from the cupboard for lunch. She couldn't do that now without thinking how appalled Hillary would be if she knew it wasn't something like coq au vin.

"We? You mean I'm going to the police station with you and Buddy?"

"Why not? New experiences are good for you."

"Wow! Wait till I tell Shakura."

Sarah's level of excitement remained high all through their lunch of peanut butter and jelly sandwiches, apples, and milk, as well as during the drive to the police station. When Jane walked in, holding Sarah's hand, she saw the look of surprise on the faces of both Beau and Buddy. Obviously, neither had expected Sarah to be there.

"Hey there, Sarah," Buddy said. "How's it hangin'?"

Jane flinched at Buddy's language, but beyond that, it bothered her that he had a worried frown on his face. She had hoped for his usual confidence.

"I'm fine, Buddy. Hello, Mr. Jackson," Sarah said. "I hope you don't mind that I came along with Mom. New experiences are good for me."

"I'm sure they are, Sarah," Beau said. "Would you like to see the dispatch room?"

"Cool! And could I see the jail, too?"

Beau gave Jane a quick glance that seemed to be a question about her approval. At the same time, Buddy said, "That ain't no place for kids, Sarah."

Jane knew he was right. She had done a stint as a newspaper reporter one summer at the end of her junior year in college. She remembered the lewd catcalls of the prisoners when she'd covered a story at the jail.

"I've got one section where all the cells are empty," Beau said, as if he were reading her mind.

"All right then," Jane said. "Just one more experience for her, I guess."

"Right this way, Miss Sarah," Beau said, taking her hand and leading her away.

"You sure you trust him with her?" Buddy asked when they were alone.

"I think so. Do you know something I don't know?"

"Well, he's a cop, ain't he?"

"Aren't we supposed to trust policemen?"

"Ha!" Buddy said.

"Do you have the note?" There was urgency in her voice. She didn't know how much time they'd have before Beau returned with Sarah.

Buddy patted his breast pocket. "Sure."

"How are you going to do this, Buddy? How are you going to get it back inside the safe without Beau seeing you?"

"I'll figure out something," Buddy said. "I'm a professional, ain't I?"

"I hope so, Buddy. I hope so," Jane said, but it bothered her that the worried frown was still on Buddy's face. "We could be in very serious trouble if Beau finds out we were in that house and you took that note."

"Don't worry. He ain't never going to know. It's a sleight of hand thang, you'll see."

Jane didn't have time to reply or to express any more of her worry before Beau and Sarah returned to the room.

"Neat, Mom. You should see it. Beau showed me a place where one of the prisoners dug a hole in the wall with a fork. And all they have are these little toilets and a sink and a bed. It is so creepy and neat.''

Only a ten-year-old would use creepy and neat in the same sentence. Jane also noticed that within the few minutes they'd been gone, Sarah had gone from addressing him as Mr. Jackson to Beau. Jane let it pass without a comment, though, and offered Sarah her hand. ''Shall we go?'' She glanced at Beau. ''We'll meet you at Sylvia's house.''

''Want to ride with me in the police car?'' Beau asked, smiling at Sarah.

''Wow! Can I, Mom? Please?''

Jane was hesitant. This was going a little too far. ''Sarah, I don't know.''

''Oh, Mom, please. Why not?''

Jane glanced at Beau. Could she trust him not to try to use Sarah somehow to get what he wanted out of this investigation?

''Come on, Mom. I need the experience.''

Jane hesitated a moment longer. ''All right,'' she said finally, but without enthusiasm. She gave Beau what she hoped he would interpret as a warning glance.

''Wait a minute!'' Buddy took a protective step toward Sarah. He pulled her aside gently and spoke to her in a low voice while Beau and Jane waited. Jane found it touching that he would want to take such good care of Sarah. But she was, after all, Jim Ed's daughter.

They left the station with Buddy in the car with Jane and Sarah in Beau's police car. ''Don't let 'em outta your sight,'' Buddy said, his eyes trained on the police car and a grim expression on his face. ''I ain't sure Jim Ed would like this. He don't like cops no more than I do.''

It was true, criminal lawyers and policemen weren't the best of friends, Jane knew, but she also knew that for Jim Ed, criminal law as well as his day-to-day concern for Sarah were things of the past. Nevertheless, she wasn't going to let Sarah out of her sight, and it had nothing to do with what Jim Ed might think about it.

Beau led the way in his police car with the siren screaming. That, Jane was sure, was for Sarah's benefit.

They arrived at Sylvia Davis's house at the same time, and Sarah got out of the car, jittery with excitement.

"Did you hear the siren, Mom? Isn't it neat? This is an official investigation, did you know that? I probably shouldn't even be along, should I? But it's a really good experience for me, don't you think? Shakura's not going to believe this! Mom, can I—"

"Hold on a minute, Sarah, I think Mr. Jackson wants to tell us something," Jane said. She'd noticed the way Beau kept opening his mouth as if he was about to say something, but Sarah's excited chatter made it impossible.

Beau gave her a grateful nod. "I just want to remind you that this *is* an official investigation. I've brought you along, Jane, because you discovered the body and might be able to provide me with information. Sarah's here because you don't happen to have a reliable baby-sitter at the moment, right?"

"Right," Jane said. Beau, it seemed, was covering his butt. If his logic was sound, however, Hillary should be here as well, since she also was in on the discovery of the body. Now was not the time for a discussion about logic, however. It was probably best that Hillary was not around. That would only increase the risk of a slip of the tongue that would make Beau suspicious about them being in the house.

Beau started for the front door with Jane at his side while Buddy lagged behind. Jane glanced over her shoulder once to see him holding Sarah's hand in a protective manner, and he was once again speaking to her in hushed tones. Probably questioning her about what had been said in the police car. Odd, Jane thought, that an ex-con should be the one who gave her a feeling of security.

Beau stopped at the door and waited for Buddy and Sarah to catch up. "I want to caution you all not to touch anything, do you understand?"

They all three nodded with gravity, and Beau unlocked the front door. Jane was loath to be in the house again. She didn't like the uneasy feeling it gave her. She didn't like remembering the sight of Sylvia Davis lying in the middle of her living room floor, dead. As she stepped into the foyer, however, she couldn't help glancing to her left into the living room. The body was gone, of course, which gave the room a strangely empty look. The place had been dusted for fingerprints, and black powder clung to almost everything.

Sarah walked beside her, holding her hand now, and with the reverence of being in a holy place. Buddy stayed close behind.

"Is that where you found her?" Sarah whispered, tugging at Jane's hand and nodding toward the living room.

"Shhh," Jane said. She was shushing Sarah, she realized, not because there was any real reason why she shouldn't be talking or asking questions. Rather, it was because Jane didn't want to answer them, and she was now having serious doubts about the wisdom of bringing Sarah along on a mission relating to murder.

"The safe is upstairs," Beau said, "in a little room just to the right of the landing. You wait here, and I'll go up and make sure everything's all right. Don't touch anything while I'm gone."

Jane, Buddy, and Sarah stood at the foot of the stairs and watched Beau go up. Beau had told them the location of the room with the safe as if they didn't know. Was that a good sign? Did that mean he didn't suspect that they'd been up there?

"Oh God, Buddy, is this going to work?" Jane asked.

Buddy gave Jane a wink. He looked different, as if his old confidence had returned.

Beau appeared at the top of the landing and called down to them, "OK, you can come up, but don't touch the banister."

Beau unlocked the door. "It's over there," he said, nodding toward the safe. "It's been dusted for fingerprints, so it's a little messy," he said, indicating the black powder that had been used to lift the prints.

"Have you found anything? Prints, I mean, that might give a clue as to who did this?" Jane asked, all the while trying to comfort herself by reminding herself that she had been very careful not to touch anything both times she'd been in the house, and Buddy had worn gloves.

"I'm not at liberty to discuss the case." Beau's voice was terse and his face stern.

Buddy walked to the safe and put his ear to the door, turning the dial with his gloved hand. It should be easy for him to open this time, Jane thought, since he'd done it once before, but he was pretending to have a difficult time. He shifted positions, gave Jane a conspiratorial look, put his ear back to the safe, turned the dial again. It was a good show.

"What's he doing, Mom?" Sarah asked.

"Shhhh," Jane said again. "He can't hear the tumblers unless we're very quiet."

"Tumblers? What are tumblers?"

"I'll explain later, Sarah." She glanced at Buddy, who shifted again, put his ear back to the safe, closed his eyes. He was playing it for all it was worth.

Sarah seemed to grow bored with the wait. She walked around the room looking at everything, her hands stuck under her armpits to make sure she didn't touch anything. Another minute passed; Sarah had inched toward the window. Finally, Buddy moved slightly away from the safe, wearing a big smile. "Got it," he said, with another quick glance toward Jane.

Jane was tense. Now was the crucial time. Buddy had to get the paper back in the safe *now*. And without Beau seeing what he was doing. But nothing like that was happening. Buddy was still turned away from the safe, looking at Jane with a triumphant smile on his face. Beau moved toward the safe with intense interest.

"Look, Mom, there's someone down there," Sarah said. She was bending over, peering out the window. "I think whoever it is, is coming into the house."

Beau glanced at her, moved quickly to the window, and Buddy took the paper out of his pocket and slid it underneath the stack that lay in the safe.

13

"Stand back, Buddy. Don't touch anything." Beau turned away from the window and moved aggressively toward Buddy and the safe.

"OK, OK." Buddy backed away obediently.

"Oh, it's just Hillary," Sarah said, still staring out the window.

"Hillary?" Jane asked.

"Yeah," Beau said. "She'll probably be ringing the doorbell any minute."

In that very second, the doorbell rang. "What's she doing here?" Jane asked.

Beau made no response. He had picked up the papers from the safe to go through them, and had, no doubt, found the blackmail note.

"I'll get it," Buddy said. He started for the door.

"No!" Beau barked. "We'll all go together." He placed all the papers inside an envelope marked EVIDENCE and walked to the door as if he expected no one to question that he was in charge and he would lead the way. The two notes of the doorbell continued to sing repeatedly.

"Is this all there is to an investigation?" Sarah asked. She sounded disappointed.

"That's all there is to this part of it, at least," Jane said. She was ecstatic with the relief she felt at having the ordeal come off so well, and it had been Sarah who provided the necessary diversion. She gave her hand an extra squeeze. By the time Beau opened the front door, Jane was smiling.

Hillary moved inside in a bluster. "I saw your car outside, Jane, and the police car, too. I *knew* something was going on. And nobody told me? How could you . . ." She saw Buddy, then looked at Jane. "Oh," she said, comprehending. "Is everything—I mean, did you—"

"Everything's fine," Jane said. "Just the ongoing investigation. Nothing to worry about."

"Oh," Hillary said again. She nodded, comprehending, then turned to Beau. "Did you find anything interesting?"

"We'll see," he said. "It will all have to be evaluated."

Jane was trying to send Hillary mental telepathy to keep her mouth shut before she gave something away. It didn't work.

"I thought maybe you'd find something to help you establish a motive," Hillary said. Curiosity was almost oozing from her pores.

"Like what?" Beau said.

Hillary did her best to look innocent. "I don't know. You know more about that kind of thing than I do. What are some of the reasons people get killed? For money? For power? Because they're being blackmailed?"

"Blackmailed?" Beau said. "What made you think of that?"

Jane got a sinking, sick feeling. She looked around for something to cram into Hillary's perfectly made-up mouth.

"Yeah," Buddy said. "What?"

"What made me think of blackmail?" Hillary said. "Oh, I don't know. Just a guess."

"Do you know any reason anyone would have to blackmail Sylvia?"

"Oh, course not," Hillary said. "I told you when you dragged me into your office for questioning, I'd hardly spoken to Sylvia Davis at all, except about decorating her house."

"That's right, she never spoke to her," Buddy said, as if he knew.

Beau didn't respond, but he was writing something in a notebook he'd pulled from his hip pocket. Jane did her best to see what he was writing, but it was impossible.

Sarah tugged at Jane's hand. "Was Sylvia being blackmailed?" she asked, eyes wide. "Is that why she got killed?"

"Hush, Sarah. I don't know," Jane said.

"It could happen," Buddy said.

Beau moved past everyone to the door. "All of you follow me out, please. I'm going to take this evidence to the office to be analyzed. Mrs. Scarborough, I'd like you to come with me to answer just a few more questions."

Jane felt the sinking sensation in her stomach again. Hillary had put her foot in her mouth, and now she and Buddy could be in serious trouble, along with Hillary. She felt torn. Part of her wanted to offer to go with Hillary to the police station, not only for moral support, but to try to make sure she didn't do them all even more damage. But she had promised to meet with Cy, and the meeting seemed important. She'd also promised Sarah dinner and a movie. That was important, too. There seemed to be no stopping Hillary, anyway. All she could do now was worry and wait for the fallout.

Jane, Buddy, and Sarah watched as Hillary got into the police car with Beau. She was still chattering. "What I would have told her, if I'd gotten the chance, is that the carpet and drapes both have to go. We'd replace them with something lighter to give the room an airy look, and then the furniture, of course, oh my lord, what can I say . . ."

Buddy pushed his baseball cap back, scratched his head, and looked perplexed. "We're gonna have to do something about that woman," he said as he watched them drive away.

"Buddy, I am not even going to ask you what you mean by that remark," Jane said. "Especially not in front of Sarah."

Buddy gave a guilty glance in Sarah's direction and got into the car. "Think she'll keep her mouth shut?" he asked.

"If she does, it'll be the first time," Jane said. She tried not to think about it. She tried, instead, to concentrate on getting Buddy dropped off to pick up his car and then driving to Montgomery to talk to Cyclone Malone and treating Sarah to dinner and a movie.

Sarah chose a film starring Brad Pitt, in spite of the fact that Jane tried to talk her into seeing an animated Disney feature. Dinner was to be at McDonald's. Sarah was unusually quiet during the drive to Montgomery. Normally, she would be chattering about school, Shakura, soccer, and her latest adventure in a police car with the siren turned on. Instead, she mostly stared out the window.

Finally, she spoke. "Beau invited you and me out to ride his horses this weekend." Rather than excited, she sounded almost grave.

"Oh?" He'd mentioned the horses before, but what did the invitation mean? Maybe she was being paranoid. It could be, simply, that he liked Sarah.

"Can we go?" Sarah asked, still grave. No enthusiasm.

"We'll see."

"I know what that means. You always say 'We'll see' when you don't want to do something." Her tone was edgy and combative.

"No, it just means I don't know yet if it will be all right."

"Why do you have to be like that? You never let me have any fun."

"What's wrong with you, Sarah?"

"Nothing." She turned her face away from Jane and stared out the window again.

Jane cast a quick, worried glance at her. "Is something troubling you?"

There was no answer.

Several seconds passed before Sarah spoke again. "You're worried about what Hillary's going to say to Beau, aren't you?" It sounded more accusative than sympathetic.

Jane gave Sarah another quick, surprised glance. "What makes you think that?"

"I just know." Sarah had her face to the window again. There was another brief silence, then she turned suddenly and asked, "You don't think Hillary really killed Sylvia Davis, do you?" She looked as if she was about to cry.

"Of course I don't think Hillary killed Sylvia." Jane was growing more and more worried about Sarah.

"Does Beau?"

"Beau? I thought he was Mr. Jackson to you."

Sarah shrugged. "We're friends now."

Jane said nothing. She was hoping Sarah wouldn't be disappointed and disillusioned when Beau Jackson decided he no longer needed them. After a while, she became aware of Sarah staring at her.

"Well?" Sarah said.

"Well, what?"

"Does Beau think Hillary did it?"

"I don't know, Sarah. You would know better than I. He's your friend, after all."

"That means he does. Why don't you just tell me the truth?"

"Sarah! Why are you trying to read more than there is into everything I say?"

"Because I know there's something going on that you're not telling me. I can just tell. 'Cause if there wasn't, then Buddy wouldn't have asked me to . . ." She turned her face suddenly toward the window again.

"Buddy asked you to do what?"

"Nothing."

"Sarah." There was a cautionary sound to that.

Sarah kept her face turned away.

"Sarah," Jane said again, a bit more demanding this time.

Sarah turned to face her. "I'm not supposed to tell."

"You have to tell me. I'm you're mother."

"I just wanted to help you and Buddy, that's all." Sarah sounded near tears again. "Buddy said it would be easy, and it was, only now I'm worried that maybe I shouldn't have, because I don't know if it was honest." Tears were streaming down her face. "I mean, I could even get arrested, and that's why I have to hurry and ride Beau's horses because, what if I go to jail? Do you think Daddy would—would defend me?" She was crying even harder now.

Jane slowed the car and turned off the highway into the parking lot of a small roadside stand with a hand-painted sign advertising boiled peanuts. She turned toward Sarah, her arm along the back of the seat. "All right, tell me what's going on." Sarah shook her head, still crying. Jane reached for her and pulled her close. "Nothing you do could be so bad that I wouldn't love you and protect you," she said, stroking her hair. "Not even if you tell me *you* killed Sylvia Davis."

That remark elicited a little giggle, along with the tears. Jane was thankful for that. She still held her daughter close, still running her hand along the silky length of her hair, but all the while her mind was searching for something Buddy could have asked Sarah to do. She was certainly going to give him a piece of her mind when she saw him, because whatever it was had upset Sarah.

She was thinking, again, that she was the one truly at fault, though, for bringing Sarah along to get mixed up in this. She never should have allowed her to come along when Buddy opened that safe. The memory of that playcd across her mind, and she sucked in her breath quickly.

"That's it!" she said aloud. "Buddy asked you to create a diversion when he opened the safe."

Sarah pulled away from her and looked at her, wide-eyed. "How did you know?"

"It's a long story, Sarah, but you don't need to worry. You acted in complete innocence."

"Are you sure? I mean, are you sure I won't get into trouble? I didn't think it was so bad at the time. Buddy just said that I was to keep an eye on the window, and then, as soon as he got the safe opened, I was supposed to say there was something down there. He said to say that, even if the only thing I saw was shrubbery. It just turned out to be Hillary instead of shrubbery, and everyone got so excited. That's when I figured it out. Buddy wanted me to do that so he could steal something out of the safe while everyone was looking somewhere else. I didn't mean to commit a crime, Mom, really I didn't."

Jane reached a hand to her face and wiped away the new tears that had begun to fall. "Don't worry, hon, you didn't commit a crime, and Buddy didn't take anything out of the safe. I can guarantee you that." She was going to give Buddy a piece of her mind, though. She'd been worried about Beau using Sarah, never dreaming Buddy would stoop so low.

"Really?" Sarah asked.

"Really."

"Then it's all right? I mean, Beau won't be mad at me or think I'm a criminal or something?"

"Not at all."

"Good. So can we go tomorrow maybe and ride his horses? Do you think he'd let Shakura come along, too? Maybe we could have riding lessons. I know they're expensive, but do you think Beau could teach us? Do you think he would?" It was the old Sarah talking now.

"Hold on! One question at a time, please," Jane said,

laughing. She was relieved to have the conversation turn away from what had happened with Buddy at Sylvia's place, so relieved, in fact, that she found herself promising to take Sarah to Beau's place the next day.

Crazy Dan's car dealership, where Cyclone Malone worked, was just off the southern end of the loop that connected all the roads leading into Montgomery. Jane planned to stop there first, before they drove to the suburban shopping mall where the theater with the movie Sarah had chosen was located. As she approached the sprawling lot filled with cars, she saw the nervous red pulsations of lights that warned of danger or disaster. Four police cars and an ambulance were parked in front of the office. Jane stopped her car next to one of the police vehicles and got out, telling Sarah, over her shoulder, to wait there.

Jane ran to the door, only to be stopped by a policeman. "You can't go in, ma'am, please stay back," he said. Behind him, Jane saw another policeman stringing out yellow tape with CRIME SCENE imprinted on it.

"What happened?" She felt suddenly breathless.

"There's an investigation going on, please stay back."

Tiffany was visible through the window, clutching something to her breast and crying while another policeman with a notebook interviewed her. Tiffany seemed to sense that Jane was looking at her. She turned to meet her gaze.

"Mrs. Ferguson!" she called from across the distance. Jane was surprised that she recognized her. "Oh, Mrs. Ferguson, it's just so awful!"

The policeman who was interviewing her must have given her a warning. Tiffany turned her attention back to him, nodding and sniffling, but she gave one more nervous glance toward Jane. At the same time, the policeman who had met her as she approached said again, "Please step back, ma'am."

Jane moved away, with a glance over her shoulder at Tiffany. Jane stood several feet away from the yellow tape roping off the area. She felt stunned and uncertain about what to do. Tiffany, it seemed, had wanted to talk to her. But that was impossible, since the police were keeping Tiffany in and her out. What had happened to Cyclone? Was he in the ambulance? If so, had someone done something to him? Whatever the reason for all the commotion, it scared her. *They don't put up crime-scene tape when someone has an accident or a heart attack,* she thought. She turned away to go back to Sarah, who was waiting for her in the car. She turned back one more time toward the roped-off opening, then back to Sarah again.

She had taken a few steps toward her car when a voice stopped her. "Mrs. Ferguson!" She turned and saw it was the policeman who had told her to move away. "The receptionist said to give you this." He handed her a slip of paper. "It's a phone number," the policeman said. "She wants you to call her. Says you're her friend." Jane was momentarily caught off guard. The policeman gave the paper another thrust in her direction. "Take it," he said. "She can probably use some comforting."

Jane nodded and took the note. "What happened in there?" she asked.

"Looks like a one-eighty-seven."

"A what?"

"Homicide."

Jane didn't remember taking her leave of the policeman, walking to the car, or even getting inside, but Sarah's voice was coming to her from the opposite side of the front seat.

"What's wrong, Mom? Why are all those police cars there?"

Jane turned toward Sarah, coming out of her daze. "There's been an accident," she said. She dropped the note with Tiffany's telephone number on it inside her handbag and started the engine. The worn tires on the old Toyota screeched as she pulled away. She wanted to get Sarah as far away from there as she could.

They went first to a McDonald's, a few blocks from the movie. Jane was working hard at having a normal conversation with Sarah and at not letting her know how unsettled she felt, but she found she couldn't eat all of her Quarter Pounder and only a few French fries.

She excused herself, pretending that she needed to go to the rest room, and dropped a quarter into the telephone positioned in the hallway between the men's room and ladies' room. She dialed Tiffany's number, but there was no answer, except for her machine asking for a message.

When they got to the movie, Jane called again when she got up to get popcorn. This time, Tiffany answered in a strained voice.

"This is Jane Ferguson, Tiffany, tell me what happened."

"Mrs. Ferguson! Oh, Mrs. Ferguson." Tiffany could say no more. She could only sob.

"Tiffany, please, tell me what happened," Jane pleaded, glancing over her shoulder. The movie would start soon, and Sarah would be wondering what had taken her so long.

"I—I was the one who found him," Tiffany managed to say between hiccuping sobs.

"Cy? Is that who you're talking about. You found Cy?"

"Yes. In his office. His face was—blue." She sounded near hysterics.

"The police said it was murder."

"It was! It was! They told me he'd been smothered. He was on the floor—a sofa pillow—his face was blue."

Jane felt as if she'd been struck a blow. A sofa pillow. The same way Sylvia had died. It was beginning to sound like the work of some weird serial killer. She felt an even greater urgency to get back to Sarah.

"Listen, Tiffany, I've got to go. Do you have someone who can come stay with you?"

"Yes, yes, my mother's coming. But you have to come, too."

"Tiffany, I'm sorry, I—"

"No, you don't understand. You have to come pick

something up. It's what he was going to talk to you about when you came. Only he died before you got there." She choked on another sob, then seemed to force herself to speak calmly. "He had me get it out of the file. That's when I found him, when I went in to put it on his desk. I didn't tell the police about it. I saved it for you."

"What is it?" There was an urgency in Jane's words, both because she was curious about what Cy had wanted to show her, and because she was becoming increasingly anxious to end the conversation so she could get back to Sarah.

"It's newspaper clippings," Tiffany said.

"Newspaper clippings? About what?"

"Football games. You know, scores and things like that."

"But why?"

"I don't know. I was hoping you would know. Listen," she said, her voice becoming strained again. "You don't think I'll get into trouble with the police for this, do you? I mean, should I have given this file to them?"

"Don't worry about it," Jane said. "I'm sure it's all right." In truth, she was not at all sure it was all right. She was not sure of anything any longer. "Listen, Tiffany, I've got my daughter with me, and I promised her a movie. I'll be over to pick up the file as soon as it's over, OK?"

Tiffany gave her directions to her house, and Jane went back into the theater, forgetting to buy the popcorn. Later, when the film was over and they were walking out, Jane remembered nothing about the movie except that the soundtrack was loud enough to give her a headache.

"Can we stop at Dairy Queen?" Sarah asked when they were in the car.

"Sure," Jane said, with a little too much forced gaiety in her voice. "I've got to go by someone's house over on Chestnut Street. We'll see if there's one on the way."

"What are all these errands for?" Sarah asked. "Are they for Hillary?"

"Yes, yes, they are. For Hillary. For my job." She gave Sarah an uneasy smile. She wasn't lying, of course, she told herself. It really was part of her job. Hadn't Hillary told her she wanted her to do what she could to clear her name? Hadn't she raised her salary to entice her? But, worst of all, hadn't she gotten in too deep now to pull out?

Jane left Sarah sitting in the car in clear sight as she rang the doorbell at Tiffany's house. She declined Tiffany's invitation to come inside. She wasn't about to let Sarah out of her sight. Dealing with murder, she now knew, makes a person paranoid.

"Just a minute," Tiffany said. "I'll go get the file." She disappeared briefly and came back carrying a manila folder. "He said it was awfully important, but I can't for the life of me see why, unless . . . You're not some kind of sports writer, are you?"

"Sports writer? No, why—"

"I didn't think so. But this file—well, I don't know what the connection is, but just by the way Cy was acting, I think he thought you might know something about Miss Davis's murder. She was murdered, you know. And Cy took it hard."

"Yes, I know."

"Well, do you?"

"Do I what?"

"Know something about her being murdered?"

"No, I'm afraid I don't."

Tiffany shrugged. "Well, anyway, I know he wanted you to have this." She handed her the file folder. "Maybe you'll know what it means when you see it."

"Thanks," Jane said, taking the folder. The temptation to open the folder while she had the advantage of Tiffany's porch light was almost overwhelming, but she resisted. It was better to review whatever was in the folder away from Tiffany in case she asked any more questions regarding what she knew about Sylvia's death.

When she was in the car, though, she left the dome light on long enough to have a peek inside the folder. What she saw answered no questions for her, however. It only created more. The folder was full of clippings from the *Prosper Picayune*'s sports pages. They were all stories about Rashaud Young.

14

Jane pitched the folder into the backseat and backed her car out of Tiffany's driveway.

"Are you OK, Mom?" Sarah asked.

Jane tried to appear unruffled. "Of course. Why do you ask?"

"When you looked at that folder, you got a funny look on your face."

"Did I?" She tried a little laugh. It came out sounding fake. She thought she saw, out of the corner of her eye, Sarah roll her eyes. They drove in silence for a while before Jane finally got the courage to ease into all that was on her mind.

"Sarah, did you ever—you know, talk to Shakura's brother before he died?"

"Rashaud you mean? Yeah, I guess."

"What did you talk about?"

"I don't know. Stuff. I was just a kid then. I don't remember."

"Just a kid? You're still just a kid. It would have been just a little over a year ago that you would have talked to him."

"I was only nine years old a year ago."

"So you were." No point in pushing it, Jane thought, but then she couldn't help herself. "Do you think Rashaud knew who Sylvia Davis was?"

"Oh, sure."

That quick, confident response surprised Jane. She glanced at Sarah. "He did?"

"Um humm. She called him up once."

"Sarah! Why didn't you tell me this before?"

Sarah turned her head quickly to face Jane. "Why? Is it important?"

"I don't know. I mean, no. No, it's not important." Jane was trying to stick to her resolve not to drag Sarah into all the problems surrounding Sylvia's death, and she didn't want to say anything that would make her worry. She wanted, badly, though, to know why Sylvia would have called Rashaud.

"Aren't you going to ask me why she called?" Sarah asked, after a while. Before Jane could respond, Sarah continued, "It was because she said she wanted him to be on her show. That's why I watched it a few times, to see if he was on. But he never was. Shakura says she never called back. So I just didn't watch her show anymore. Just boring stuff, anyway. Politicians, ugh. Hillary's show's better, even though she's totally mental."

"Sarah! You shouldn't talk about Hillary that way."

"Well, don't you think she's a flake?"

"Hillary is a very generous, kind person, who is very good at what she does."

"Oh, you mean all that Martha Stewart kind of stuff? Yeah, I guess she's good at that. And she's a nice lady, too, but she's still a flake."

"Sarah, you will not use that word in reference to Mrs. Scarborough ever again. That's disrespectful."

"Yes, ma'am," Sarah said, and lapsed into another silence. Whether the silence was born of petulance or contemplation, Jane wasn't sure. Jane kept giving her surreptitious looks, but it was becoming too dark to see her face.

Finally, in spite of herself, she asked, "Why did Sylvia want Rashaud on her show?"

"Because he was the town hero. Everybody knows that, Mom. Everybody except you, because you don't like football. People said he was going to be a star for the Crimson Tide." She giggled. "You remember what I told you Shakura said those newspaper writers called him?"

"No, what?"

"A little ripple headed for the Crimson Tide. No, it was a little wave headed for the Crimson Tide. Something like that. Isn't that weird? I mean newspaper writers are *really* mental."

Some unknown reflex made Jane's foot touch the brake. "They called Rashaud a what?"

"What's wrong, Mom? Why are we stopping?"

Horns were blaring as Jane pulled over to the roadside. "What did you say they called him in the newspaper? A little wave? Did you say a wave?"

"Geez, Mom, what's wrong with that? It's not disrespectful like flake, is it? And besides, it wasn't me that called him that, I was just telling you what they wrote in the paper. Don't be mad at me."

Jane reached a hand across to touch Sarah's face. "I could never be mad at you, Sarah. And of course it's not disrespectful. It's just that I'd never heard anyone referred to that way before—as a wave."

"Does it mean something bad?"

"Not that I know of. Just some sports writer getting carried away with his metaphors," Jane said, trying once again to appear nonchalant as she started the car and pulled onto the highway again.

Sarah's question, "Does it mean something bad?" kept playing over and over in Jane's mind. Just what did all of this mean? Was the blackmailer referring to Rashaud when he mentioned "the wave"? That did seem likely, but why? What did Rashaud's death have to do with Sylvia? And how could Rashaud or his death be related to blackmail? Jane knew it was all related somehow, and that it did, indeed, mean something bad.

As soon as Sarah was in bed, Jane went through the folder of newspaper clippings Tiffany had given her. It was nothing more than story after story about Rashaud's prowess as a running back along with photos of him in action, as well as the story about his death. She could see nothing that could relate in any way to Sylvia's death, except that there were, indeed, stories in which a writer referred to Rashaud as "a little wave headed for the Crimson Tide." But what was the connection?

Maybe Hillary would have some ideas. She wanted to talk to her, anyway, to find out about the questions Beau might have asked her when he took her in to the police station. When she called, the maid answered. Mr. and Mrs. Scarborough had gone out to a dinner party and weren't expected back until quite late. At least that meant Beau hadn't found cause to throw her in jail, Jane reasoned.

When she finally went to bed, she was restless and slept very little. She kept trying to imagine how Sylvia's interest in high school football could lead to her death. First thing in the morning, she resolved, she would call Thelma to see if she could give her any insight.

It was past midnight when the telephone rang. Hillary was on the line, and she was upset.

"Hillary, calm down. Take a deep breath. You say your house was burglarized? Have you called the police?"

"Of course I've called the police. They're on their way. But Jane, I think there's something you should know." Her voice was screechy and breathless.

"Something I should know? What, Hillary? What are you talking about?"

"I can't tell you on the phone. You'll have to come here."

"I can't just leave Sarah, Hillary. Tell me what you think I should know."

"No," she said in a whisper. "I'll come to your house. After the police leave."

"Hillary, there's no need—"

"Oh, Jane, it was so scary to come home and find my

home violated like this. Billy and I came back from a dinner party at Regina Conyer's house—the mâche wasn't fresh enough, should be bought on the *day* it's served—and that's when we found it. The house, I mean. Broken into. It was awful.''

"Did they get everything? All your valuables, or did you get there in time to—''

"Get anything? Why, no. Not a thing is missing. It's just that my back door—you know, that door that leads into the garden room—was smashed.''

"But Hillary, if nothing is missing, you can't call it a burglary. It was just a break-in.''

"Jane, you know I can't stand it when you get into these little legal nuances. I've been violated! That's all I know, and—I'll call you back, Jane. The police are here.''

She hung up then, and Jane lay back with a thud on her pillow. A dull ache was crawling across the inside of her forehead. She got up and took two aspirin with a cup of warm milk and went back to bed. When the doorbell rang at seven in the morning, she had been asleep one hour.

When she opened the door, Hillary was there, wearing Liz Claiborne slacks and a silk shirt. Her makeup looked as if Mary Kay herself had done it. Jane had thrown on a cotton robe with the pocket half ripped off and hanging by one corner. She had washed her face and given her hair two strokes with the hairbrush.

Hillary came in with a bluster, hardly noticing Jane at all. "Oh, Jane, I have to talk to you. I didn't tell the police about this. I wanted to talk to you first. I'm just so glad it wasn't that Beaumont Jackson who came. He asked me all those questions down at his office, and I didn't know the answer to any of them. How would I know about Sylvia's house? Her safe? I don't know a thing about Sylvia. Oh, but I was very calm, Jane. I didn't say a thing about that blackmail note. It's been such an awful twenty-four hours. First the questioning, and then the burglary.''

Hillary took several steps into the living room, and she stopped, looked around, taking in the secondhand furniture, the disarray of magazines and Sarah's school papers, along with an almost congealed half cup of yesterday's coffee sitting on one of the lamp tables.

"Homey," Hillary said. After she'd made her pronouncement, she moved a stack of papers and sat with finishing-school grace on the sofa. She didn't sit back and relax, though. Instead, she sat on the edge, her back straight, fishing in her purse, pulling out a slip of folded paper, which she handed to Jane.

"This!" she said.

Jane looked at the paper, a small sheet with sticky glue along one side. It had been folded over so that the sticky side was stuck together. She looked back at Hillary, puzzled.

"Read it, read it," Hillary said with a flick of her rose pink–tipped hands.

Jane unstuck the paper, turned it over, then turned it over again. It was completely blank on both sides. She gave Hillary another puzzled look.

"Don't you see?" Hillary said. "At the bottom? That little bitty imprint?"

Jane held the paper closer for a better look, and there, in tiny letters at the bottom of the paper, were the words, "Church of God's Riches, Rev. Chester Collins, Pastor."

"I don't get it," Jane said.

"Of course you do! That came from Rev. Collins's office."

"So?"

"So, I found it on the floor in my house. *I* didn't put it there. Whoever broke in must have dropped it. It had to be that preacher."

"Good lord, Hillary, why didn't you tell the police?" She was remembering his muddy shoes at the country club after someone had attacked her in the wooded area.

Hillary shook her head. She had a worried frown on her face. "I didn't know if I should. I couldn't go through more of that questioning. I mean, I feel as if I'm on the FBI's Most Wanted list. I tell you, Jane, everything I do turns against me. Even that phone call I got."

"What phone call?"

"Oh, I didn't tell you last night, did I? But I didn't want to upset you any more than I already had. It was right after we got home and found the mess. The phone rang, and when I picked it up, there was this voice that said, 'Back off, or it'll be worse next time.' " Hillary's voice shook. It was obvious she was very frightened. "I told Billy about that, of course, and he said we had to tell the police. So I did, and all they did was question me over and over again about who I know who might have made that call. They gave me a feeling that they think I'm up to something. You know, shady business of some kind, and that's why I got the call. Oh, I know that phone call must be because you and I have been doing a little of our own investigating, but I couldn't tell the police all about that, could I? And that's why I couldn't tell them about this piece of paper. They'd turn it against me somehow."

Jane sat down next to Hillary. "You should have told the police everything, including about this paper you found. The whole thing is getting out of hand."

"I couldn't. Not until I talked to you. I couldn't tell anybody. Not even Billy. I thought you would know what to do." She moved closer to the edge of the sofa. "When I found that paper, I asked myself, *Why would that crazy preacher be breaking into my house?* And then, when I thought of the phone call, I knew. He's trying to scare me, of course. The same way he tried to scare you with all those awful things that have been happening to you: your car sabotaged, run off the road, someone grabbing you in the woods. It was that preacher, wasn't it?"

Jane stood and paced the floor. "I don't know, Hillary. Something's not right about this. I just can't put my finger on what it is."

"Of course, something's not right. It's not right that he killed poor Sylvia for tattling on him, and it's not right that he's now trying to kill us. It's sure enough not right for Beaumont Jackson to be making me his prime suspect." Hillary was becoming more and more distraught.

"I know, I know." Jane reached for Hillary's hand and

gave it a squeeze. "Try not to worry. So far, all anyone has done to us is try to scare us. But I do think you should tell the police about the paper you found." But would that be all? She was thinking about Cyclone Malone being dead. She would have to tell Hillary about that, but she would have to break it to her gently, upset as she was.

"I can't believe you, Jane!" Hillary snorted. "You're telling me to tell the police everything? You know you don't trust Beau Jackson. You *told* me you didn't."

"Well, all right, I'm still not sure about him, but Beau Jackson isn't the entire Prosper police department. We'll call and ask for the patrolman who investigated the break-in."

"Oh sure," Hillary said in her best sarcastic tone. "He already thinks I'm part of some crime family because of that phone call I got."

Jane had already picked up the telephone and was about to dial, but she hesitated, then put it down again. She couldn't follow Hillary's logic in that telling the police about the note paper would somehow incriminate her, but there was, she decided, more that needed to be discussed. "What do you know about football, Hillary?" she asked.

"Football? For heaven's sake, Jane, do you have attention deficit syndrome or something? I don't want to talk about football when my life is threatened."

"Just tell me, Hillary, do you go to the high school football games?"

"I don't have any children, Jane. Why would I go to high school football games? I leave that to Billy."

"Billy? Your husband goes to the high school games?"

She gave a dismissive wave. "It's one of those Y chromosome things."

"Did he by any chance follow Rashaud Young's football career?"

"For heaven's sake, how should I know? You'll have to ask Billy. What's this all about?" She hesitated a moment. "Rashaud Young? That boy who got killed?"

"Yes. He's—was—a high school football player. I

think he was the wave that was mentioned in the black-mail note we found.''

"What? How did you figure that out?"

"It's a long story, Hillary, but what could a dead high school football player and the minister of the Church of God's Riches have to do with murder?"

"You're not making any sense," Hillary said.

"You're right. It doesn't make sense. I don't know how all the pieces of this puzzle fit together. Let me tell you what happened last night in Montgomery, and you see if you can figure it out."

She told Hillary about Cyclone's death and about the folder Tiffany had said he wanted her to have, and that it was supposed to have something to do with Sylvia's murder. Hillary, however, was just as puzzled as she was about what it all could mean. She looked at the clippings about Rashaud Young that were collected in the folder and could only shake her head.

"I don't know. Maybe it would make sense to Billy, but it doesn't make sense to me."

"Before we ask Billy about it, I think we should talk to Rashaud's mother. See what her take is on this."

"You know her? The boy's mother?"

"Very well. Sarah and her daughter are friends."

"That's a brilliant idea, Jane. Billy would make us go straight to the police with everything. Mr. Law and Order. He voted for Bush and Reagan both, you know."

Before Jane had a chance to tell her she wanted to go talk to Thelma immediately, Sarah came bounding down the stairs, still in her pajamas.

"Oh, hi, Mrs. Scarborough," she said when she saw her perched on the edge of the sofa.

"Hello, Sarah."

"You know, I meant to tell you when I saw you at Mrs. Davis's house yesterday that I watch your show. I enjoy it very much," Sarah said. She was obviously in one of her grown-up moods.

"Brilliant child," Hillary said. "And she looks just like Jim Ed, doesn't she?"

Jane turned away toward the stairs. "I'll get dressed." There was a note of resignation in her voice. "Then we'll go talk to Rashaud's mother."

Sarah, who had started toward the kitchen for her morning cereal, turned back quickly. "Mrs. Young? You're going there? Can we pick up Shakura while we're there so she can go with me out to Beau's place?"

"Beau's place?" Hillary gave Jane a cynical, questioning look. "Aren't we getting a little chummy with the enemy?"

"Hillary!" Jane said, cutting her eyes toward Sarah to caution her.

"Beau's not the enemy, Mrs. Scarborough," Sarah said. "He's really pretty cool."

"Oh, I'm sure he is," Hillary said.

"Go eat your breakfast," Jane said.

"But what about Shakura? Can we take her with us?"

"Yes, yes, at least we'll ask," Jane said, shooing her out. "Hurry along now. You promised Mr. Jackson— Beau—you'd be there early."

"We'll have to wait for Shakura to get out of Sunday school," Sarah said over her shoulder.

Jane had temporarily forgotten about Sunday school. Virtually everyone in the South, she had learned, goes to church on Sunday. She was trying to develop the habit herself, for Sarah's sake, by taking her to the Episcopal church at least fairly often. Murder had been on her mind more than religion lately, however, and made her forgetful, it seemed. Not only had she forgotten that it was Sunday, she'd also forgotten about her reluctant promise to take Sarah out to Beau Jackson's place.

"So, what is this?" Hillary asked when Sarah was out of the room. "If it's not consorting with the enemy, what is it?"

"For heaven's sake, Hillary, we don't *know* he's the enemy."

"He's the enemy if he's trying to pin a murder on me."

"Don't you see? He's just doing his job. You had an apparent motive, and—"

"Whose side are you on, anyway?"

Jane sat down wearily on the sofa. "I'm on your side, of course, Hillary." She put her head in her hands. "I just don't know what to do. We've gotten into this deeper than I ever wanted to. I don't know if I'm supposed to trust Beau Jackson or anyone else. I just don't know *what* to do anymore."

"Oh, hon." Hillary's drawl now sounded sympathetic. "I don't know, maybe it'll be all right," she said, relenting. "Maybe if you go out to his place, you can pick up some information about him. Something that will give you a clue about what he's up to. You know, if he's on the up and up. Why he wants to pin the murder on me. That kind of stuff."

"Yeah, maybe you're right," Jane said, sounding weary. "Maybe we're both wrong to be suspicious of him. Maybe he really is just trying to do his job. I mean, at least, I didn't pick up on anything out of order any of the times he's been here." She had said more than she'd meant to say, but it was already too late.

"He's been here? More than once? And now you're going out to his place?" Hillary cocked her head, eyeing Jane, nodding. Her suspicion had returned.

"Don't read anything into that, Hillary."

"Oh, of course not. Next thing I know, *you'll* be telling me I killed poor Sylvia."

"Hillary, I know you didn't kill Sylvia. Why do you think I've been knocking myself out trying to find out who did?"

"Well . . ." Hillary sounded a little hesitant, a little petulant.

"Look, go home. Have a nice brunch with Billy. Then, after Thelma and her family have had time to get home from church, we'll go over and talk to her. See if she can shed some light on this."

Hillary stood and slung her Dooney bag across her shoulder. "You know, Jane, my life was never this interesting or scary until I met you."

"I could say the same thing about you, Hillary. I was

a quiet law student until I met you. Never saw a murder victim in my life.''

"Well, it certainly wasn't *my* idea to get mixed up in murder. It's all that Sylvia Davis's fault.'' Hillary headed for the door. Just as she placed her hand on the knob, she turned back to Jane. "You know, a little bamboo would work,'' she said, moving her eyes to the living room. "It's *très artistique,* and it's not too expensive. Excellent to balance plain furnishings.''

15

"Why yes, I have all these stories about Rashaud, myself. Right there in his scrapbook," Thelma Young said when she saw the folder Jane brought her. "And this one, too, about the accident. But why did that man have them? What does it all mean?"

"I was hoping you could tell me," Jane said. "He left me a message telling me he wanted to talk about Sylvia Davis's murder, but he was killed before I could meet with him. His office girl said he had planned to show me these."

Truly, who had been standing behind Thelma looking over her daughter's shoulder at the clippings, shook her head. "Don't know why this is all comin' up all over again. Just be more trouble, that's all. More trouble for us."

"But why, Mama? Why would it mean more trouble for us? It just doesn't make sense. Rashaud didn't even know Sylvia Davis. None of us did."

"Hmmph," Truly said, hobbling away on her cane. "That's what my cousin Bessie Lee say when her baby died in his sleep. It don't make sense, she say. That's what my daddy say when he took a whippin' for something a white man done. It don't make no sense.''

Thelma shook her head. "There's no reason to think—"

"Don't need no reason," Truly said.

"Mama! It's not like you to be like this. You're getting to where you sound just like Dushawn. Suspicious all the time."

"Hmmmph," Truly said again and plopped down heavily into her chair.

"She's right," Hillary said. "Trouble doesn't have to make sense."

"Well, you're smarter than I thought you was," Truly said. Jane had introduced Hillary to Thelma and Truly when they arrived. She'd met Shakura, as well, who was now out in the backyard with Sarah, playing on the swings.

"Say what? Grandma sound like me? You be crazy, Mama?" Dushawn said, moving his long, lanky frame into the room. He was smiling.

"Don't talk that jive talk in front of me, boy," Thelma said.

Dushawn glanced at Hillary. His expression changed to an uneasy look, as if he had just that moment noticed there was a stranger in the room. Jane introduced the two to each other. Dushawn told her, in a surprisingly shy manner, that he was happy to meet her. It was his inbred Southern politeness showing through, in spite of his sometimes rebellious attitude.

"What's this?" Dushawn asked, glancing at the folder. He seemed immediately to lose some of his shyness as soon as he turned away from Hillary, and he had slipped into standard English. "Ah, Mama!" he said, when he saw the clippings. "You got to quit that. You got to quit dwelling on the tragedy."

"I'm afraid I'm the one who brought it up," Jane said.

"And me," Hillary said. "We're trying to figure out how your brother's death and Sylvia Davis's death might be related."

"You got to be kiddin'." He looked at Jane. "I told you there was no way."

Jane once again went through the story of Cyclone Malone calling her, his death, and Tiffany's contention that what he had planned to talk to Jane about was in the folder.

Dushawn listened, his expression stony. Then he glanced back at the clippings strewn across his mother's kitchen table. "Man!" he said. "It makes no sense. Only connection she had was she was one of his fans. Just like the rest of the town. Was even gonna have him on her show. She never did, though, and I tried to get her to do an investigative piece after it happened, but she wouldn't do that, either."

"Yes, but you're right, none of that seems to be enough of a connection," Jane said.

"Gonna have our Rashaud on that show?" Truly asked. "I never knew that. Thought all she had was politicians she could hang out to dry."

Hillary gave a little snicker. Everyone else ignored Truly's remark. Dushawn was fingering through the clippings. "Oh yeah, I remember this one," he said. "It's the one where they first started calling him a little wave moving toward the Crimson Tide."

Hillary's well-made-up eyes widened. "Yes," she said. "That's exactly what we wanted to talk to you about. About the fact that they called him a little wave."

"Why?" Dushawn asked. He sounded defiant.

"Because it might be a clue to Sylvia Davis's murder," Jane said, deciding it was best to be completely open. She told them about the blackmail note. "We're not supposed to know anything about that note," Jane said, "so please don't say anything to anyone else."

"If you ain't supposed to know about it, then how come you do?" Truly asked. She seemed to have a way of living up to her name. The blunt and naked truth was what she spoke and what she demanded.

"It sort of just fell into our hands," Jane said.

Truly gave her a look that cut through her soul. "Yeah,

and I'm the new Miss Universe,'' she said.

"So, the question is, why would anyone who was blackmailing Sylvia make reference to the fact that Rashaud was dead?'' Jane asked, hoping to avoid giving away too many details of her investigation.

Thelma could only shake her head. Dushawn looked troubled. "Could be that whoever killed that Sylvia chick killed Rashaud too, and then killed Cyclone because he knew too much,'' he said.

"That's a logical conclusion, of course,'' Jane said.

"It is?'' Hillary sounded surprised. "Because, that's just what I was thinking.''

"And the next logical conclusion is that if anybody else gets to know too much, then that person is gonna be dead, too,'' Dushawn said.

"Don't think I haven't thought of *that*,'' Hillary said. "Could I have a glass of water? I need to take an aspirin.'' She was digging in her handbag. "I tell you, it's a real strain, being a murder suspect *and* a potential murder victim.''

"Suspect?'' Dushawn said. Thelma gave her a quizzical look.

"Hillary, for heaven's sake . . .'' Jane began.

"Well, I am, you know. That Beaumont Jackson. He thinks I did it. Can you imagine? Just because Sylvia and I had this little teeny rivalry going with our TV shows.''

"Speakin' of your TV show, that green bean casserole you cooked on your show last week,'' Truly said, with an attention-demanding tap of her cane. "It woulda been better if you'd a-cooked them beans down.''

"What?'' Hillary gave her a surprised look.

"That's right,'' Truly said. "Put 'em in a big pot and cover 'em with water and add a chunk of fatback. Cook 'em all day. Now *that* be the way to cook beans.''

"Mama!'' Thelma said.

Truly was rising, with difficulty, from her chair. "I could teach you a thing or two 'bout cookin', I reckon,'' she said. "Now, you take that stuff you call po-lenta. Ain't nothin' in the world but grits, honey, and if anybody

knows how to cook grits, it be me!'' She studied Hillary
with her eyes for a moment. ''That po-liceman think you
done it, do he? And that got yo' nerves fried? Well, you
come with me,'' she said to Hillary. ''I'm fixin' to give
you somethin' to calm yo' nerves down. And it sho' nuff
ain't aspirin.'' She was laughing to herself as she hobbled
toward the kitchen. She turned around once to see if Hillary was following. When she saw that she was, instead,
staring after her in stunned silence, she motioned with her
hand to follow.

Hillary glanced from Truly to Jane to Thelma, then
back to Truly again, looking uncertain, but she got up and
followed the old woman to the kitchen door. Truly turned
back once again before she reached the door and pointed
her cane at Jane.

''That Davis woman. You ever think about she might
be the one doin' the blackmailin'?''

''What?'' Jane said.

''Mama! Why would you say a thing like that?''
Thelma said.

''Well, it seems like y'all been lookin' up a lot of blind
alleys. Ever stop to think it could be *she* was the one
threatening to ruin somebody? Been lookin' into ever'
corner but that one, so why don't you put that in your
pipe and smoke it awhile?''

''Mama!'' Thelma said again, but Truly ignored her.
She had a stunned Hillary by the arm, leading her toward
the kitchen.

''No, wait!'' Jane said. ''You're right, Truly. I hadn't
thought of that possibility before. She could have had that
note there because she was going to send it to someone.''

Truly nodded her head, still making her way slowly
toward the kitchen. Thelma tried to protest again. ''But
Miss Davis would have no cause to—''

''We don't know that,'' Jane interrupted. Her voice was
full of the excitement she felt at the possibility of a new
angle to study. ''What do you think, Truly? What reason
would Sylvia Davis have for blackmailing anyone?''

''There ain't no way I could know that.'' Truly stopped

her slow walk and again turned to Jane. "The Lord didn't give me the second sight. Didn't git no education, either, but it don't take much to know it had somethin' to do with Rashaud and his ball playin'."

"But what?" Jane said.

"Sylvia? A blackmailer?" Hillary was finally able to speak, but she still wore a stunned expression.

Truly simply shook her head and started toward the kitchen again, mumbling. "I don't know what, Miss Jane. I don't know nothin'. I'm just a poor old woman that don't know nothin' but hard work. You're the smart ones. Y'all figure it out," she said with a dismissive wave of her hand. When she finally reached the kitchen door with her slow, hobbling gait, still with Hillary in tow, she turned back once more to look at Jane. "Ever watch them *Matlock* reruns on TV?" she asked.

Jane felt disoriented for a moment. Was the old woman's mind wandering? "Uh, once or twice," she said, deciding to humor her. She didn't want to be rude.

"Well, ever' time he has a blackmailer on there, it's on account of somebody knowing something the other feller don't want him to know." She gave Hillary's arm a gentle tug. "Come on, honey, I'll get you that nerve medicine." Truly and Hillary disappeared into the kitchen.

Jane sat wide-eyed, looking at the empty space where Truly had stood. She glanced at Thelma and then at Dushawn, who both stared back, momentarily speechless.

Finally, Dushawn shook his head. "Man, oh man! You know what she's sayin'? My old grandma? You know what she's sayin'? She sayin' Sylvia Davis was blackmailin' whoever killed Rashaud."

"Who would want to kill my boy?" Thelma said, agony making her voice sound fragile. "He was a good boy. He wasn't mixed up in anything that would get him killed. He . . ."

"Mama, you said yourself over and over again he was killed. Murdered. You said that yourself," Dushawn said.

Thelma could only shake her head and sob. Jane moved

next to where she sat on the sofa and put her arms around her. "Wait, Thelma. Maybe Rashaud wasn't mixed up in anything. Let Dushawn talk."

"I don't know, Mama," Dushawn said. He was pacing back and forth across the living room. "Maybe he was. Maybe not. I don't know. But you always said yourself he was framed somehow. That he would never get drunk."

"He wouldn't! You know that, Dushawn. You know your brother—"

"I know, I know," Dushawn said, holding his hands in front of him, as if to ward off his mother's pain. "But something happened that night. Something unusual. Something that got him killed."

"His car ran off the road," Thelma said. "Maybe somebody—"

"Right," Dushawn interrupted. He had stopped his pacing, but he was still charged with energy. "His car ran off the road. Maybe someone forced his car off the road. And somehow Sylvia Davis knew about it, and she was blackmailing that person. Or maybe Sylvia Davis did it herself, and someone was blackmailing her."

Thelma shook her head. "I don't want to think about any of this. I don't like to think about Rashaud in that car. I don't want to think about anybody hurting my boy."

Dushawn sat down next to his mother, opposite Jane. He picked up Thelma's hand and spoke in a gentler tone. "We got to think about this, Mama. You want to know the truth, don't you? The truth will set you free."

Hillary hummed a tuneless melody half under her breath as Jane drove her back to her car, which was parked in front of Jane's house. Sarah and Shakura were in the backseat, singing "One Hundred Bottles of Beer on the Wall." Shakura had persuaded her mother to let her go with Sarah to ride Beau Jackson's horses.

Jane glanced at Hillary as she drove. "It must have worked," she said.

"Hmmm?" Hillary looked happy.

"Truly's nerve medicine. It must have worked."

"Bourbon," Hillary said. "Good old straight bourbon. Truly had a couple of shots herself."

"Uh huh. Took all your worries away, did it?" Jane was still watching her out of the corner of her eye.

"Well, I only had two teeny little shots. Or maybe two and a half. Truly was right. It's very relaxing."

"I can see that."

"You're still thinking about the murders, now, aren't you?" Hillary pointed a slightly unsteady accusing finger at Jane. "You should relax a little bit, too, you know. 'Cause I wasn't even thinking about being a murder suspect anymore till you brought it up." There was a hint of a slur to her speech.

"I didn't bring it up, Hillary."

"Maybe not, but that's what you were thinking."

"What I was thinking, Hillary, is that maybe Truly was right. We haven't looked at this from all possible angles. We hadn't considered that Sylvia could have been the blackmailer instead of the one being blackmailed."

"Well that *would* explain why someone would want to kill her. Maybe you should talk to Beau Jackson about that."

"How am I going to do that without bringing up the blackmail note?" Jane asked.

"Oh, Jane, honey, you are so clever. I know you'll find a way," Hillary said and then hiccuped loudly. She put her hand to her lips and giggled.

"Forty-eight bottles of beer on the wall, forty-eight bottles of beer."

Jane dropped Hillary off at her house after convincing her that Truly's "nerve" medicine and driving did not go well together. She promised to deliver her car to her later in the day.

Beau Jackson had a small mare saddled for Sarah and was waiting outside his stable when they arrived. As soon as he saw Shakura, he brought out another horse for her— bigger, but old and gentle.

"It's really very nice of you to do this for the girls. Are you sure you don't mind?" Jane asked.

"Mind? Uh, no. No, of course not," Beau said. He had been oddly distracted ever since they arrived.

"I'll be back for them in about an hour, then, if you're sure it's all right," Jane said, preparing to leave.

"Be back?" Beau looked disappointed. "Why don't you just stay here? By the time you drive all the way back into town, it won't be long before it's time to come back, anyway."

"Well . . ."

"Look, I'll give the girls a quick riding lesson, then when we finish, you and I can have a glass of tea and relax while the girls play with Bessie. It's Sunday, after all. The day of rest."

"Bessie?"

"My Sheltie. She just had pups."

"A dog?" Sarah said. "You have a dog, too? With puppies? Oh, Mom, say yes. Please, please, say yes."

"Well . . ." Jane said again. She glanced at Shakura, who, though she was too polite to ask, was pleading as earnestly as Sarah with her eyes. "OK," Jane said, finally. "For just a little while."

Beau smiled. "You can wait right there. In the shade," he said, pointing to the lawn chairs in his backyard.

Jane walked over to the chairs and sat down to watch as Beau, mounted on his own horse, a beautiful sorrel gelding, took the girls a little way out into his pasture for a riding lesson. Beau's backyard garden, though not as elaborate as Hillary's, was, nevertheless, well kept and fragrant with roses in myriad colors and sizes. Jane remembered the beautiful yellow, pink, and red roses she'd seen in a canning jar on his desk the day he'd called her and Hillary into his office for questioning about the murder. Did he grow these roses himself, she wondered. Or did he have a gardener? A gardener wasn't likely, she thought, not on a policeman's salary.

The September afternoon was unusually pleasant for Alabama, with the humidity and the temperature both low

enough not to be oppressive. Jane found herself enjoying
herself as she watched the girls learn to use their legs to
signal a change of gait for the horses and to use gentle
tugs at the reins for turns and for stopping. In a little
while, Bessie wandered over and placed her head con-
tentedly in Jane's lap. It was the first time Jane had felt
truly relaxed since Jim Ed left. She'd been so busy with
law school, and now with making a living, there was little
time to slow down. But this time, she had, in fact, even
dozed a little by the time the girls came running up to
her, flushed with excitement and full of chatter about what
they'd learned.

Beau disappeared into the house while they talked, and
then came out in a little while with a pitcher of sweet
Southern ice tea. He poured a glass for everyone, including the girls.

"Want to see the puppies?" he asked the girls.
"They're over there." He pointed to a shed just beyond
the rose bushes. "If you're quiet and gentle, Bessie won't
mind."

Jane was glad for the momentary distraction. She had
just been explaining to Sarah for the second time that no,
she couldn't afford a horse and that the backyard was too
small for one, anyway. Now, she supposed, there'd be a
demand for a dog as well. She watched the girls walk to
the shed, with Bessie following behind, then turned back
to Beau just in time to see him glance quickly at his
watch.

"Oh, we should be going," she said. "You probably
have plans."

"Plans? No. No plans," Beau said. But once again he
sounded distracted.

Jane set her unfinished tea on a metal patio table and
stood. "Really, it was very nice of you to spend the time
with the girls, but I'm sure we need to be getting back
to—"

"Sit down. Please," Beau said. "I don't want you to
go. Not yet."

Jane sat again. "OK, but you've got to tell me what's

on your mind. Why do you keep looking at your watch?"

"I didn't look at my . . . OK," he said, when he saw her face. "Maybe I am a little distracted. I got a phone call just before you got here. From the chief of police in Montgomery."

"Oh?" Jane took a sip of her tea and set it down carefully.

"Cy Malone has been murdered. Smothered with a pillow. Same MO as Sylvia Davis."

"Really?"

"I guess that's what's on my mind. Trying to figure out the connection."

"I can understand that."

"Mom! Mom, look!" Sarah said, running toward her, carrying one of Bessie's pups. "Look, isn't he cute?"

"He is, Sarah, yes," Jane said, looking at the little black ball of fur.

"He's the friskiest of all of them. You know, kind of athletic," Shakura said. "We're going to name him Wavy."

"Yes," Sarah said. "We decided that. We're going to name him after Rashaud. I hope that's all right, Beau."

"Wavy?" Beau said.

"Yes," Sarah said, "my mom got these newspaper clippings from a man in Montgomery who died. Well, not the man really, his secretary, 'cause he was already dead when we got there, and they were all about Rashaud. The clippings, I mean. And they called him a little wave," Sarah said.

"Yeah," Shakura said. "My mom has those clippings, too. That's a funny name, huh?"

"Oh yes. Funny," Beau said.

Jane wished she could just disappear somehow.

"Do you want to hold him?" Sarah asked, offering the puppy to Jane.

"I, uh, I think you should put him back in the shed now. We really need to be going."

"So soon?" Sarah said.

"Yes," Beau said, "so soon?"

Jane gave him a weak smile. He seemed to be enjoying her discomfort. "Put the puppy back, please, Sarah," she said. Sarah and Shakura turned away, reluctantly, toward the shed. Jane, realizing she was about to be left alone with Beau, stood up. "I'll help you," she called to the two girls.

"They don't need any help," Beau said. "Sit down." This time his tone was more demanding than cordial. Jane sat down, feeling edgy.

"You knew about Cy Malone," he said. "But most important, you knew about 'the wave.' In the note, I mean."

Jane looked at him, not daring to respond, certainly not daring to admit anything.

"I don't know how you knew about Malone, but I *thought* you'd been in the Davis house. Now I'm sure of it. That day you were parked on Sylvia's street. The day your air conditioner quit working. I was pretty sure of it then."

"But how could you have surmised that just because—"

"I told you. You can't eat the fruit of chinaberry trees, Jane. They're poison."

Jane shrugged. "Well . . ."

"And Buddy Fletcher. I saw him on the street that day you were parked there. He turned away from me, like he wanted to avoid me before I caught up with him again and asked him to open that safe. He opened it just a little too easily. Like he'd opened it before. That's illegal, Jane—breaking and entering. I'm sure you know that."

"It's not like you think. Let me explain."

"Do you want a lawyer present?"

"Do you think I need one?"

"You should know that better than I do."

Jane thought about it, took a deep breath, and then took a chance. "Just let me tell you how it happened," she said.

She told him everything, down to the details of tearing her hose in the tree and even falling out of the tree as well as how she found out about Sylvia and Cy's ro-

mance and about Cy's telephone call to her, then she told
him about the scrap of paper from Chester Collins's office
Hillary had found in her house after the break-in and reminded him about Chester's muddy shoes at the country
club after she'd been attacked.

Beau was silent for a long time after she finished speaking. She was aware of the girls, still lingering as long as
they could in the shed with the puppies. She wished
they'd come out and become the distraction they were
capable of being—anything to relieve the uncomfortable
moment.

Finally, he spoke. "You should have told me this a
long time ago." His expression was grim. "What you've
done. Breaking into that house. There's the possibility of
some serious charges here."

Jane felt the familiar knot forming in her stomach at
the same time she tried to form a reasonable defense in
her mind. "Actually," she began, "I don't believe I've
broken any laws. When I entered the house it was not by
force, and I tried on several occasions to . . ." She stopped
speaking, staring at Beau, who was starting to smile, and
the smile grew to become a laugh.

"I have to hand it to you. You got guts," he said.
"Climbing up in that tree and then falling out. By God,
I wish I'd seen that." He laughed again.

"It wasn't *that* funny," Jane said.

"Just don't ever do it again," Beau said, still laughing.
"Enter a house illegally like that or interfere with an investigation, I mean. You can fall out of as many trees as
you want to."

"Well, thanks a lot."

"Now, tell me everything you know about Cy Malone
and his death."

"I've told you everything I know. I just don't know
why he would have wanted to talk to me about Rashaud."

Beau, his expression serious now, looked at Jane. "If
there is some connection to his death and Sylvia's, then
it's because they both knew too much, and that means it
could be dangerous for you, Jane. I want you to back off.

No more snooping around. Do you understand?"

"But what about Chester Collins?"

"I said, back off, Jane."

"Oh, of course, of course," Jane said.

16

"And so you told him you would back off, did you? Promised him we wouldn't do any more snooping?" Hillary asked the next morning when Jane met her at the office.

"I'm sure I left him with that impression."

Hillary laughed. "Oh, you're clever, Jane. But of course we *can't* back off. We've got to solve this murder. I'm still not completely in the clear, you know."

"Maybe not, but if we keep sticking our noses in it, and Beau finds out about it, it could make things worse for you."

Hillary raised a wary eyebrow. "What does that mean, Jane? You're not going to chicken out, are you?"

"Hillary, I just think that we should—"

"Because if you are, I'm going to have to fire you, and how can I do that when I've got another affair to cater? It's the political season, Jane. Barbecues and receptions are popping up everywhere. Democrats, Republicans, Independents, Libertarians—they all call me because they all want the best, of course, so how could you think of leaving me now when I need you most?"

"I'm not thinking of leaving, Hillary. You threatened to fire me."

"Well, I'm sure I had good reason," Hillary said with a wave of her hand. "But I don't want to talk about that now. We've got work to do."

"Yes, I'm sure we do," Jane agreed. "The Regina Conyers political rally. We've been planning it for days."

"And we're not finished yet. A barbecue is nothing fancy, of course, but it does have to be done right. Did I tell you it will be at the community center?"

"Several times."

"So it will be indoor-outdoor, and the decor will be red, white, and blue bunting, of course, and checkered tablecloths so it looks, you know, grassrootsy. Now, as for the menu, it doesn't have to be fried chicken. We'll do a pig on a spit, and I can make a wonderful grilled chicken with a sauce of mora peppers and cider vinegar and unsulfured molasses. And I think I'll do next week's show on how to plan a picnic based around this menu, so I'll need you to make sure we can get everything I'll need."

Hillary went on, planning the catering for the political rally and the television show in tandem. Jane was busy taking notes and looking up sources for the various props and ingredients Hillary said she would need. When the telephone rang late in the day, she expected it to be another food supplier or the television station replying to Hillary's request to film the segment outdoors. She was surprised when it turned out to be Tiffany.

"Ms. Ferguson? Oh, I'm so glad it's you. I just had a terrible time finding you. I called information to get your home number, but you weren't there, of course, and I just didn't know what to do, but since your last name is Ferguson, I thought you might be related to Jim Ed, so I called him in Birmingham, and he told me he thought you had gone to work for that woman on television that cooks and stuff, so I called the television station, and they told me—"

"You know Jim Ed?"

"Well, of course I do. I went out with him once or twice four or five years ago."

"Of course," Jane said, remembering that she was still married to him four or five years ago. "What is it that you needed to talk to me about, Tiff?" she asked, deciding it was all right to be informal with someone when you had, in a manner of speaking, shared the same bed.

"Well, I just feel awful about this, but there's something I forgot to tell you, and well, I'm not real sure how important it is, but . . ."

There was a long pause, which made Jane edgy. "But what, Tiff?"

"It's probably not important, but besides telling me to get the files I gave you, Cy said something I thought was real funny. I mean funny odd, not funny ha ha." There was a nervous giggle from Tiffany and another pause.

"Yes, Tiffany, what did he say?" Jane was trying hard to be patient.

"Well, he said he wished he hadn't destroyed the records for that car the body shop repaired June of last year. We have a full-service dealership here, you know—new and used cars, body shop, mechanic shop."

"Uh huh." Jane was wondering now where this was leading.

"Well, Cy got kinda mad because he couldn't find them, the repair records, I mean, but gosh, it wasn't my fault. He *told* me to delete them out of the computer. He just got real weird that day after that boy got killed, and I mean, he didn't even know him. It was Sylvia that knew him, so I don't see why—"

"Wait! Wait, Tiffany. You say he asked you to destroy some records on car repairs in June?"

"Yes, but I—"

"June? After Rashaud Young died in an automobile accident?"

"Yes, that's what I was trying to tell you, but I—"

"And you destroyed them?"

"Why, yes, he told me to, but Ms. Ferguson—"

"Are there any backups?"

"Backups? You mean, like, copies?"

"That's right, copies."

"No, uh uh, I didn't save any copies."

Jane hesitated, wondering if she should just drop it now and turn it over to Beau as she had promised, but she couldn't seem to stop herself. Cy Malone having records of body work destroyed soon after Rashaud died in an automobile accident was undeniably significant. It could mean someone Cy knew had been responsible for the accident and wanted it covered up. It could mean both Cy and Sylvia were involved somehow. But Jane knew she would get nowhere unless she could find out whose car had been repaired and then had the records destroyed.

"Tiffany," she said, "do you think any of the repairmen in the body shop would remember anything about the work they did June of last year?"

"Oh no, I don't think so. They do so many cars, you know, and besides, the turnover in the body shop is so fast, I doubt if the same guys are even there."

Jane was silent for a second, trying to think of another way to get the information she wanted, but nothing would come to her. She would just have to give it some more thought. "Thank you, Tiffany, this information is important, and I'm glad you called me. If you think of anything else, anything at all—"

"There is one more thing, Ms. Ferguson. That's what I was trying to tell you just now. I remember something about that car. The one he had me destroy the records on, I mean."

Jane's heart skipped a beat and she sat up straighter. "Yes, Tiffany, what do you remember?"

"Well, I remember that it belonged to a woman named Regina something. I remember the name Regina on the work order because I have a cousin named Regina. She lives down in Mobile. She's a second cousin once removed, actually. On my mother's side, and she—"

"Could it have been Regina Conyers?"

"Conyers, Conyers . . . Why, yes, I think that's what it was . . . Regina Conyers. I guess she must have been one of that crowd that was out there at Moody's that night. You know, I always did wonder what was going on out there that night and why Cy got rid of those records. I mean, I never heard of that Regina woman having an accident, but then, she lives down there in Prosper, so maybe I wouldn't hear, but I always wondered what happened to her. Is she the same Regina whose running for some office or other? If she is, I guess whatever happened was just politics, and you know how that is—''

"Tiffany! Tiffany! Slow down. What do you mean Regina was one of the crowd at Moody's? What's Moody's?''

"Oh, everybody's heard of Moody's. It's that roadhouse that's just off the main highway between here and Prosper. It's real popular. They have those guys that play and sing the blues. Sometimes they even have some of them come down from Beal Street in Memphis. When you go out there to Moody's, you always see a lot of—well, I would call them high-powered people, you know, politicians and guys that own big businesses and stuff like that. I guess that's why Sylvia liked to go out there. Because that was the kind of people she always had on her shows, you know. Cy was out there that night. He met Sylvia there. She came up from Prosper, and he came down from Montgomery.''

"That night?'' Jane asked. "What night do you mean?''

"The night before we got that Regina woman's car in here to be fixed.''

"Do you remember the date, Tiffany?'' Jane asked.

"You know, it's funny that you would ask that, because I do remember the date. And the reason is because it was the first date I had with this fellow I'm going with. His name is Leo McPherson. *Doctor* Leo McPherson. He's a chiropractor? I tell you, if you never have dated a chiropractor, you should. The things they can do to your body is just out of this—''

"The date, Tiffany. You were going to tell me the date.''

"Oh yeah. That was June twenty-fifth."

"The night Rashaud Young was killed," Jane said, half under her breath.

"What did you say?" Tiffany asked.

"Never mind," Jane said. "Is there anything else you remember about that night or about the car?" Jane was thinking about what Tiffany had said about the location of Moody's near the highway between Montgomery and Prosper. That's where the restaurant where Rashaud had worked was located.

"Ummm, let's see. Oh yeah, I remember that I wore a white crepe dress that is backless and has these teeny little buttons down the front."

"Sounds lovely, Tiff. How about Regina? What time did she leave?"

"I don't know. I mean it was so crowded, you just couldn't tell who was coming and who was going, and I guess I really don't know what she looks like, but she had to be there, didn't she? I mean it was her car we got in here to be fixed, and I did see the car there that night. In the parking lot when me and Leo came in. I mean, how could you miss it? It was a gold Lincoln, and it had a license plate that said Regina. You know, one of those specialty kind of license plates?"

"But you don't know what time she left," Jane said, trying to make sense of all that Tiffany was telling her. "Did you see her car in the parking lot when you left?"

"Ummm, I don't remember, but I don't think so. I mean, me and Leo left kind of late, and I think most people had already gone. Oh, I do remember when Cy left. Well, not *when* he left really. I just remember that he left before Sylvia did, and so Sylvia went over and sat at a table where these two guys were."

"Two guys? Do you know who they were?"

"Cy introduced me and Leo to them. He said one of them was the mayor of Prosper, but I don't remember his name, and the other guy was a preacher."

"Arnold Sedgewick and Chester Collins?"

"Hey, I think that's right. You're really good at this,

Jane. You ought to be a detective or something."

"Thanks for your help, Tiffany," Jane said. "Oh, and if you think of anything else, please give me a call. Even if it's late. You can call me at home."

Jane gave Tiffany her home telephone number and hung up the phone. Then she sat for several minutes, unable to work while she tried to comprehend all that Tiffany had told her. It came down to a few simple facts. Regina Conyers, Arnold Sedgewick, Chester Collins, Sylvia Davis, and Cy Malone were at a roadhouse nightclub on the night of June twenty-fifth, which was the night Rashaud Young died in an automobile accident. Rashaud, Regina, Sylvia, Sedgewick, and Collins all would have taken the same road back to Prosper, and the route would have taken them along the edge of the lake into which Rashaud's car plunged. Regina Conyers was in some sort of accident that night and took her car to Cy Malone's place in Montgomery to have it repaired. Could that mean that Regina was involved in the accident that caused Rashaud to go off the embankment? Could it also mean that Sylvia witnessed the accident and was blackmailing Regina, threatening to ruin her political career if she didn't pay up? Could Regina then have killed her to stop the blackmailing and to silence her? And what, if anything, did Chester Collins have to do with it?

It was all speculation. There were no concrete facts she could turn over to Beau Jackson that would implicate anyone. Jane sat at her desk for several minutes more. The pencil she held loosely with the fingers of her right hand made a tap-tap-tap sound as she flipped it, absently, on her desktop.

Perhaps the best place to start, she thought, was with Regina. Maybe she could ask her in an offhand way about what happened that night after she'd been to Moody's. She began by calling Regina's campaign office, only to be told she was not available and was not expected to be in for the rest of the day. She looked for her home number, but it wasn't in the telephone book, and when she tried to get her number through directory assistance, a recorded voice told her the number was unlisted. She called Chester Collins's office as well and met with a similar response. He was out of the office and would not return until later in the day. Jane left a message for him to call her.

She tapped her pencil some more. Eventually, a plan began to take shape in her mind. She could set the plan in motion as soon as she saw Regina Conyers at the barbecue later in the week. If everything worked the way she had it planned, Regina would be trapped into confessing what happened on the night of June twenty-fifth when Rashaud Young died, as well as in the early-morning hours a few weeks ago when Sylvia Davis died. The Reverend Chester Collins would be at the barbecue, too. Beau would be keeping an eye on him. Maybe he had already questioned him. Maybe she could also get something from Regina about how he figured into this.

Before she did anything else, though, Jane wanted to talk to Thelma Young again. She wanted to get a clear picture of everything Thelma remembered about the night her son died. It could be important in helping her understand where all the players were.

"Regina Conyers? Sure, I know her," Thelma said. She was sitting across from Jane in the booth of the snack bar next to the JC Penney store where she worked as manager. "She's that woman running for Congress. Doesn't have a chance, if you ask me. Alabama's not that emancipated yet. Not enough to have a woman in Congress."

"What do you know about her? I mean, has she ever tried to contact you? Has she ever said anything to you about Rashaud's death? Did you see her at any time just before or after Rashaud was killed?"

Thelma took a sip of her ice tea without taking her eyes off of Jane. "What's this all about?" she asked, setting the tea glass down carefully.

"I think I may be on to something, Thelma. I just need your help," Jane said.

"On to something? Like what?"

"I'm not sure. If you could just tell me anything at all about Regina for now, maybe it will all come clear."

Thelma seemed to think about it for a few seconds. "Well, all right," she said finally. "Let me think. Has she said anything to me about Rashaud? Yes. She wasn't at the funeral, of course, but I remember seeing her a week or so later. She was kind. Said she was sorry it happened. Said she couldn't even imagine how I must feel. Said she had a son of her own. I remember there were tears in her eyes."

Thelma paused a moment, obviously trying to deal with the painful memory.

"You said she wasn't at the funeral. In fact, you said 'of course.' Why of course?"

"She was out of town," Thelma said. "I remember that because—well, you ask if she'd ever called me. Actually, she had called me once. It was just before Rashaud died. I had volunteered to work on her campaign, and she called to tell me she was going to Europe on a vacation. She was leaving the first of June, and she was going to be gone the whole month. Said she'd get in touch when she got back. Well, of course Rashaud got killed that month, and when she got back, I wasn't up to doing any kind of volunteer work, so . . . Why is this important, Jane? Why are you letting me ramble on like this?"

Jane felt now as if she'd had the breath knocked out of her, and she had to take a moment before she could speak. "She was out of the country? Is that what you said? That she was out of the country when Rashaud died?"

"That's right," Thelma said, nodding. "Why is that important?"

"Thelma, there is something very strange going on," Jane said. She told Thelma, then, what she had learned from Tiffany about Regina's car. "I just don't understand this. How could Regina be in two places at once?"

"She couldn't, of course," Thelma said. "But I'm sure she was out of the country. I saw a story in the paper about her trip. Did you see it? It was a Sunday paper, I remember."

"No, I don't remember," Jane said, shaking her head.
"And I just don't understand why Tiffany said she saw
her at that roadhouse." Jane thought a moment, trying to
remember everything Tiffany had said. Finally her eyes
widened with realization. "Of course!" she said. "Tiffany didn't say she saw Regina. She said she didn't know
what she looked like. She said she saw her car. But who
would be driving her car? She doesn't have a husband,
and there are no children at home."

"I don't know," Thelma said. "But, Jane, if we could
just get to the bottom of this . . ." Her face still showed
her agony. "I need to put some closure on this. I need to
understand what happened to my boy that night, and I
know in my heart that the whole truth has never come
out."

Jane reached across the table to cover her friend's hand
with her own. "We have to talk to Regina," she said.
"I've tried to reach her by phone, but her office tells me
she's not available, and her home number is unlisted. She
must be getting her speech ready for the rally later this
week. We'll just have to try to snare her there."

"If I can help, I will," Thelma said.

"There's one more thing," Jane said. "The Reverend
Chester Collins. Do you know him?"

"Well, I know of him, of course. He's on the city council. But I don't go to his church. It's an all-white church,
you know."

"Has he ever called you? About Rashaud or anything?"

"Never," Thelma said. "Why?"

"No particular reason," Jane said evasively.

"You mean he's a suspect, too?" Thelma asked, seeing
through her.

"At this point, I'm suspicious of almost everyone,"
Jane said, using Beau's tactic.

The Prosper Community Center was located on city-
owned land next to Woodland Hills Municipal Park and
Golf Course. The barbecue was to be held in an area of
the park adjacent to the community center building.

Workers had prepared the pit for roasting the pig the day before, and Hillary had started the roasting early that morning before Jane arrived to help.

"I just couldn't do it without Billy," she said when Jane arrived. "Thank God he didn't have to leave for Birmingham until after he helped me get the pig on the spit."

"He's already gone to Birmingham?" Jane said with disappointment. She had yet to meet the elusive Billy.

"Oh, you know, some kind of business trip," Hillary said with a wave of her hand. "Now, I think that bunting should be draped all the way across the stage. Not just on the sides," she said, tilting her head to study the angle of the bunting. "If you'll get the workmen to change it, Jane, I'll get the chicken in the marinade. It was so clever of you to get the TV crew to do the filming while I'm here. It really will work better than my own backyard. Does my hair look all right?"

"It looks fine, Hillary," Jane said. She had dozens of details to see to before the crowds would begin arriving at six that evening. She wanted to have it all done well before then, with the expectation that Regina would get there ahead of the crowd. Jane wanted to be free to talk to her. Even if she had been out of town when Rashaud was killed and in a meeting with the mayor and Reverend Collins when Sylvia was killed, her car was involved somehow. She wanted to find out how Collins was involved as well.

All the preparations were made by three that afternoon, which gave Jane time to drive home, change clothes, drive Sarah's baby-sitter home, and then drive herself and Sarah back to the community center. Jane was used to having her Saturdays free to be with Sarah, and she would have liked to have spent some time with her daughter, but Sarah saw some of her schoolmates in the playground area in the park, and she left Jane's side immediately to be with them.

The TV crew had just finished filming Hillary at the spit where the pig was roasting and was now indoors with cameras trained on Hillary while she talked about toasting mora and cascabel peppers for making barbecue sauce. Jane waited outdoors where the tables had been set up and the stage was ready. A bluegrass band arrived, plugged in a few speakers, tuned their instruments, and began playing "Orange Blossom Special." Then the crowd started trickling in, looking for the food and drinking the beer and the soft drinks that workers sold out of large tubs of ice.

Hillary finished the filming and came outdoors to oversee the food service. Jane helped, tracking down the napkins, the plastic forks, her eyes sweeping the crowd constantly, looking for Regina. She saw Thelma, holding Shakura's hand. Thelma waved and mouthed, "Where is she?" Jane shrugged and shook her head.

Reverend Collins arrived with his wife and the mayor and his wife. She saw Beau over near the beverage tubs talking to Buddy Fletcher, but he kept glancing toward Collins. When at last Regina arrived, she went immediately to the biggest group of people and began shaking hands, talking, playing the part of the politician.

Jane wove her way through the crowd, trying to reach her. There wouldn't be much time, since it would soon be time to start serving the food, and Hillary would need her to help oversee all of it. She had almost made it to Regina's side when a big hand fell on her shoulder, stopping her.

"Miz Ferguson, I thought you might be here." It was Buddy, grinning down at her.

"How are you, Buddy?" Jane said, trying to keep Regina in her view.

"Mighty fine," Buddy said. "This is some crowd, ain't it?"

"Yes, it is." Regina had moved to another group. Jane glanced quickly at Buddy. "What were you and Beau Jackson talking about?"

"Nothin' much, but I think he's on to us. We got to be careful."

"On to us?"

"Yeah. He's actin' like he knows we was in that Davis woman's house. But I was bein' cagey. He ain't about to get nothin' out of me."

"Good for you, Buddy. Now, if you'll excuse me, I have to—"

"Man, I love these crowds. The whole town's here. That's when I do my best work."

"What do you mean by that?" Jane asked, although she was afraid of his answer.

"There ain't hardly nobody at home. It just makes it so easy. I could have a couple a TV sets, half a dozen VCRs in nothin' flat. Man, it would be so easy."

"Buddy!"

"Now, I ain't sayin' I'm goin' to do it. I'm just sayin' it would be easy. Know what I mean?"

"Promise me, Buddy. I've got enough to worry about. Promise me you won't try anything."

He paused a little too long, then finally said, "Yeah, sure. I promise."

Jane gave him a nervous smile. "OK," she said, with a quick pat on his arm. "Now, if you'll excuse me, I've got to speak to someone."

"Sure," Buddy said. As Jane moved toward Regina, he called her back. "Miz Ferguson!" She turned to face him. "If I was to, you know, give it a try, you want in on it?"

"Buddy!"

He shrugged. "Well, you was pretty good at it that time when we was in you-know-who's house, and I just thought—"

"Don't even think it, Buddy," Jane said, pointing a warning finger at him.

He shrugged and stuck his hands in his pockets. Jane turned back to Regina, feeling uneasy.

Regina was moving away again, and Jane called to her. She turned to look at Jane, who was waving broadly to her. Regina smiled and walked toward her.

"Jane, I looked for you when I got here. It's so good to see you." Regina offered her fine-boned hand. She was casually dressed in chinos and a soft cotton shirt, but she still looked elegant.

"I only have a few minutes. I've got to start serving the food soon, but I was hoping you'd have some time to talk to me," Jane said.

"Sure," Regina said. "There's an empty table over there. Let's grab a couple of sodas and we can sit and talk." She sounded more like a good friend than a killer. Her kindness, her amiability, her elegant look, all were intimidating and unnerving to Jane, but she hurried to the beverage tubs with Regina, pulled out one of the cans, and was about to head for the empty table when Beau stopped her.

"Jane, can I talk to you a minute?" He, too, was dressed casually in jeans and a T-shirt, but his expression was serious, almost grim.

"I'll be with you in just a minute," Jane said. "There's someone I have to talk to." She sensed that he was about to try to stop her, but she moved away quickly, with Regina following her. Thelma should be here, she thought, as they made their way through the crowd. She looked around, but could not spot her. Sarah and Shakura were standing next to a man dressed as a clown blowing up balloons and twisting them into animal shapes, but Thelma wasn't with them.

"Hello, Regina, dear." It was Nancy Sedgewick stopping them this time. She smiled at Regina, but ignored Jane as if she weren't there. "Your committee has done a wonderful job organizing this. It's so primitive. It seems all the common folk are here." She looked at Jane when she said those words.

"I hope so," Regina said with a little laugh.

"Common folk?" Jane said when Nancy had moved away.

"Oh don't mind Nancy," Regina said. "She can be a little tiring at times, but she's been very helpful to me. She's a wonderful organizer, and she's taught me so much. She's always been the mayor's representative at the charity committee meetings I chair, and I swear I couldn't have done it without her.''

They had, at last, reached the tables, and Regina sat down at one of them. ''Now, what was it you wanted to talk to me about?'' she asked.

Jane sat down, too, and toyed with her soda can a moment. ''I want to talk to you about Rashaud Young,'' she said, deciding to be as direct as possible without scaring her off.

''Rashaud Young? Oh yes, that was such a tragedy. Such a promising young man, but I'm afraid I don't know much about him. Why do you ask?''

''Do you remember where you were when he was killed?''

''Yes, I was in France with a group of friends. I decided to take a vacation before I started the heavy campaigning. But I don't understand why you—''

''Have you ever been to Moody's Bar?''

''Jane, what is this?''

''Just answer me, please, Regina. This is important.''

Regina hesitated a moment, then said, ''Well, all right, yes, I think I was there maybe six or seven years ago.''

''Six or seven years ago? Not last year?''

''No, but why are you . . .''

''What did you do with your car while you were in France?''

''I loaned it to a friend.''

''A friend? Who?''

''What are you two girls doing over here all by yourselves? Planning to overthrow the country?'' Mayor Sedgewick laughed at his own joke and put his hand on Regina's shoulder. He was holding a can of beer with his other hand.

''I don't want to overthrow the country. I want to help run it,'' Regina said with a chuckle.

''Then take it from an old politician, you ought to be out there shaking hands, not hidin' in a corner,'' the mayor said. ''Come here, there's somebody you ought to meet.''

Regina glanced at Jane. "Will you excuse me?" she said, getting up.

"But . . ." Jane began, but it was too late. The two of them were moving away, the mayor holding Regina's elbow. His voice trailed off as he spoke to her. "This ol' boy's been a big contributor for my campaign in the past, and if you play your cards right . . ." They disappeared into the crowd, and Jane watched them go, feeling frustrated.

Jane looked around for Chester Collins, hoping maybe she could worm some information out of him and come back to Regina later, but he seemed to have disappeared. She caught sight of Hillary, signaling to her from near the building.

"It's time to start serving the food," Hillary said when Jane walked up to her. "I could use your help."

Jane tried to keep her mind on following Hillary's orders and helping the kitchen staff serve the food to the crowd, but she was having a difficult time of it. She kept remembering her conversation with Regina. Several minutes later, she could see, from the window, Regina and Mayor Sedgewick on the stage, the mayor introducing her, Regina making her speech. Thoughts and questions were a turbulent roil in her mind. And then a realization came to her. An epiphany. Sylvia Davis's murderer was out there in that crowd, and she knew who it was. Something Regina had said had brought it all together. She knew, too, that someone had to keep that person from killing again. Possibly tonight.

It was growing dark outside, and the colored lanterns that lined the stage were shining like bright dots on the lavender fabric of twilight. People were still eating, and there was more food to be served, but Jane untied her apron and threw it aside, heading for the door with no thought in her mind except to stop another murder.

She was almost to the door when Thelma stepped inside, holding Sarah's hand. Sarah was pale and holding her arm across her stomach. Shakura walked beside her, looking frightened.

"I'm sick, Mommy," Sarah said. "I think I'm going to throw up."

"Too many chocolate chip cookies, I think," Thelma said.

Jane saw the look on Sarah's face and knew what was coming. She took her hand and hurried toward the rest room.

"Did you talk to Regina?" Thelma asked, following.

"Yes, she told me she loaned her car to someone that night. She didn't tell me who it was, but I think I know, Thelma," Jane said over her shoulder.

"Who?" Thelma asked.

Jane didn't have time to answer. They barely reached the rest room before Sarah literally tossed her cookies. When they came out, Sarah looked pale and weak. Thelma and Shakura were still waiting just outside the door.

"I've got to take her home," Jane said. Her heart was pounding, no thought in her head now except keeping Sarah and Shakura safe. "Listen, Thelma. I'm going to leave her here with you while I go get my car. Don't let the girls out of your sight until I get back."

"What's wrong?" Thelma asked. "You look as pale as Sarah."

"I'll explain later," Jane whispered, hoping the girls wouldn't sense the danger. "Please, just do as I say."

Thelma was placing a wet paper towel on Sarah's forehead. Her own forehead was creased with worry. "All right, Jane, I'll trust you."

Jane squeezed her arm. "OK," she said. "I'll just be a minute. I'll meet you at the east door."

Although Jane had parked her car as close to the community center as possible, there was a large expanse of the park she had to cross. The park was well lighted near the building and along the street, but as she ran across the darker, wooded area, she began to wish she had brought a flashlight. She found herself looking over her shoulder, remembering the night at the country club when she had been attacked in the woods.

She picked up her pace, running toward the street, remembering how the attacker had suddenly been there behind her and the arm had come around her neck, choking
her. She heard a voice behind her.

"Jane! Wait. We have to talk." She knew the voice.
She'd heard it before on Sylvia's answering machine. She
tried to keep running, but a hand on her arm stopped her.

"Lordy mercy, gal, why in the world are you in such
a hurry?"

"Hello, Mayor." Her breath was coming in gasps from
the exertion of her run.

"I saw you runnin' out across the woods, and I thought
somethin' was wrong. Thought I'd better see if I could
be of some help." He still held her arm, and he was guid-
ing her toward the street where the cars were parked.

"I'm just going to get my car. My daughter's sick, and
I'm taking her home."

"Your daughter's sick? Well, now, why don't you let
me drive her home for you."

"No. I'll just . . ." Jane glanced over his shoulder,
looking into the darkness, hoping to see Beau. Or anyone.

"Just get in my car."

"No, my car is just down the street. I'll . . ."

"I said, get in my car." She felt cold steel boring into
her ribs. She walked toward his dark sedan and got inside,
catching a glimpse of a pillow in the backseat—the same
pillow, perhaps, that had killed Cy Malone. Sedgewick
kept the gun trained on her the whole time as he walked
around to get into the driver's seat.

"I've known for a while that you were on to me, and
you're not getting away this time," he said when he was
seated next to her, the gun still trained on her. "Just tell
me this, how did you know?"

"I didn't know, Arny. Not for sure. At least not until
I found out from Regina you never attended those charity
committee meetings. Your wife attended them for you,
and that meant you didn't have an alibi for the morning
Sylvia died. And it must have been you in Regina's car
when it hit Rashaud. Sylvia knew about it and was black-

mailing you. If that was true, then you had a motive.''

"You're too smart for your own good. It didn't have to come to this, you know. I tried to scare you off, but you wouldn't stop. You just wouldn't stop.''

"It was you trying to run me off the road, messing with my car, attacking me at the country club.'' Jane's voice trembled as all the pieces fell into place in her mind, and the fear of what was to come intensified.

"Of course it was me, Miss Smart-Ass Lawyer. I got scared when Hillary said you had solved the murder. I thought you'd found something at that TV station. I knew there was a connection with Cy Malone there, and I was afraid he knew too much and you found out, somehow. I even thought maybe Sylvia wasn't dead when you found her, and she told you something. I just couldn't take any chances. I would have had you that time out by the country club, if that big hick hadn't stopped me. Then that damned preacher saw me. He was out there slogging through the grass to meet some woman. At least he was as nervous as I was, so I didn't have to worry about him asking me why I was out there. It would have been so perfect. Everyone thought I'd gone to the men's room after my speech. I could have gotten it over with right then if it hadn't been for the preacher and the other big fool.''

"But it didn't have to come to this.''

"No? Well it wouldn't have come to this if you hadn't kept up your snooping. I thought I could deal with you just by scaring you in your car, but you wouldn't back off. Not even when I messed with your car.''

"You could have killed me and my daughter both when you messed with my car, you jackass,'' Jane said, her protective nature making her bold.

"I didn't want to hurt anybody,'' Sedgewick said, but he raised the gun until it was even with her head. Jane saw his finger tightening on the trigger. "You just keep forcing me into it, just like Sylvia did. You even got Cy Malone suspicious. He called me up with all those questions about the car Sylvia had him repair. I knew then he hadn't figured it out until he talked to you. But he knew, nevertheless, and that's why I had to go all the way to Montgomery and kill him.''

He moved the gun closer to her; then, the hand that held the gun seemed to relax slightly. ''I didn't mean for it to be this way, but I can't let any of you ruin my career. There's so much good I can do for this town, for this state. It's not right for you to ruin that.''

He used his left hand, awkwardly, to start the car, still pointing the gun at her. ''I kept hoping I wouldn't have to do this, Jane. I thought that little piece of paper I dropped in Hillary's house would throw you off my scent. I knew you were probably suspicious of Chester because Sylvia had exposed that mess he got himself in, so why didn't it work? Why didn't you back off?''

Jane didn't bother to tell him that it had worked, for a little while at least, or that there had been numerous blind alleys she'd followed.

''I heard you talking to Regina, asking her about that night, and I heard you ask her about loaning someone her car,'' Sedgewick said, using one hand to maneuver the car out of its parking space. ''She told you it was me, didn't she? Well, she did loan it to me, told me to drive it a few times while she was gone to keep it running right. It was a favor I did for her. But when I heard you talking to her, I knew for sure you were on to me, and I'm not about to let it get out of hand the way it did with Sylvia. I should never have taken her with me that night, the bitch. But she came on to me, leading me on. I should have known she just wanted to find a way to ruin me.''

''Then you did it,'' Jane said. ''You killed her and you killed that boy.''

''She deserved to die,'' Sedgewick said. ''I'm sorry about the boy. That was an accident. I did my best to make it up to the family. Even got the oldest girl a scholarship. Can't you see, I—''

''It all fits together now. It was your voice on her answering machine, saying you had to talk to Sylvia. I didn't recognize it at first, but now I know.''

Sedgewick laughed, a cold sound. "You listened to her answering machine? By God, you *are* nosy. Sure, I called her and wanted to talk. I gave her every opportunity to back off." He was continually glancing from the road back to Jane, while he still held the gun trained on her. "But I didn't kill that boy. Not the way you think," he said, his attention divided between her and the road. "It was an accident. I'd had a little too much to drink, and Regina's car was unfamiliar to me. I hit his car. He was hurt bad. He was going to die, anyway. I just did what I had to do. Even Sylvia said that. She said we had to cover it up because I was drinking. She said if the press got hold of it, it would ruin me. I knew she was right."

Sedgewick glanced nervously in his rearview mirror. "It was her idea to pour the whiskey on him and down his throat. And she was with me in Regina's car when I pushed the boy's car off the embankment. Even helped me get it repaired and said she'd fixed it so nobody would know about it. I had a few scratches myself, but nothing I couldn't hide." Once more, he glanced at his mirror. "Even Regina doesn't know about her car being smashed up to this day." He wiped quickly at his eyes with the hand that held the gun. "Then the bitch started black-mailing me. Writing those damn notes." He shook his head. "Everybody thought she was rich, that she had a rich daddy footin' the bills, but there was no rich daddy. There was just Sylvia and her greed."

"You didn't have to do what you did," Jane said. "You just let Sylvia scare you. She helped you with the cover-up. She would have implicated herself as well. You could have just gone to the police and avoided all this."

"No, no, it would never have worked. Sylvia would have denied everything. Left me holding the bag. It would have ruined me." The gun in Sedgewick's hand waved unsteadily as he spoke. "Sylvia said if word got out I was drunk that night, that I was on the wrong side of the road, that I hit that boy, then it would be the end of me, and she was right, of course. It would ruin my chances to be governor, to govern and serve this great state the way it should be. That's why I had to get rid of her. You can see that, can't you? And now I've got to get rid of you."

They were on the edge of town now, nearing the lake. "It happened here." His voice was unsteady. "Right here." He wiped quickly at his eyes again. "God, I didn't mean . . ." He took his eyes off the road to glance at Jane. "You have to believe me. I tried to help that boy's family, Jane. I'm a good man. A good man for this state, a good man for . . ."

Sedgewick glanced once again in his mirror. "What the—" He sped up, swerved, sped up again. Jane dared to look behind them and saw the lights of a car swerving back and forth, very close. Then the car bumped Sedgewick's car, backed off, hit it again. Sedgewick tried to speed up, but another jolt sent his car careening to the side and into a tree. Jane felt her head hit the top of the car, then her head was thrown back as Sedgewick's car climbed the tree, front tires and hood first.

Jane felt stunned and disoriented for a moment, then she heard a tapping sound to her right. She turned and saw Hillary's face pressed against the window. Behind her stood Buddy.

"Are you all right?" Hillary tugged at the door. Jane glanced to her left and saw Sedgewick slumped over the wheel. The gun lay on the seat next to them. She picked it up and used her shoulder to force the door open. It came open with a jolt, pushing Hillary back against Buddy and almost making both of them lose their balance. Jane tumbled out of the tilted car.

Hillary and Jane embraced spontaneously, Jane shaking with emotion, and Hillary asking over and over again, "Are you all right?"

"I'm all right. I think," Jane said. "But how did you . . . ? I mean, what made you follow . . . ?"

"You sure you're OK?" Buddy asked. "What was that guy doing holding a gun to your head? I swear, Miz Ferguson, you're a hard woman to see after. But I gotta do it. I gotta do it for ol' Jim Ed."

"Thanks, Buddy. I thank you, and Jim Ed thanks you.

Now, tell me what the two of you are doing here?''

"I went out to my car to get a sweater," Hillary said, "and I saw you getting into the mayor's car. I thought that was kind of odd, and then I saw the gun. Lord, I was scared to death. I didn't know what to do. I saw Buddy walking toward one of those big houses. You know the ones I mean. Across from the park? So I yelled at him and I told him what I saw."

"Yeah," Buddy said, "so I told her we better foller you."

Hillary nodded. "I was afraid, though, at first, to get too close, afraid Arnold would shoot you. Then when he turned off on that dark road, I just thought, *I've got to do something. I can't just wait to see what happens.* So I . . . well, you know the rest."

"That woman's a hell of a driver," Buddy said.

Jane gave Hillary another hug. "Thank God you came when you did," she said. "Buddy, I don't even want to know why you were walking toward those houses, but I'm glad Hillary saw you and brought you along." She hugged Buddy as well.

"What's this all about? Why did he have a gun? Did he hate that coq au vin recipe that much?" Hillary asked.

"He killed Sylvia, Hillary. He thought we were on to him."

"Arnold killed Sylvia? Oh, my God! And to think I was in his house all those times." She bent down to glance at Sedgewick again, who was still slumped over the steering wheel. "What do we do with him?"

Jane stuck her head inside the open door of the almost perpendicular car. "He's still breathing," she said, "but I don't know how much longer he'll be out. Do you have your cell phone?"

"Of course, lamb," Hillary said, handing it to her.

Jane took it and dialed the number for the community center. When one of the kitchen staff answered, she asked for Thelma.

"Jane, where are you?" Thelma asked, sounding worried.

"It's a long story," Jane said. "I'll tell you all of it later tonight, but first I want to know how Sarah is."

"Sarah? Oh, she's fine. Got her color back and everything. Just a few too many cookies, that's all."

"Can you bring her to my house? I'll meet you there. I've got a lot to tell you."

"Well, sure. This party is breaking up, anyway. I'll just call Mama and Dushawn and tell them where I'll be."

"OK, but before you do that, could you walk outside and find Beau Jackson for me?"

"Uh oh, this sounds serious," Thelma said.

"Yes, Thelma, I would say it's serious. You and Beau both are going to be very interested in what I have to tell you."

"Well I can hardly wait," Thelma said. "Just hold on a minute, I'll go get Beau."

It was only a short time before Beau picked up the phone. "Jane, is that you? Where the hell are you?"

"I'm out on Lakeview Road. I think you'd better get out here."

"Are you all right?"

"Yes, I'm fine."

"Are you alone?"

"Not exactly, I—"

"I'll be right there. Having trouble with that old Toyota, I'll bet. But listen, before you say anything else, let me tell you what I've been trying to say all evening."

"What, Beau?"

"Watch out for Arnold Sedgewick."

"Really? Why?"

"He's dangerous, Jane. I've spent a long time investigating what went on that night Rashaud was killed, and I think I have it linked up with Sylvia Davis's murder. I'm not going to say any more than that because this is police business. Just do what I say, and stay away from him. You got that?"

"I've got that, Beau."

"All right, I'll be there as soon as I can." There was a pause, then Beau said, "Oh, and there's another reason

I wanted to talk to you. I guess I'd better ask you now because getting your full attention isn't easy.''

"Yes, Beau?''

"Would you like to drive into Montgomery with me for a movie tomorrow night?''

"Beau, I think you'd better get out here. We'll talk about that later.''

"Just say yes or no.''

"Maybe, Beau. Maybe. But first, I have something to tell you.''

"What?''

"I—uh, think I'd better tell you when you get here. It's a long story, Beau, but you're gonna love it.'' She turned off Hillary's phone and handed it back to her. She breathed a long sigh that ended in a laugh born of relief and exhaustion. "You know, Hillary,'' she said, slapping her playfully on the back. "Buddy's right. You're one hell of a driver.''

Don't try Jane's coq au vin recipe at home, but Hillary's recipe makes an elegant and easy dish. She likes to serve it with a red Côtes du Rhône and thick slices of French bread fried in butter.

HILLARY'S COQ AU VIN

4   slices bacon, cut in small pieces
2   tablespoons chopped onion
1   2½- to 3-pound broiler-fryer chicken, quartered
1   tablespoon flour
1   clove garlic, minced
1   bay leaf
¼   teaspoon thyme
12   small white onions
1   cup mushrooms, sliced
½   cup coarsely chopped carrots
¾   cup red wine (Hillary uses Burgundy)
½   cup clear chicken broth

In a large, heavy skillet, brown bacon pieces and chopped onion. Remove bacon bits. Add chicken pieces and brown slowly in bacon drippings. Stir in flour and cook until well browned. Add remaining ingredients. Heat to boiling and stir to loosen the crusty brown bits. Simmer for 45 minutes or until meat is tender.

CARROLL LACHNIT

MURDER IN BRIEF   0-425-14790-8/$4.99

For rich, good-looking Bradley Cogburn, law school seemed to be a lark. Everything came easy to him—including his sparkling academic record. Even an accusation of plagiarism didn't faze him: he was sure he could prove his innocence.

But for ex-cop Hannah Barlow, law school was her last chance. As Bradley's moot-court partner, she was tainted by the same accusation— and unlike him, she didn't have family money to fall back on.

Now Bradley Cogburn is dead, and Hannah has to act like a cop again. This time, it's her own life that's at stake...

A BLESSED DEATH   0-425-15347-9/$5.99

Lawyer Hannah Barlow's connection to the Church is strictly legal. But as she explores the strange disappearances—and confronts her own spiritual longings—she finds that crime, too, works in mysterious ways...

AKIN TO DEATH   0-425-16409-8/$5.99

Hannah Barlow's first case is to finalize an adoption. It's a no-brainer that is supposed to be a formality—until a man bursts into their office, claiming to be the baby's biological father. So Hannah delves into the mystery—and what she finds is an elaborate web of deceit...

Prices slightly higher in Canada

PENGUIN PUTNAM

online

Your Internet gateway to a virtual
environment with hundreds of entertaining
and enlightening books from
Penguin Putnam Inc.

While you're there, get the latest buzz on
the best authors and books around—
Tom Clancy, Patricia Cornwell, W.E.B. Griffin,
Nora Roberts, William Gibson, Robin Cook,
Brian Jacques, Catherine Coulter,
Stephen King, Jacquelyn Mitchard,
and many more!

Penguin Putnam Online is located at
http://www.penguinputnam.com

PENGUIN PUTNAM NEWS

Every month you'll get an inside look at our
upcoming books and new features on our site.
This is an ongoing effort to provide you
with the most interesting and up-to-date
information about our books and authors.

Subscribe to Penguin Putnam News at
http://www.penguinputnam.com/ClubPPI